ALL I WANT IS YOU THIS CHRISTMAS

ALSO BY CODI GARY

Standalones

How to be a Heartbreaker

All I Want is You this Christmas

Moonlight Ridge

Under the Moonlight

Can't Fight the Moonlight

The Something Borrowed Series

Don't Call Me Sweetheart

Kiss Me, Sweetheart

Be Mine, Sweetheart

Bear Mountain Rescue

Hot Winter Nights

Sexy Summer Flings

The Men in Uniform Series

I Need a Hero

One Lucky Hero

Hero of Mine

Holding Out for a Hero

The Loco, Texas Series

Crazy for You

Make Me Crazy

I Want Crazy

The Rock Canyon, Idaho Series

The Trouble with Sexy

Things Good Girls Don't Do

Good Girls Don't Date Rock Stars

Bad Girls Don't Marry Marines

Return of the Bad Girl

Bad for Me

Good Girls Don't Kiss and Tell

Good at Being Bad

ALL I WANT IS YOU *this Christmas*

CODI GARY

Printed by Codi Gary's Books, Inc., in the United States of America.

First printing, 2019.

ISBN: 978-1676392927

For all of the people is this world who love
Christmas as much as I do, this one's for you!

One

"Jared! Whoohoo! Do you mind helping me?"

Jared Cross turned to find Rachel Walsh, standing next to a six-foot Christmas tree secured in bright white mesh, flagging him down. Her short silver hair was brushed back from her face, revealing a wide smile, and large sunglasses. Rachel's bejeweled hand waved like a flapping bird, her rings twinkling in the afternoon sunlight.

"Sure thing."

Jared walked across the garden center, passing the holiday wreaths and rows of snow-covered Christmas trees. The outdoor garden center didn't offer much cover from the weather and although it was still early December, Snowy Springs had experienced a decent snowfall already.

"You're a sweetheart." Rachel let him push the cart, walking alongside him. He slowed his pace so she could keep up while avoiding the lingering patches of ice on the asphalt parking lot. "They are slammed today and I've got to get home to Dave. He's been a bear since he broke his leg and he still has another month to go in his cast. I swear, he's going to drive me to drink with all that griping he's doing."

Jared chuckled. "Dave's an active guy. I'd be cranky if I had to sit around, too." He leaned over and whispered, "But I'm sure no one would blame you for pouring an extra bit of brandy in your eggnog."

She laughed. "Probably not. After twenty-five years of marriage, my patience is wearing a little thin. You'll understand when you find *the one*. They may be your soulmate, but they'll still get on your one last nerve."

"I bet." Even though he loved his Labrador Rip, his rambunctious dog was irritating enough. He couldn't imagine sharing his house with another human. His foster parents' home had been a loud, lovable, chaotic mess and it'd been fun, but as an adult, he relished his solitude.

Jared stopped the cart next to Rachel's F-250 and hefted her Christmas tree onto his shoulder.

"Oh, by the way, did you hear who's back?"

Jared grunted in response as he set the Douglas Fir in the back of Rachel's truck. "Nope. Who's back?"

Rachel put her hand over the front of her purple peacoat, her eyes twinkling with excitement. "Anna Beth Howard! Can you believe it? I thought she was bound for bigger and better things when she married that tech tycoon but, apparently, he died. Poor thing. Widowed so young."

Jared kept his expression benign, even as his heart galloped in his chest. Anna Beth was back in Snowy Springs?

"You used to be friends, right?" Rachel asked.

"Yeah, when we were kids. We haven't spoken since she moved to California years back."

Not since her wedding day, when he'd made an ass of himself.

"Oh, well, maybe the two of you will catch up." She opened the door of her truck and climbed inside. "Thanks for your help with the tree. You probably have better things to do than assist an old lady."

"It was my pleasure, Rachel. Tell Dave I said, hello."

"I will. Bye."

She closed the door and Jared headed back into the garden center, barely acknowledging the bustling crowd around him. As he loaded his cart with Ice Melt, his mind wandered.

Anna Beth was back. What could she be doing here? The last Jared heard about Anna Beth was when he'd overheard a conversation between her aunt and the station dispatcher. He hadn't meant to eavesdrop, but the minute her name was mentioned, he couldn't help himself. He and Anna Beth hadn't exactly parted on the best of terms.

"Apparently, she's doing well for herself. Writing for some sitcom. She sends me cards on holidays, but otherwise, I don't hear from her much."

Jared wasn't surprised by the statement, as Anna Beth had never been close to her aunt. Having her come back here after five years left him shaken.

He paid for the supplies and headed out to his truck. As he filled up the bed of his Dodge Ram, memories surfaced, unbidden memories he'd rather stayed buried.

Anna Beth standing in the middle of an empty bridal suite at Snowy Springs Church, the same one her parents had been married in. The white off-the-shoulder gown molding her curves. Her blonde hair loose under a white veil that skimmed past her shoulders like a lace waterfall. Her green eyes filled with tears as he confessed everything he'd been holding back from her for so long.

Obviously, it hadn't gone well for him.

Despite how things ended between them, Jared hated hearing about Ian's death. She must be devastated to come back here, where life hadn't been the easiest for her.

Jared returned the cart to the store front and climbed up into his truck. He'd barely gotten the door shut when someone tapped on his driver side window. He jumped in his seat. Then, seeing his friend Vance Shepard standing there, rolled down his window, and held his hand out to him.

"Hey, man. What's going on?"

Vance took his hand in a firm shake. "Nothing much, brother." He pushed back his Broncos hat, his gray eyes meeting Jared's. "I just saw your truck and ran over to check on you."

"Check on me? Why?"

Vance shrugged. "I heard Anna Beth is back in town."

"And?"

"And I thought you might not be taking the news so well."

"I'm cool. Why wouldn't I be?"

"Come on, man. You can't play dumb with me. You forget I was your drinking buddy that whole year after she left. It being Friday…I just wanted to make sure I didn't need to keep my eye on you."

Jared ran a hand through his short hair. "It was a long time ago. I'm over it. Besides, I'm working tonight."

"Good. Cause we're too old to go on a weekend bender."

"Speak for yourself," Jared said, attempting to lighten the mood. "I'm younger than you."

"Only by a couple months. You're no spring chicken."

"Twenty-seven is not too old to bar hop, but I have no interest in that. I haven't thought about Anna Beth in years. The sight of her is not going to send me into a bottle of Fireball. Cross my heart."

"Fireball? Fuck, you are such a girl-drunk. Drink some real whiskey, ya sissy."

"Screw you! I didn't hear you complaining."

"That's because you were too distraught to handle any razzing. Since you're over it, I can tell you to man up."

"Eat me."

"Not today, my friend. I gotta run. Mom asked me to put up their Christmas lights this year so Dad doesn't have to get up on a ladder."

"If you need help, just holler."

"Will do. Later."

Jared watched Vance lope across the parking lot to his truck, glad he hadn't asked how Anna Beth looked. Vance would have read too much into it, mistaking curiosity for interest. He'd lied when he said he hadn't thought about her over the years. He'd wondered about Anna Beth from time to time, but hadn't had the stomach to do a Google search on her. Not because he was still in love with her, but seeing her would have just dredged up all the emotions from her wedding day. The embarrassment. Guilt. Anger. Loss. He'd never been one to handle his feelings well, so avoiding painful memories served him just fine. He'd come close to looking her up when Ian Crawford's letter arrived in his mailbox, but didn't. Having the husband of the woman he loved send him a letter out of the blue two years ago left him sweating bullets. Jared waited months before he read it and when he did, it didn't make a lick of sense.

Until now. Because Anna Beth came back, just as Ian predicted she would.

Jared turned toward the heart of town instead of heading straight home. Almost a foot of dirty snow had been plowed to the side of the roads, creating narrow strip of road between the buildings on either side. Despite the black sludge crowding the sidewalks, the layers of sparkling white snow on the roofs of local businesses and trees were picturesque.

Had Anna Beth been surprised to find the small town hadn't changed? Was she back for good? Did she still slip and slide driving in the snow because she took the turns too fast?

Jared smiled as he remembered the only time he'd let her drive his truck. They'd slid off the road into a snow drift. She'd cried and apologized a dozen times before he'd pulled her across the seat and onto his lap, holding her as they waited for the tow truck, stroking his hand from the top of her head to the middle of her back while she'd sniffled against his jacket. He could still smell the body spray she wore that reminded him of sugar cookies. When help arrived, he'd actually been disappointed to let her go.

In that moment, Jared realized he loved his best friend.

He'd been too scared to tell her and before he'd worked up his courage, she'd left for college. Two years later, she'd come back engaged and then he…well, he was a romantic idiot with incredibly bad timing.

She'd been right to tell him no. What kind of moron walks into a girl's bridal suite on her wedding day and asks her to run away with him? He'd been a fool to think she'd say yes.

It taught him another valuable lesson about love. It sucked.

He slowed down to twenty-five as he came up to the city park. The cherry red classic Chrysler in the driveway across the street caught his eye.

Seeing that car was like being kicked in the nuts. Nausea tied his stomach in knots. Sweat drenched him like a cold shower. Anna Beth was really back.

Shit.

Suddenly, a few drinks didn't seem like such a bad idea.

Two

"I'm surprised you called. You haven't been back to see me since you ran off with that city boy."

Anna Beth Howard sat down on the couch, holding the gift box she'd brought in her lap. She knew her aunt wouldn't waste any time before jumping in with a guilt trip. It'd been her favorite tool of manipulation when Anna Beth was a kid. Like the rest of Snowy Springs, Sarah Driver hadn't changed.

"I didn't run off, Sarah. I got married."

Her aunt never liked to be called aunt or auntie, always insisting that Anna Beth use her given name. A few of the ladies from her aunt's craft circle had admonished Anna Beth for it, until Sarah had told them she preferred it that way.

Just another way for her aunt to keep her at a distance.

Sarah set the antique tea tray on the coffee table. Although she was only fifty, everything about her screamed classic. Even the décor in her home was like stepping back into a parlor from the early 1900s. Everything vintage, expensive. Perfect.

Having an eleven-year-old move into her home couldn't have been easy for her aunt. A precocious child, several of her aunt's cherished antiques met their demise at her hands. Accidentally, of course, but it hadn't stopped Sarah from berating her at every turn. Her favorite terms of endearment for Anna Beth had been *oafish child* and *clumsy elephant*. Even breaking one of her own dishes as an adult could bring back the cold sweat and embarrassment.

Her aunt sat down on the floral couch and patted her perfectly coiffed dark hair. Her green eyes, just a shade lighter than her dress, and the one feature they shared, sparked with annoyance. There were hardly any signs of age on her face.

"Yes, I know you got married, but you could have visited."

"We had a guest room. You could have come to see us."

Sarah sniffed. "You know I don't like the city. All that noise and pollution."

"Yes, and it's all about—" Anna Beth sighed. "I didn't come to fight."

"What did you come for, Anna Beth?"

With only a moment's hesitation, Anna Beth held out the box to her. "This is for you."

Her aunt lifted the lid and her eyes went wide. "Oh my… what…"

Anna Beth's heart hammered as Sarah pulled the emerald green goblet out, memories rushing back. She'd been washing dishes and an identical glass had slipped through her fingers, shattering on the kitchen floor. Sarah screaming at the top of her lungs. Anna Beth shaking, having only been living there for a few weeks and, while her mother had yelled occasionally, it was different coming from a virtual stranger. The moment set the stage for their entire relationship and for the millionth time, Anna Beth asked herself why she'd come back.

For Ian. You have to do this for him.

"I don't know if you ever replaced it, but I know how devastated you were when I broke it." Anna Beth swallowed, pushing through the short speech she'd practiced dozens of times since making the decision to come. "I just wanted to give you something to show you how truly sorry I am for everything. I would like to start fresh and have a closer relationship with you. What do you think?"

Sarah cradled the goblet in her hands, blinking her eyes rapidly. Was she trying not to cry? In all the years Anna Beth had known her, she'd never seen her aunt cry.

Sarah placed the goblet gently back into the box with a cough. "I appreciate the gesture, but it wasn't necessary. Accidents happen. I know I wasn't the easiest person. By the time you came to me I was set in my ways. And I'd never been good at relationships, so our difficulties weren't all your fault."

Anna Beth quirked a brow. Maybe the years had softened her aunt. That green goblet had been the topic of conversation many times over the years, usually in reference to Anna Beth's clumsiness. Anna Beth wondered many times growing up how her loving, affectionate mother could have been so different from her sister.

Her mother and aunt grew up on a dairy. When their parents sold the franchise, each of them ended up with a healthy trust. Anna Beth's mother married and moved to Idaho. Her aunt remained a spinster, only visiting them briefly for holidays. Before her parent's death, Anna Beth had never visited her aunt's home. When she'd moved into the guest room of the two-story Victorian, Sarah made it clear with every action that her niece being there had inexplicitly derailed her life.

The only thing they'd ever agreed on was Anna Beth's car. Formally her dad's project, he'd never finished it before the car accident. Anna Beth took a part time job at Kirk's Auto Body answering phones after school. In exchange, Kirk taught her everything she needed to know to keep her baby running. Her aunt surprised her by purchasing the parts she needed and even having it painted her favorite color for her sixteenth birthday. It was the only time Anna Beth remembered hugging her.

If she were honest with herself, Anna Beth hadn't made it easy for Sarah. At fifteen, she'd pushed boundaries and gotten into quite a few scrapes, embarrassing her aunt. She figured Sarah would be relieved when she went off to college. At least then Sarah wouldn't have to worry about the local police bringing her home in the back of a squad car.

"What brought on the need to make amends?" Sarah asked, picking up her tea cup. "Ian has been gone a year. You could have come sooner."

Anna Beth wasn't about to tell her the truth, that it was at Ian's behest that she returned to Snowy Springs. Without him, she'd never have come back, but she couldn't disappoint him, even if he wasn't here to call her out.

Ian Crawford was the epitome of goodness and Anna Beth's estrangement from her aunt pained him. After losing his father to cancer when he was nine and his mother at sixteen, he had no family members to take him. His mother had granted guardianship to her best friend, and Ian moved to Ireland to live with her family He'd never understood how Anna Beth could just give up on family. Insisting on their reconciliation in his posthumous list of last wishes had been a genius move on his part to make the reunion happen. Ian's happiness had always been her weakness and she could deny him nothing.

Even when it meant losing him.

Anna Beth realized her aunt was still waiting for an answer and pulled the easiest excuse out of her butt. "With the holidays, it got me thinking about forgiveness. We are both alone in this world and it would be nice to have a relationship, as adults, based on mutual respect and understanding."

Her aunt lifted her tea cup to her lips with a non-committal, "Hmmm." After a few delicate sips, Sarah set her cup down and folded her hands in her lap. "I suppose if you'll be staying for a while, we could spend some time together. I'll make up the bed in your old room."

When Sarah started to stand, Anna Beth held up a hand. "You don't have to do that. I got a room at The Peaks. I'll only be here until the day after Christmas."

"Staying at a hotel for three weeks will be awfully expensive." Before she could say anything, her aunt continued, "People will think you're flaunting your wealth, you know."

Anna Beth knew people assumed she'd married Ian for his money. He'd been twenty-two when they'd met at UCLA, and he'd already sold three successful gaming apps for millions. The tabloids crucified her, calling her a gold digger. It stung that her flesh and blood believed the worst of her, too.

Normally, Anna Beth would've snapped back to defend herself. But that wasn't what Ian wanted. Being here was a way of honoring him and she loved him too much not to try. She pasted a painful smile on her lips, reminding herself of how happy it would've made Ian to see her with her aunt.

Even during this awkward exchange.

She could hear his voice even now, encouraging her. *It's a start, honey. It takes time to heal old wounds.*

Ian the optimist.

"I've never really cared about what people thought of me,

but I understand your concern."Wanting to change the subject, she pointed towards the edge of the room. "By the way, when did you get the china hutch? It's beautiful."

Sarah glanced at the edge of the living room where a robin's egg blue cabinet sat. "Three years. I needed a place to hold my special occasion dishes. I finally pulled them out of storage and decided to display them. It doesn't make sense to own something so beautiful and hide it away."

"Especially since I wasn't here to destroy everything anymore."

Anna Beth meant it as self-deprecating, but could tell by her aunt's expression she hadn't taken it that way.

"I know I wasn't always the kindest to you. There are many things I wish I could take back. I suppose I have my own amends to make."

Anna Beth had a feeling if she kept blathering on, everything she said would be misconstrued. Although it soothed Anna Beth that her aunt genuinely felt remorse for the lack of compassion she'd displayed while Anna Beth was growing up, she hadn't come here to make her aunt feel remorseful.

She was beyond ready to head to the hotel room and spend the rest of the evening with a bottle of wine, but that was no longer in the cards.

Sarah poured Anna Beth a cup of tea and held it out to her. "If you really want to begin anew, a good start would be to cancel that reservation and stay here. We are family; if you are staying in Snowy Springs, then you should be with me."

What could Anna Beth say to that? If she argued, it would just cause more friction and be counterproductive.

She raised her teacup and held it up with a nod of her head. "You're absolutely right. I'll pick up my luggage and come back. I will probably need to find a quiet place to work, though."

"Are you still writing for that television show?"

"No, I left when my contract came up."

Sarah reached across the table and patted her hand sympathetically. "That show was a grotesque bit of fluffery. You're better off."

It was slightly condescending, but it seemed as though her aunt was trying. Though *The Darcy's* writer's room toxicity had left Anna Beth never wanting to work on another TV show, she'd learned a lot in the two years she'd written for it.

"Thanks. I wasn't happy there, so it all worked out."

"Are you writing for another show?" Sarah asked.

"Actually, I'm developing my own screenplay."

"Good for you. What is it about?"

"It follows a blended family that falls apart when the matriarch dies and how they come back together." Anna Beth took another sip of her tea, a sheepish smile on her lips. "A major departure from fart jokes and innuendos."

Sarah retrieved her cup once more. "I'm proud of you. You deserve to work on your own ideas instead of someone else's. Despite our struggles, I always knew you were smart and talented."

Surprised, Anna Beth stuttered, "Th-thank you."

"Although, it sounds awfully dark. I hope that the family at least gets a happy ending."

Anna Beth blinked. "I'm not sure yet. Happy endings aren't realistic." She knew from experience, since Anna Beth lost the man she loved at twenty-five.

Her aunt clicked her tongue. "Yes, but people watch movies to be entertained, not depressed."

Anna Beth bit the inside of her cheek. The screenplay wasn't depressing. Emotional and ultimately uplifting, absolutely. Gut wrenching moments, sure. Just because it wasn't going to be a bit of holiday fluff sprinkled with candy canes and glitter, didn't mean it wouldn't be entertaining.

"I'm only a quarter of the way in, so we will see how it goes."

"I am sure it will be wonderful and I don't want to discourage you. I just thought I'd give you my opinion as a consumer."

"I appreciate it," Anna Beth lied.

"On a happier note," Sarah said, while pouring herself some more tea, "you don't have to worry about finding a quiet place to write. Between working at the police station part-time and helping at the community center, I'm hardly home. You'll have the place to yourself."

"What are you doing for the Snowy Springs PD?"

Her aunt's face twitched, which was as close to she'd ever come to smiling. "I run the front office. After you left, I found myself at a loss, being here alone, and they needed someone to answer phones and do paperwork a few days a week. It's a win-win."

Anna Beth couldn't believe it. Growing up, her aunt had enjoyed various clubs and charity work, but the majority of the time, she preferred to avoid the public.

Could someone really have such a major personality progression without aliens or robots being involved?

You've spent way too much time in Hollywood.

"That's great. I'm happy for you."

"Yes, I've even grown fond of that young man who used to sneak into your window at night when you thought I was asleep."

Anna Beth choked on her tea. "Jared? Jared works at the police station?"

"He's an officer now." Anna Beth's mouth dropped and her aunt shook her head. "Close your mouth, dear. I know it's a surprise. I expected him to go the other way, but he's really made something of himself. He bought a house off River Road a few months ago and has done a wonderful job renovating it, all on his own. You should see the before and after pictures. Extraordinary."

Anna Beth's mind raced. Jared was a police officer? He owned a house? Was he married? Kids? She didn't dare ask. It would make her seem invested. She'd let Jared walk out of her life years ago. It didn't make sense for her to care about his life now.

"Anna Beth?" Her aunt watched her curiously and she cleared her throat.

"I'm listening."

"Have I said something to upset you?"

"No, I'm fine. I just...I guess I assumed Jared would have left town."

Her aunt's green eyes narrowed. "There is a lot Snowy Springs has to offer. It's not glitzy and glamorous, but we have a community here that cares. For many, that's enough."

Anna Beth knew that. As far as small towns went, she could have done worse.

She'd spent her adolescence going with her aunt to various charity functions. She'd helped prepare holiday dinners for families who couldn't afford them and wrapped toys for the Angel Tree project. Her aunt taught Anna Beth how to sew so she could assist the women's auxiliary with repurposing donated clothes into stuffed animals. It's how she met Jared in the first place. She'd been helping her aunt at a clothing swap when Jared came in with a woman and her four kids. He was wearing pants several inches too short for his gangly legs, a winter coat with a gaping hole in the side, and his brown hair in desperate need of a cut. Yet, Anna Beth's eleven-year-old heart still skipped a beat the moment she saw him.

Before Anna Beth could stop herself, she'd blurted, "*I can sew that for you.*"

He swung his angry brown eyes her way, piercing Anna Beth with a scowl. "*Who are you? The sewing fairy.*"

As dreamy as his outside was, she hadn't been a fan of his rudeness. "*No, smart mouth, I'm just being nice to your ungrateful butt.*"

"*Ungrateful butt, huh? I've been called worse.*" His twelve-year-old face split into a wide grin and he shrugged out of his coat. "*How long will it take?*"

Anna Beth took the jacket from him, examining the tear. "*Give me fifteen minutes.*"

She'd sat down with his coat in her lap and pulled a needle and thread from her craft bag. It hadn't taken Anna Beth long to stitch up the coat and when his family came back to make their exchanges, she'd handed him his jacket with a smile. He'd examined it in awe and to her surprise, he'd held out a tiny wooden bear to her.

"*Payment for you fixing my coat. And my mom said you could come to our house for dinner. If you want.*"

It was the first invitation she'd received since moving in with her aunt and she'd responded enthusiastically. "*I'd love to.*"

Sarah sighed loudly, jerking Anna Beth from her memories. "Anna Beth? You haven't changed a bit. Your mind drifts faster than the snow."

She shook her head with a laugh. "Sorry, I always have dozens of thoughts rolling around in here." Anna Beth stood, smoothing down her gray cable knit sweater. "I should probably get going anyway. I don't want Ernie at The Peaks to be upset with me for bogarting one of his rooms for too long."

"Ernie Michaelson is a pussy cat," her aunt said fondly. "I'm sure he'll be fine with it."

The familiar way Sarah spoke of the hotel owner gave her pause. "You know Ernie?"

Sarah's cheeks turned a brilliant shade of red. "Of course, I know him. We went to high school together. We've lived in the same town for fifty years." She stood abruptly and took Anna Beth's tea cup from the coffee table. "Go, get your errands done, and I'll make up your old room. No need to worry about a thing."

"Sure, Sarah." She watched her aunt bustle out of the room with the tea tray and she shook her head. The relaxed energy surrounding her aunt had to come from somewhere.

Maybe she'd started yoga?

Three

Jared sat in his cruiser off the Snowy Springs Highway, watching the snowflakes fall on his windshield. He hadn't seen another car for over thirty minutes. Most likely because they were expecting eight inches of snow tonight. He'd hoped to get at least one speedster, but it seemed like a quiet one.

He wasn't a fan of slow nights. They always took a turn.

His radio crackled. "Officer Cross, this is dispatch, over."

He pushed the button on his radio. "Hey Margo, it's Cross. What do we have?"

"Mr. Salvatore just called. He caught a couple of shoplifters trying to make it out the door with a cart full of beer."

Jared chuckled. "Typical Friday night shenanigans. Does he want me to come down there and scare the snot out of them?"

"Actually, he wanted to give you a heads up. One of the kids is Casey. Thought you'd want to handle it."

Jared's jaw hardened. "Thanks, Margo. I got it."

"Ten-four."

Jared released a heavy sigh as he twisted the key in the ignition. Over the years, his foster parents had taken in dozens of kids. Some, like him, aged out, but still considered the Jeffries' four-bedroom house their home. Others had gone back to their biological parents or been removed from the Jeffries for various reasons. Casey Harlow was the Jeffries' last foster child. They'd had him for five years and, although he'd been a good kid for the most part, Casey's attitude took a massive turn several months ago. This was the third time Jared had gotten a call to bail him out of a jam. The first time, he'd been caught smoking pot after school. The last time, he'd gone paintballing houses and cars around town. Now, stealing from the local grocery store? Jared tried to keep things under wraps for Karen, but maybe it was time to loop his mom in on everything.

In all honesty, he'd wanted to save her the headache as much as shelter Casey from the trouble. Social Services placed Jared with the Jeffries when he was eight years old and they'd been his only foster home. Most kids went through at least five of them, but Karen was an old hat with traumatized kids. Her husband, Mike, owned a trucking company and drove an eighteen-wheeler, so he wasn't home much but when he was, he'd always been willing to toss a ball around or play video games. Other families would have called Mike the fun parent.

Jared didn't remember much about his birth mother, and the memories he did have were better left alone.

Karen tried to be everything Jared needed after his mom left him at a neighbor's and never returned. He'd been a challenge at first, but Karen hadn't given up on him. Even when the principal called her in because he'd gotten into another fight, she'd ask Jared what happened as though she might actually believe him when he told her the truth. Jared never started the fights, but he wasn't afraid to finish them. It was comforting to have someone give you the benefit of the doubt when most adults, upon hearing the words *foster kid*, automatically thought you were the cause of the trouble.

Of course, at twelve he'd gone through a rebellious stage. He never wanted a haircut. He loved this old coat he'd found at a yard sale that was two sizes too big and had a hole in the side. And he shot up several inches that winter, outgrowing all his new clothes by December.

If he hadn't been such a pain in the ass, he'd have never met Anna Beth that day at the clothing exchange.

He'd never been friends with a girl before, besides his sisters, but Anna Beth's sweet personality combined with her smart mouth drew him in. His behavior even improved once they started hanging out. Probably why Karen liked Anna Beth so much.

Karen and Mike offered to adopt him but, by the time they'd jumped through every hoop to make him legally available, he'd been fourteen. He'd convinced them that if he stayed in the system, they'd continue getting state money and he'd be able to take advantage of special grants and education programs. Besides, he hadn't needed a piece of paper to know who his family was.

On his high school graduation night, Karen presented him with a savings account she'd been depositing the state checks into and letting the interest accrue to pay for his education. She taught him to budget while he was in college, then invest what money remained. While most adults his age were drowning in debt, he wasn't, thanks to everything she taught him.

He owed Karen so much for being a selfless and amazing mother. She'd been dealing with a lot because of Mike's prostate cancer scare this year and, although he was out of the woods now, they'd been through hell the last few months. Knocking some sense into his punk ass little brother seemed like the least he could do.

Jared parked right next to a cherry red classic Chrysler.

Son of a bitch.

Anna Beth. She was inside the market. What would he say? What was the likelihood of avoiding her in such a small space? Minuscule.

"Hi, A.B., how've you been? Sorry about being a douche on your wedding day and not talking to you for five years. Mint?"

God, he wasn't ready for this.

Despite the thirty-degree weather outside, he wiped his sweaty palms on his pants before slipping on his winter gloves. He couldn't avoid her forever, especially if she was back in town for good. He grabbed his jacket and climbed out, locking the car behind him. He shrugged into the black police coat as he crossed the parking lot and stepped through the electric doors of Snowy Springs Market and Deli. His gaze scanned the front lobby, but there was no Anna Beth.

Maybe he'd actually make it out of here without having to face her so soon.

He caught sight of Henry Salvatore ringing up groceries for Tammy Cain. Tammy waved at him as he approached, her jingle bell necklace ringing when she moved. Tammy was what people called "extra." In her early forties, she never passed up a piece of jewelry or an article of clothing if it sparkled. From the top of her glittery blonde mohawk to her silver snow boots, Tammy's outfits were always eye-catching and it worked for her.

"Hey, Jared. Whatchu up to?"

Jared winked. "Got a complaint about someone being too fabulous and you're my prime suspect."

Tammy's blue eyes twinkled and she held her wrists out to him. "Oh, does that mean you're going to use the cuffs on me?"

"If you give me any trouble, you bet."

In a southern accent, Tammy said, "I do declare, Officer Cross, you've made me blush."

"Then my work here is done."

"Not quite," Henry said. He placed the last of Tammy's items in the bag and tapped a few keys on the register. "Your total is forty-two dollars and fifty-three cents. If you can stop flirting with Officer Cross, that is."

Tammy laughed. "Don't be jealous, Henry. You're still my favorite grocer."

Henry took her money, fighting a grin. "Oh good. I was worried."

"Unfortunately, neither of you can compare to the knight in shining armor I have waiting for me out in the car." Tammy's husband, Nick Cain, was her polar opposite. A camo-wearing introvert who preferred hunting in the woods to hanging with people, while Tammy adored attention and beautiful things. Somehow, they made it work, which should be inspirational for anyone.

"Nick's a lucky guy," Jared said.

"'Course he is." She picked up her bag and hefted it onto one curvy hip. "You gentleman take care."

"Have a good night, Tammy," Henry called after her. When she was out of sight, the older man faced Jared with a frown. "I guess you want your brother?"

"I'll take them all, if you need me to."

Henry pulled his keys out of his pocket. "I've already called

Devon and Finn's parents. They should be here soon. I was going to call Karen, but I didn't want to put any undue stress on her with everything else going on."

Living in Snowy Springs was both a blessing and a curse. On one hand, everyone knew everyone else's business and the whole town helped out the Jeffries whenever they could.

On the other hand, no one could keep a secret either.

Jared nodded. "I appreciate that."

Henry heaved his short, round frame from behind the register and opened the door to his front office. He glared at someone out of Jared's sight.

"Your brother's here to get you. Do not come back into my store unless you're with your mother."

"My mother's dead, asshole."

Jared recognized Casey's voice and clenched his jaw. The teen walked past Henry and stopped in front of Jared. His curly brown head barely reached Jared's shoulder and he glared up at him with defiant brown eyes.

"Well? Let's go."

When Casey started for the door, Jared grabbed him by the back of his hoodie. "Not until you apologize to Mr. Salvatore."

"For what?"

"Stealing from him? Calling him an asshole? Take your pick."

Casey scoffed, "This is such bullshit."

Jared took Casey's shoulders in his hands and glared down at him. "Say it, or I'm calling Mom."

"Call Karen. Tell her I said hi."

Jared turned his brother around and before he could get a reign on his temper, he jerked him toward the exit.

"Henry, call my mom and let her know to meet us at the station."

"You're seriously arresting me because I won't apologize?"

"No. I'm not arresting you...yet. But if you keep mouthing off, I may be tempted."

"Blow me, Officer Douchebag."

"Let's go." Jared headed for the exit with his brother dragging his feet. He caught a flash of blonde hair out of the corner of his eye and nearly stumbled. Green eyes held his as Anna Beth stood alongside the book rack, clutching a paperback with a Christmas tree on the front.

Time slowed as he passed her, taking in every change to her face, her body.

Then she smiled, that sweet, shy lifting of her lips. It used to drive him crazy.

Still did, if his racing heart could testify.

"Hi, Jared," she said.

Her breathless whisper rushed over him like a summer breeze. God, had her voice always been that husky?

His tongue swelled. He couldn't speak. So many things came to mind, every scenario he'd ever imagined, but nothing made it past his lips except...

"Ma'am."

Her eyes widened for a moment. Then, without another word, she turned away from him and set the book in her cart. She probably thought he deliberately pretended not to know her, but that wasn't the case. His brain couldn't keep up with his mouth.

He would have called out to her, but Casey chose that moment to break out into loud guffaws. The world went back to it's normal speed and Jared cursed himself for being caught off guard.

"Smooth moves."

"Shut up." Jared pushed a laughing Casey out the door,

wishing he could strangle the obnoxious punk. If he hadn't been so keyed up by his foster brother's behavior, he'd have been prepared for running into Anna Beth.

She'd looked good too. Damn it. Same shimmering hair and smooth skin. She'd put on some weight since he'd last seen her, but it only made her sexier. Curvier. More grown up.

"So, who's the hottie?"

"Knock it off, Casey."

"Seriously, is she an old girlfriend or something?" Casey snickered. "You called her ma'am, but the way she looked at you makes me think you might actually have balls. Congratulations."

Jared leaned him against the cruiser as he opened the door. "You are this close to spending the night in the tank."

"Yeah, right."

"Keep running your mouth and see."

The kid snapped his mouth closed. Jared helped him into the back seat and closed the door behind him.

"This back seat is cramped."

"It's a three-minute drive. You'll live."

"Police brutality."

Jared climbed into the front and buckled his seat belt. "Trust me, Case. This little trip to the station will be a cake walk compared to what will happen the next time you get into trouble."

"Oh, scary."

Jared caught his brother's gaze in the mirror. "You keep going the way you are and it will be. You do not want to end up in a juvenile center or prison, do you?"

He looked away. "Why do you even care? You're not really my brother."

"Close enough. We don't have to be blood to be family."

"I am so sick of that crap. You barely know me and just

because you're one of Karen and Mike's golden children, doesn't mean you're anything to me."

Jared glanced at the sullen kid in his rear-view mirror and tried again. "You know—"

"I'm done talking."

Jared sighed. *It's not shaping up to be a good week.*

"Alrighty then."

He backed out of the parking spot and watched Anna Beth's Chrysler disappear in his rearview mirror. Of all the ways for their reunion to go, it could have been worse.

Or so he told himself.

Four

Ma'am? Five years without so much of a "hey, how you doing," and that's all I get?

"Anna Beth?"

She glanced up at her aunt. "Huh?"

The morning light streamed into the kitchen through the French doors, gleaming off the clean dining room table. Anna Beth had come down a few minutes ago, exhausted and grouchy. Her aunt set a plate of food in front of her and started chatting away, but Anna Beth couldn't stop dwelling on her brief encounter with Jared.

"Is there something wrong with the eggs?"

She poked the scrambled eggs with her fork. "No. They're great."

Her aunt sat down across from her, sliding a gorgeous coffee cup toward her. "Then please stop stabbing them. You're going to scratch my plate."

Anna Beth set the fork down next to her plate and picked up the cup of creamy coffee with a sheepish grin. "Sorry, Sarah. I was lost in thought."

"So it would seem. What's on your mind?"

"Just a little writer's block. It'll pass."

"I'm sure it will." Sarah scooped up a bite of eggs with her fork, holding it in front of her as she asked, "Did you sleep well?"

"Like the dead." Being back in her old room hadn't been as weird as she'd thought it would be. If only her brain had shut up long enough for her to enjoy the soft mattress and cozy bedding. "You know how I love flannel sheets. I haven't used any in years. It doesn't get cold enough in LA."

"I imagine it doesn't." Her aunt took a sip of her green tea. Sarah wasn't a fan of coffee and vehemently disapproved when Anna Beth started drinking it junior year of high school.

"I'm surprised you still keep coffee in the house."

Sarah's cheeks reddened. "I have a friend who takes it the same way you do?"

"Which friend?"

"Just a friend."

Anna Beth quirked a brow. Did her aunt have a boyfriend? Preposterous as it may seem, she *was* being cagey.

"What are your plans for today?" Sarah asked, changing the subject.

"I'm going to take a shower and get dressed. Work a bit. Then I'm not sure."

"Well, I'm headed to work for a few hours this morning and then I'll be making stockings at the community center this afternoon if you want to help out. I am sure everyone would like to see you."

Back to a large room full of middle-aged women and the hum of sewing machines?

"I'll see where the day takes me."

"Alright." Sarah stood up and poured her tea into a silver travel cup she'd taken out of the cupboard. It was so ordinary and not at all something she'd ever imagined Sarah using.

"I'm heading out. We will be at the community center until five and then we're going out for dinner."

"We?" Anna Beth prodded.

"Yes, the fundraising committee."

"Of course."

Sarah stood in the doorway, seemingly at a loss for words. "I just...I wanted to say how glad I am you decided to stay."

"Me, too."

Anna Beth meant it. Other than a little awkwardness in the beginning, she enjoyed this softer version of her aunt. She seemed happier. More relaxed.

"Good. I'm off then. Don't hide here all day."

Anna Beth waved. "I won't."

When the front door closed, Anna Beth took another sip of her coffee. The rich, warm brew slid down her throat and settled into her stomach. She stared out the back door as several birds feasted at the large bird feeder hanging from the porch ceiling. It was amazing what you witnessed in the quiet of the morning. Ian had never been a morning person. He used to stumble down after nine like a zombie, giving her loud kisses until she would squeal with laughter.

December twenty-eighth would mark a year since his death, but in all honesty, he'd been a different person long before that.

He would have been thirty last month. Instead of spending the evening celebrating it with a party, she'd flown overseas with Ian's ashes and dispersed them in his favorite spot overlooking the ocean. Then, she'd spent Ian's birthday reminiscing his too-short life in the Irish Pub his best friend owned.

Picking up her coffee cup, Anna Beth headed back up the stairs to her room. She swallowed, her throat clogged with emotion. God, she missed him.

Last night, she'd been shocked to find her room relatively untouched since she left for college. She'd come back for a few school breaks and then her wedding, but stepping into it after five years was like taking a ride in the DeLorean. The pink glittery cork board above the full bed with its collage of pictures, detailing her life from age eleven to eighteen. Seven years of pictures with Jared next to her, smiling, in ninety percent of them.

She set her cup down on her nightstand and pulled her computer bag off the hope chest at the foot of the bed. As a teenager, she'd never imagined her life this way. At eighteen, she'd gone off to college hoping Jared would show up one day and tell her he loved her. Like they were starring in their own sappy rom-com. She'd throw herself into his arms and confess her affection, they'd graduate from college, get married, and then live happily ever after in Snowy Springs.

Instead, she'd met Ian in her philosophy class. Incredibly selfless and giving, even to strangers, he'd swept her off her feet with his honest charm, and she'd fallen harder for him every day.

Anna Beth studied the pictures of her and Jared again. She still thought about what happened on her wedding day from time to time, wondered what her life would've been like if she'd made a different decision. When the bridal suite door opened, she'd turned, expecting her aunt.

Instead, Jared stood in front of her in his best suit. He opened and closed his mouth several times.

"*You look beautiful, A.B.*"

The way his brown eyes traveled from her face down to

her toes, left her breathless. He'd never looked at her that way before.

"Thanks."

He took another step toward her, sweat beading on his forehead and she remembered the way her heart leaped in her chest.

"Jared? What's up? You look like you're going to hurl."

"No, I'm just..." He sucked in a breath and smiled nervously. "I love you."

Anna Beth gave him a puzzled smile. "I love you, too."

Jared shook his head. "No, Anna Beth. I love you. I wish I'd said something sooner. I love you, like I want you to take my hand and run out that door with me. I love you, as in I want to spend the rest of my life with you."

Tears stung her eyes, spilling over onto her cheeks. For years, she'd imagined that moment. Of being with Jared. Taking their friendship to the next level. Holding his hand. Kissing him. But...this was the moment he'd chosen to tell her?

She swiped at her cheeks. She'd spent years pining for Jared, wishing he'd make a move. Say something.

But on her freaking wedding day?

Her temper flared to life, her fists clenching. "How dare you?"

"What?"

"You come in here, on my wedding day, to bare your soul? You've had years to tell me how you feel. You pick today?"

"Better late than never?" It was a lame attempt at humor she did not appreciate. "I figured since you haven't taken your vows yet, I needed to tell you before it was too late."

"It was too late the moment I met Ian. This isn't a movie, Jared. If you'd told me how you felt before, maybe things would be different, but I'm in love with Ian. He's the man I want."

She'd never forget the pain on Jared's face as he turned

and walked out the door without another word. It had taken everything in her not to chase after him, but what good would it have done? She'd chosen Ian and Jared made the choice to walk out of her life. So many times, she'd thought about calling him, but she had no idea what to say to mend their broken friendship.

She didn't regret marrying Ian. She'd loved him. She still did.

Anna Beth pulled her laptop out of the bag and Ian's journal fell to the floor with a slap. She set her computer aside and picked up the leather-bound book. She flipped it open, smiling as her gaze scanned the first page.

There was a doodle of two people hugging, a red heart above their heads. At the bottom, he'd written their names.

For Anna. Please read it and check each item off as you complete them. I promise I'm not just making you do crazy shit every month for the fun of it. Well, maybe for my entertainment. Ghosts gotta get their rocks off some way. I love you.

Her hand skimmed over where he'd signed his name, a tear falling on the page. Ian had always been dramatic and goofy. Even as his illness progressed, he still seemed so full of life and in good humor.

His first seizure occurred on their two-year wedding anniversary. They'd been out to dinner, laughing about his nearly raw steak. He'd been making the hunk of meat *moo* and she bent over to catch her breath. When she'd straightened up, Ian fell to the floor, convulsing. She'd never forget the terror of seeing her vibrant husband curled on his side, shaking with the aftershocks.

Dozens of tests and several weeks later, the doctor diagnosed Ian with a fast-growing brain tumor, in the middle of his frontal lobe. The minute he'd heard cancer, Ian lost the spark that made people flock to him. She'd jumped into research mode, asking the doctor questions about their next steps and, when he'd suggested surgery, Ian protested.

"I want to stay me, An. What if they cut into my brain and I come out a vegetable?"

"What if they get it all? What if the medication works and you live another eighty years?"

"It's in my genetics, baby. My dad had a brain tumor. Mom's moved so fast there was nothing they could do for her. The doctor said, even with surgery and radiation, there's a good chance it will come back. I don't want to be sick for years just to buy us a few months. I want to enjoy every second I have left with you."

Still, for two years he'd seen every specialist she'd found, but by the time he finally agreed to surgery, the tumor was too invasive to remove. They told Ian he had a year, three if they were lucky.

Anna Beth lost it. She'd railed against him for being so stubborn, screaming and cursing in the middle of the hospital room like a banshee.

And he'd let her do it, lying in his hospital bed with gauze wrapped around his head. He sat there listening patiently and, at the end of her tirade, her body wracked with sobs, he held out his arms to her and she climbed up onto the bed next to him.

It wasn't long after, he'd started writing in the journal, and although she'd been curious about what he wrote, Anna Beth never invaded his privacy.

When their attorney went over Ian's will, and handed her the leather-bound book, she realized it was so much more.

She flipped through the pages of lists, a different one for every month, and she'd crossed off nearly every item. In between the lists were letters, explaining each list, even the most bizarre tasks.

Ian left her one hundred and eighty tasks. She now had fourteen items left to finish.

Then she could read his final letter.

Taped to the inside of the back cover was an envelope with Ian's blocky script.

Anna Beth: Open Upon Completion of the Last List.

She went back to her final list and groaned.

1. *Mend fences with your aunt.*

She'd been here a little over twenty-four hours and, after breakfast this morning, Anna Beth crossed that one off the list. She and her aunt were well on their way to a reconciliation. Anna Beth studied the next item on the list:

2. *Deliver Christmas gifts to the local hospital... dressed as The Grinch.*

Ian's favorite movie. They'd watch every version at least a dozen times during the holiday season. She wasn't quite ready for that one yet.

Her finger slid down the list, stopping on number eight:

8. *Visit an old friend.*

Jared flashed through her mind. That one didn't seem likely to happen. Avoiding Jared was probably best for both of them.

Three weeks in a small town...How hard could it be?

Besides, she had someone else in mind.

Five

Jared opened the doors to Foam Capped Java a little after ten, the bells above jingling over the hum of the crowded coffee shop. While he really wanted to go home and get some sleep, he'd promised to help his mom do some Christmas shopping this morning. At least he had tonight off to recuperate.

He spotted his mom in line and walked up, sliding an arm around her shoulders to give her a hug. She turned her head and her round face split into a broad grin.

"Sorry I'm late."

"That's okay. I just got here a few minutes ago myself." She waved her hand towards the line. "They're hopping today."

"Always are on Saturday mornings. Where's Casey?"

"Mike is keeping him busy. He finally has his strength back, so he's catching up on log reindeer and snowmen orders. You know how your dad loves to create things."

Jared frowned. "He shouldn't be lifting anything. Are you

sure Casey will actually help and not just sit around like a lazy little shit?"

She poked his side. "Hey, now. Watch your mouth. I know you two aren't on the best of terms, but Casey processes grief differently that you or me. Mike retired right before social services placed him with us and they're very close. It was hard for him when Mike got sick, especially after losing his mom. I'm not saying I condone his behavior, but he's a good boy. We just need to be patient."

Jared released a deep breath. "I know the kid had it rough, but he called Mr. Salvatore an asshole."

"Which we'll deal with." She pinned him with a pointed look. "If you'd told me about the trouble to begin with, we could've handled this sooner."

"I didn't want to add to your stress."

Karen gave him a hug. "I'm a parent, sweetheart. It's all stress. I worry about you constantly."

"Why?"

"Your work. Snowy Springs may be small, but I'm still concerned you'll pull over the wrong car one night."

"I'll be fine."

"Your love life is also concerning...all the girls you're dating." His mom clucked her tongue disapprovingly. "You should really find a nice girl and not do all this bed hopping."

Jared groaned. "I'm not hopping anywhere and besides, I'm twenty-seven. I'm supposed to take my time and see what's out there and not have my mom chiding me for it."

"Well, I go to church with the mothers of those women you're seeing."

The line finally moved and he took a step forward. "What does that mean?"

"It means, I hear about whose heart you're breaking."

"For the love of…I'm not breaking hearts. I go out with a girl to see if we click and if we don't, I move on." Jared shook his head. "I need to get out of this town. It's absurd people can't seem to mind their own business."

"Oh, stop being so dramatic. You're quite the catch. Any girl would be devastated to lose you."

They reached the counter and Olive Waters greeted them with a sunny smile. "Hi, Karen. Jared. What can I do you for?"

"Hi, Olive. You wanna go out with my son? He's still single."

Jared glared at his mom until Olive started laughing. "What's funny?"

"The thought of actually dating you. He's pretty, Karen, but I remember when he used to wipe his boogers on the monkey bars."

Karen turned his way in horror. "Jared Tyler!"

"I did not!"

Olive scrunched up her nose. "Pretty sure you did. The image is seared into my brain."

Jared shook his head. Olive had been a year behind him in school and when Anna Beth had moved to Snowy Springs, she and Olive became best friends. Because of Anna Beth, Jared and Olive spent a lot of time together in middle school and high school, but as adults, they didn't run in the same crowd.

"Can I get a large coffee with room for cream, and fewer embarrassing lies being spread about me?" Jared asked.

"Not a lie, but I can still get your drink. How about you, Karen?"

"A medium coffee, black."

"I love you, but you're boring."

Karen laughed. "And you're mouthy! I'm going to tell your mama when I see her later."

"Where do you think I get it from?" Olive tapped the register. "Alright, that will be five-thirty-eight."

The bells on the door jingled behind them and Olive squealed. Jared jumped a foot in the air as she took off around the counter and through the shop. He turned around to follow her movements and time slowed the same as when he'd seen Anna Beth at the market.

Anna Beth stood in the doorway, her face beaming. Olive launched herself into Anna Beth's arms and the two women danced in a circle.

Olive pulled back and grabbed Anna Beth's shoulders in her hands, shaking her. "What took you so long? I heard you were in town yesterday and I didn't get a phone call."

"I wanted to surprise you, but I should have known someone would spill the beans."

Their excited voices carried from the front door to the register, and Jake caught himself staring. Anna Beth's happiness shone in every feature. From her eyebrows to her lush pink lips and he couldn't help admiring her.

Karen pinched Jared's arm, drawing his attention away from the two friends. "You didn't tell me Anna Beth was back."

"Sorry, I forgot."

His mom sent him a disbelieving look, but Jared ignored it. He'd never told anyone, not even Vance or Karen, about what he'd done on Anna Beth's wedding day. Partly because he hadn't wanted to talk about it, but mostly, he knew they'd agree he'd been a romantic idiot.

Olive let Anna Beth go, backing away slowly. "Do not move. Let me clear this line and I am yours."

"Sounds good."

Olive came back around the counter, smiling sheepishly. "Sorry about that, guys."

"I understand. As soon as I pay, I'm going to go hug her myself," Karen said.

"I haven't seen her in a year."

Karen shook her head. "It's been longer for me. Not since a few days after her wedding, I think."

Jared wished he could disappear out the door without anyone noticing. Karen had always loved Anna Beth and berated him for not asking her out all through high school. If she only knew he'd laid his heart open for Anna Beth and she'd squashed it like a tomato, she'd probably have a few choice words for him about waiting too long. But relationships had never come easy for him, still didn't, which made it hard to open himself up to someone.

Jared held out his debit card to Olive. "I'll pay. You go say hello."

"Thanks, baby." Karen patted his shoulder. "Come over when you finish. I don't know what the two of you fought about, but it really should be water under the bridge by now."

When his mom took off, Olive ran his card, watching him with her left eyebrow arched. "Your mom doesn't know?"

"Know what?"

"That you confessed your love for A.B. on her wedding day, serious rom-com style, with the car still running?"

"That's not how it happened…is that what she said?"

Olive shrugged. "Not exactly. She told me the basics and I let my imagination take it from there."

"It wasn't quite that dramatic."

"Yet, you didn't share with anyone? Not even Vance?"

"No, I never told anyone."

"I see. I wouldn't either, I guess." Olive handed him back his card. "Even if the two of you were destined to be together, you telling her like that wasn't cool. Expecting her to run off with you and break another man's heart? That's just immature."

"Thanks." Jared took the receipt and signed his name with jerky motions.

"Don't forget to tip your barista."

"What happened to tips are accepted, but not expected?" Still, he wrote two dollars on the tip line. He handed her back the receipt and she blew him a kiss.

"This girl needs all the mula she can get."

"Maybe you should be a little less honest with your customers. You may find your tips increase."

"Hey, I call it like I see it. I gotta do me."

He'd forgotten what a pain in the ass Olive could be when she thought she was right.

She is right. Confronting Anna Beth that day and expecting her to choose you was a stupid move. You should have just sat in the back pew and gotten drunk at the open bar during reception on Ian's dime. At least then, you might have stayed friends.

As he crossed to the back of the shop where Karen stood talking animatedly with Anna Beth, his heart beat double time. Bundled up in a blue hooded peacoat with a yellow and blue plaid scarf, she looked so sweetly beautiful his teeth ached. Her blond curls were held back from her face in a ponytail, drawing focus to her rosy cheeks and sparkling green eyes.

"Jared, I was just telling Anna Beth she needs to come over for dinner tonight."

Anna didn't quite meet his eye as she responded, "And I told your mom, I didn't want to impose at the last minute."

"I invited you, silly! It's not an imposition at all, and I'm not taking no for an answer. Tell her, Jared."

"Hi, Anna Beth." There was no staying out of the conversation now. "You might as well say yes. Unless you've forgotten how stubborn she can be."

Her gaze finally met his. Before her wedding, he would have greeted her with his arms wide open and she would have jumped into them or burrowed herself against him, but they weren't kids anymore. They were adults and virtual strangers, so he kept his hands at his side.

Her lush mouth twitched. "Oh, so you didn't forget my name? I thought I was *ma'am* now."

"What's this?" Karen asked.

"Nothing," he said.

"Hmmm mmm, sounds like it." Karen cupped Anna Beth's cheeks. "Come by the house at six, alright? It is so good to have you back, baby."

Anna Beth's eyes shimmered. "Thank you, Karen."

Olive called out his name and before he could make his escape, his mom hurried to grab the cups. An awkward silence fell between the two of them amid the bustle of the coffee shop.

Anna Beth spoke first. "If you don't want me to come to dinner, I can make an excuse."

Jared shook his head. "No, she's excited to have you. I can skip it, if me being there makes you uncomfortable."

"Not at all. I'm fine."

Exactly how he felt. F.I.N.E.

Fucked up. Insecure. Neurotic. Emotional.

Six

Anna Beth followed Olive out of Foam Capped Java ten minutes later, a peppermint mocha in one hand, arms linked with her friend. They headed down Main Street, Olive's black, puffy coat rasping against Anna Beth's wool blend peacoat. For the first time since her return, she felt completely at ease and all the tension drained from her body.

"I am so happy you're back! I've missed your face."

Anna Beth squeezed her arm. "I've missed you, too. A year is too long between visits."

"I know. I'm a terrible friend," Olive said.

"No, you aren't. We've both been preoccupied. Will your boss be upset that you took off like that?"

"Nah, Sierra came in, so we should be good. I was just filling in today, anyway. I only work Mondays and Wednesdays to help out, but Sierra had car trouble. Every other day is spent taking pictures of adorable newborns and families."

"And your pictures are beautiful." While Anna Beth headed to California to major in screenwriting, Olive stayed closer to home to study photography. She'd always had an amazing eye, even with a cell phone camera.

"Thanks, doll. It's hard to make a living with so many people doing it as a hobby. The good news is, I have over sixty-thousand followers on Instagram and I've been selling my pictures on various stock photo sites. Every little bit helps us starving artists."

Anna Beth chuckled. "I've hardly posted on the Gram at all this year. Nothing good to post."

"I don't blame you. You've had a lot going on." Olive hugged her close, squishing their faces together. Olive was only an inch taller than Anna Beth with dark hair and blue eyes. Anna Beth adored Olive since she'd sat beside her on the bus her first day at Snowy Springs Intermediate. Despite the distance between them as adults, when they were together, they never missed a beat.

"How are you doing, by the way?" Olive asked.

"Me? I'm fine. Just plugging along."

"I mean, really. I know you miss him."

A lump formed in Anna Beth's throat. "Every minute of every day."

Olive took her hand. "I'm so sorry."

"Thanks. We had a nice celebration of life the year before he passed. Ian insisted on attending his own funeral, so to speak. A bunch of his friends flew in and they roasted him pretty good." Anna Beth signed. "I miss his laugh. The way he could get me out of a bad mood with one corny joke." She blinked rapidly, keeping the tears at bay. "Let's change the subject."

"Sure. How is the writing going?"

"You know, slow. Who knew writing could be so hard?"

Olive took her arm once more as they rounded the corner onto 2nd Avenue. "Shakespeare? Dickens? Austen? I'm pretty sure they all wanted to throw in the towel at one time or another. Just remember that you are one badass writer and you're gonna hit the big time sooner or later."

"See, I should record you saying that and replay it when I need a boost."

"Record away, boo. Now, what about Ian's lists? Is that why you're back? Tell me everything."

"Not much has changed since we talked a few weeks ago. I'm down to the last thirteen items on my list. Nope," she said, realizing that her meeting with Olive took another off the list. "Make that twelve."

"Okay then. Let's get real, here. What is it like seeing Jared again?"

Anna Beth laughed weakly. "In a word? Rough."

"I figured. Has he said anything to you?"

"Besides calling me *ma'am* and an awkward exchange where we both offered to skip dinner at his mom's house but ultimately decided we could handle it? No, it's been silky smooth."

"Easy, Sassy McAssy. Maybe if we can just get you two alone in a room, you can hash it out. Or let it go and move on."

"I'm not sure it really matters. In three weeks, I'll be out of here and my path will no longer cross with Jared's."

Olive frowned. "Really? You'd give up the snow and country charm for the bright lights of La La Land again? I always figured you lived there because of Ian and work. Can't you write anywhere now that you don't work for *The Darcy's*?"

"I can. Believe me, I do not want to go back to LA. I sold our house, per Ian's instructions, but I'm not sure what's next.

I was thinking I'd try New York. Or maybe Ireland. We have friends there and it's gorgeous."

"You have friends here, too," Olive said softly.

Anna Beth swallowed hard. As much as she loved Olive, she wasn't sure Snowy Springs should be her final destination. Even though things with Sarah were better, there wasn't anyone else besides Olive who'd miss her if she left again.

How did they keep ending up on all the tough subjects?

"Let's talk about you," Anna Beth said. "Seeing anyone?"

Olive smiled like the cat who caught the canary. "I have a casual something-something with Vance, but other than that, nope."

Anna Beth stopped in the middle of the sidewalk. "Wait, Vance Shepard?"

"The very one. We're keeping it on the down low though, so shhh."

"But...you hate Vance."

Olive winked. "I don't have to like him to enjoy him, sunshine."

"Seriously? What do the two of you even talk about?"

"We don't talk. That is the beauty of it."

Anna Beth couldn't understand sleeping with someone you didn't care about, but Olive seemed happy. "You couldn't even be in the same room together in high school. You two ripped each other apart every chance you got."

"Now, we just rip each other's clothes off," Olive said, winking. "That is the whole point of casual relationships. We do the deed, he leaves, I grab a pint of ice cream and watch whatever the hell I want. You know why I don't want a man? Because I don't want his action movies gumming up my que."

"So, find someone with similar tastes. You don't like having someone to cuddle with?"

"Not at all. Cuddling makes me hot and grouchy." Olive waved her hand. "I get that being in a relationship worked for you, but some of us enjoy being alone." Anna Beth must have winced because Olive's face fell and she squeezed her arm. "Ah, A.B. I'm sorry. I'm an insensitive prick."

Anna Beth smiled a little too brightly. "You're fine, and you're right. You're young and you should enjoy all the wonders being single in your twenties has to offer. I just want you to find someone worthy of you, instead of sleeping with someone you can't stand just to scratch an itch."

"Vance isn't so bad, now that we've both grown up some. Eventually I will start thinking of a future with someone, but until then, I'm living large. Besides, Vance is an excellent scratcher."

"Gross, no details, thanks." Anna Beth laughed.

"Suit yourself." Olive's expression turned serious. "You know, you can have some fun too. You are single in your twenties. Have you been out with anyone since Ian…passed?"

Anna Beth didn't want to think about dating. After spending months in a writer's room with six men in their late twenties to early thirties, she'd learned a lot about the way men think and she wasn't interested in being a punchline.

She'd dated sporadically through high school, but until Ian, she'd never had a serious relationship. She wasn't quite ready to swipe right yet.

"I'll get there. It's hard to date as a widow. You get the guys who are super creeped out about it and then there are the ones who ask really awkward questions or talk about their dead pets, as if that's somehow the same. I figure, if it happens naturally, fine. But I'm not really interested in actively seeking someone. Not yet."

"I completely understand, but…what about sex?

"If the mood strikes, I've got a rechargeable friend I brought with me."

"You make me feel like a horn-dog."

"You've always been a horn-dog." Anna Beth laughed.

"True. Would you like to change the subject?"

"Yes, please."

They started walking again and Olive piped up, "Have you thought about what you're going to wear to dinner tonight?"

"Jeans and a sweater. It's just the Jeffries. I've been to their house dozens of times."

"That doesn't mean you can't dress up, especially since they haven't seen you in years. I find that if I get pretty from my undies to my jacket, I am in a better frame of mind for whatever life throws at me. More confident. Better conversationalist." Olive snapped her fingers. "I'm taking you into Tammy's place. You're going to love it. She has some little black dresses, but her specialty is bling and pops of color. I got this off the shoulder purple sequin dress at home that makes my chest look huge."

"Your chest is huge."

Olive smirked. "Yes, but the dress really makes them va-va-voom."

"Olive, I packed plenty of clothes. I don't need to shop."

"Yes, you do and do you know why? Because I bet every outfit is serviceable. That's too much *able* in one suitcase. It won't hurt you to look and who knows, the right outfit can do wonders for your libido."

"Oh, good God, you leave my libido alone."

"You'll thank me later." Olive led her down to a storefront window. Tammy's Glitzy Boutique used to be a thrift store until they moved into a bigger space down the street. Glittery, fake snow covered the floor of the window and silver snowflakes hung around three stylish mannequins. One was draped in a slinky, red sequin dress with cute black boots. The second wore a white fuzzy sweater, a green wreath in the center, paired with distressed blue jeans, while the last mannequin stood decked out in an iridescent halter dress and gold heels.

"This is awfully fancy for a small-town store."

"Please! We are freaking fabulous and we need Tammy's. The big cities got nothin' on us."

Olive opened the door to the store and shooed Anna Beth inside. Several women browsed the racks of clothes throughout the store, cheery Christmas music playing overhead.

A woman sporting a blonde mohawk waved from behind the computer and walked over next to Olive, giving her a hug. Her eyes, cheeks, and even her hair were dotted with specks of glitter and she greeted them with a wide, infectious smile on her face.

"Olive, so good to see you. Did you come to check out our new Christmas collection?"

"Yes, but not for me. Do you remember my friend, Anna Beth? Sarah Driver's niece?"

Tammy's blue eyes lit with recognition. "Yes! Oh my goodness! How are you? I haven't seen you since I used to help out down at the community center. Your aunt said you were some hot shot writer in Hollywood! She is so proud of you!"

Anna Beth coughed to hide her surprise. "I'm fine, thanks. How are you? Your shop is lovely."

"Thank you. I love it. Making ladies feel beautiful is what I was meant to do, so I am fabulous."

Olive jumped in. "A.B. needs something to get her sexy back and I told her this was the place."

"You flatter me," Tammy said with a wink. "I'll let you look around while I pull some things. Size twelve?"

"How did you know?" Anna Beth asked.

"It's my job, baby. Now, you just relax. You're in good hands."

"We're actually just looking." Anna Beth ignored Olive's death stare and continued, "As beautiful as your clothing is, I don't really have anywhere to wear them. I'm a homebody."

"You make your own occasion! I never leave my house without looking amazing. But I understand." Tammy winked. "Today we're just testing the waters, but maybe in the near future, you'll take the plunge. When that happens, I'm here for you, girl."

Seven

Jared parked his truck behind Anna Beth's Chrysler on the side of the road. He'd forgotten tonight was supposed to be the family tree trimming party and his parent's driveway was packed with cars from his other foster siblings. He'd thought about telling his mom he couldn't make it to dinner since he'd only had four hours of sleep, but he didn't want to disappoint her.

Besides, he needed to see Anna Beth. Now that he'd run into her several times, he wanted to make amends. Maybe, one day, they could even be friends again.

Hopefully, she could forgive him for putting her in such an uncomfortable situation.

He should have never confessed to Anna Beth on her wedding day, but he'd been consumed with the thought of losing her. In the end, he'd lost her anyway. It was a selfish motivation, and hopefully she could see he'd grown from that scared kid into a man.

The trim around the house was lit up with multi-colored Christmas lights, flashing brightly in the dark. A ginormous blow up Frosty graced the front yard, weaving in the breeze. Jared turned the corner and jumped as an animatronic Santa by the front door moved. The eyes lit up bright blue as it sang *Santa Claus is Coming to Town*, the arms and body twitching as though possessed.

The porch light flipped on, making the Santa even more terrifying in the light, and the door opened as his mom stepped out onto the porch.

"Jared! I thought I heard someone out here."

"Yeah, Santa was coming for me. Where the hell did you get that? It's creepy."

"We ordered him from some Christmas store online. I think he's great!" She stood back, waving her hand for him to enter. "Come in before you freeze your buns off."

Jared bent to kiss her cheek as he passed. The rich smell of fresh-baked bread wafted from the kitchen, causing his mouth to water. "Speaking of buns, what did you make? Smells good."

"Lasagna, a tossed salad and a cream pie for dessert, but Anna Beth came early with this bread she bought. You just pop it in the oven for a half an hour to bake and viola, tasty bread!"

"I can't wait to try it." He slipped out of his coat and hung it up on an empty hook by the door.

"I'm going to head back into the kitchen. Go, say hi to your dad."

"I'll be in to give you a hand in a bit."

She patted his cheek playfully. "Such a sweet boy."

"Now, I feel like a toddler. Thanks."

"It's a mother's job."

His mom disappeared into the kitchen and he headed into the living room. The high vaulted ceiling with two bay windows faced east and, between those windows, stood an eight-foot-tall Noble Fir without lights or ornaments adorning its branches. Perfectly prepared for tonight's activities. His parents took in dozens of foster kids over the years, but they'd only adopted four. Isabel, Savannah, Forrest, and Grayson. Unofficially, he made five.

Isa was two years older than him. After college, she'd taken a job at Mike's trucking company running the office, where she'd met Gil, one of Mike's drivers, and fallen head over heels in love. They'd married five years ago and, along with a very sassy three-year-old niece, Alana, Isa was seven months pregnant with his nephew, Simon.

Savannah, Forrest, and Grayson were biological siblings. Savannah was the eldest at twenty-five, then Forrest at twenty-three, and Grayson rounded out the trio at twenty.

Sometimes they'd get a surprise visit by a former foster sibling, but for the most part, they were the only ones who showed up.

His dad sat in his recliner, watching an action movie with Forrest, Grayson, and Isabel's husband, Gil. His dad lost at least thirty pounds since his diagnosis and even though they'd removed his prostate and labeled him cancer free, he still hadn't quite bounced back.

Mike looked up when Jared put his hand on his shoulder.

"Nice Christmas movie, Pop."

Mike patted Jared's hand. "Hey there. Your mom said I couldn't watch any without her."

"Still only one a night?"

"I can't stay up the way I used to. I barely make it through one."

"I'm the same way, Pop. Don't feel bad." He sent a salute toward the others. "Sup, guys?"

Gil raised his beer to him, while Forrest stood up and gave him a one-armed hug. Several inches shorter than Jared's six-foot three, Forrest made up for the lack of height in breadth, the kind of stocky that genetics played a huge part in and five days at the gym created the rest. Jared spent hours at the gym for years just to put on fifty pounds of muscle.

"How's it going, bro?"

"You know me. Keeping the peace." Jared looked around. "Speaking of peace, where's Casey?"

"He's back in his room," Gil said. "He dashed back there the minute you pulled up."

Mike poked Jared in the side from his sitting position. "Maybe you could go talk to him? Clear the air?"

"I'll see what I can do, Pop."

Grayson looked up from his phone and gave Jared a nod. Although Grayson shared the same blue eyes with Forrest, his build was slight in comparison and his hair a lighter shade of blond with long strands falling into his face.

"Hey, Jared, busted any drug dealers with massive amounts of cash?" Grayson asked.

"Not recently, why?"

"Cause I was hoping you could slip a little money my way to help a poor, starving college student."

Forrest leaned over the arm of the couch and punched Grayson in the shoulder. "Maybe if you actually saved money instead of spending every dime you make, you wouldn't be so broke."

Grayson pushed his hair back behind his ear, glaring at Forrest. "I have needs."

"Get a girlfriend. Then you won't have to fill your life with video games."

"Video games are cheaper."

"Girlfriends have other perks," Forrest said, waggling his eyebrows. "You'd probably have to cut the man bun to get one, though."

Grayson climbed to his feet, and Jared jumped in to defuse the situation. "Speaking of girlfriends, is Megan here?"

Forrest's face lit up at the mention of his longtime girlfriend. "Yeah, she's in the kitchen. She drove so I could have a few beers with you guys. She's awesome like that."

"I rode with you. Can I have a beer?" Grayson asked.

Mike, Jared and Forrest answered at the same time. "No!"

"Just asking, geez," Grayson grumbled as he sat back down.

They drifted into silence for a few moments, watching the television. Jared's gaze bounced around to each of them before chuckling. "Does anyone else find it archaic that all the women are in the kitchen preparing the meal, while the men folk sit out here watching TV?"

All of them stilled, glancing around at each other.

"You don't want to go in there, man. They are plotting," Grayson said.

Forrest nodded in agreement. "I walked in to grab the beers and Isabel was talking about her pregnancy…things I am still too young to hear about."

Gil shrugged. "Your mom said they were fine when I offered."

Jared pinned Mike with an amused stare. "And you? What's your excuse?"

"I was ordered to sit down and stay out of the way. I do what my wife tells me."

Jared laughed. "Well, I'm going to go and check on them. If it gets too hairy, I'll be back."

Grayson grinned. "You just want to see Anna Beth, who is looking fiiiii—ow!" Grayson rubbed the side of his head where Forest smacked him. "What?"

Jared saluted Forest. "Thanks."

"What did I do?" Grayson asked.

Forrest folded his beefy arms over his chest. "You need to learn how to talk about women with respect."

"I'm gonna get in there," Jared said.

Mike took his hand in a firm grasp. "Thanks, son."

Jared warmed at the simple word. Making his parents happy meant the world to him, especially after almost losing Mike.

Jared headed into the kitchen, the sound of women's laughter filling the air. He stood in the doorway, his gaze immediately trained on Anna Beth. She sliced bread at the counter on one of the large cutting boards, laughing at something his sister, Isabel, said. A long blonde braid fell down her back and the red V-neck sweater she wore brought out her rosy cheeks.

When his sister saw him, Isa squealed, "Jared!"

It had been a few weeks since he'd seen her and guilt settled into the pit of his stomach. He needed to make more of an effort to visit, but he was an introvert and preferred staying home on his own than socializing with anyone, even his family.

Anna Beth glanced up for a split second then winced. She dropped the knife on the counter and stared at her hand.

"Shit," she muttered.

Jared made it around the kitchen and stood at her side before he realized he'd taken a step. He took her hand in his, frowning at the bleeding gash on her thumb.

"You might need stitches."

"I'm sure it's fine." She tried to take her hand back. He held it gently, but firmly.

Isa passed him a clean kitchen towel, hovering over his shoulder. "Here, wrap it around so blood doesn't get all over the place."

"Oh no, I got blood on the bread," Anna Beth whimpered.

Jared glanced down at the two slices with red splatters across the surface and grimaced. "We'll throw those away. Let's get you cleaned up."

Anna Beth dug in her heels. "I'll be fine, really. You don't need to help me."

His sister, Savannah sat at the counter next to Forrest's girlfriend and put her two cents in. "I'd listen to him. Jared's had a ton of stitches. Mom took him to the ER once a month when he was in school."

"Hush, Nana. There's a first aid kit in the bathroom," his mother said, cradling little Alana on her hip. "Jared will take care of you."

Anna Beth didn't argue anymore and silently allowed him to lead her down the hallway to the bathroom.

"Take a seat." He crouched down and opened the cupboard under the sink, his heart pounding. Even though she'd been hurt, being alone with Anna Beth for the first time had him keyed up so bad, his hands shook. He found the red plastic tub and set it onto the counter.

"Mom usually keeps it well stocked. Force of habit from having up to six kids under one roof," he explained, standing up.

"You don't have to doctor me. I can handle it," she said.

"After my mother gave me a direct order? Not a chance." He popped the lid on the kit open, eyeballing the contents. "I have everything we need, but I can take you to the ER, if you want me to."

"Really, I think it will be fine with a bandage. It's already stopped bleeding."

Jared removed the towel, noting the blood had slowed to a mere ooze. "It's going to hurt like a son of a bitch when I clean it."

"Go for it. I'm tougher than I look."

Her lighthearted attempt at humor put him at ease a bit. With steadier hands, Jared opened up an antiseptic wipe and cleaned the wound as gently as possible. Her hand jerked once and he blew across her skin. "Sorry."

She didn't respond and he glanced up at her, but her attention was directed past him. Either she was trying to distract herself from the pain or being alone with him disconcerted her, too.

While he was putting on the Neosporin, he tried to break the ice. "You were surprised I showed up."

Her eyes widened. "Why do you say that?"

"Because you sliced your finger right after Isabel said my name. Doesn't take a genius to realize you got spooked."

"I wasn't spooked." He shot her a skeptical look and she rolled her eyes. "Fine, yes. I was a little surprised to see you, but that's only because I figured you'd avoid me."

"It's my family tree trimming. No way I'm missing that, no matter who showed up."

"Yes, but we haven't talked since...my wedding. I didn't want to stir up the past."

"Honestly, Anna Beth, I feel like an idiot and you have every right to be angry with me. I shouldn't have put you in that position. I'm sorry."

She blinked at him rapidly. "Thank you. I know you were taking a risk and that's not your nature. I've felt horrible for hurting you—"

"Don't. You did nothing wrong." He wrapped her finger with gauze. "I should have apologized a long time ago but, honestly, I didn't think you'd want to hear from me."

"Of course, I wanted to hear from you!" The hoarse declaration threw him off guard. "You were the only person in

Snowy Springs besides Olive who ever understood me. You don't know how many times I almost called you. Especially, when things got bad. One moment shouldn't have completely derailed ten years of friendship."

"I know." Jared's chest squeezed at the pain in her voice. "I'm sorry about Ian. He seemed like a good man."

Anna Beth dashed her tears with her free hand. "He was. It's been hard. He died just a few days after Christmas last year, but he'd been unresponsive weeks before that. I still miss him like crazy."

Jared's stomach constricted at her admission, although logically he knew she had every right to miss her husband. He secured the tape around her wound and stood, praying his face didn't give away his discomfort.

Then his eyes met hers and the sadness in her green depths tore into him. She opened up about the second most painful moment of her life, and he'd only thought of himself.

Yep, you're an asshole. Now fix it.

He took her good hand and pulled her to her feet. Before he could consider Anna Beth's reaction, he pulled her into a hug.

"I am very sorry."

For several moments, she let him hold her, his hand traveling from her neck to the small of her back. Anna Beth relaxed against him, her arms going around his waist and she buried her face in his chest. It took him back and he lost himself for a moment. The sugary scent of Anna Beth's body spray still reminded him of fresh baked sugar cookies. Her soft curves molding against his body.

Damn, but it felt good to hold her again.

The door squeaked open and Jared glanced up to find Casey leaning against the door frame, a smug expression on his face.

"What's going on in here?"

Anna Beth pulled away, rubbing at her tear-soaked cheeks. "Nothing." She cleared her throat, avoiding his gaze. "I better head back out there. I'll ask your mom for an Ibuprofen."

Before he could hand her the bottle from the first aid kit, she'd darted past Casey and disappeared down the hallway.

Casey's looked after her, then back at Jared, all wide-eyed innocence.

"Something I said?"

Jared gritted his teeth. At this rate, the kid would be lucky if he made it to sixteen.

Eight

Anna Beth forgot how much the Jeffries' liked to argue.

Loudly.

Each family member tried to talk over someone else, creating a chorus of voices. Anna Beth kept biting her lip to restrain her mirth, but she didn't think she'd hidden her amusement from Jared. He sat across from her, his eyes twinkling whenever their gazes met.

It really took her back to when they were kids and she used to stay with the Jeffries' for dinner on Saturday nights while her aunt visited friends. Karen even sat her in the same chair she'd used as a kid between Savannah and Forest. Never the boisterous type, Jared used to carry on silent conversations with her throughout dinner. A smile here. An eye roll there. A silly face to make the other laugh.

Anna Beth nearly stuck her tongue out at him, just to see if he'd crack up. Jared had a great laugh. She missed it.

Where had that come from?

The Motrin she'd taken earlier helped with the pain in her thumb, but possibly made her loopy. She looked away from Jared and grabbed another piece of bread. What other reason would explain her dwelling on their embrace in the bathroom or that ever since, she watched him when he wasn't looking. His mature face, fuller than it'd been five years ago, carried a days' worth of dark stubble covering his cheeks and chin. He looked like he just stepped off the cover of one of those bad boy romance novels she read every once in a while. He was all man and it made her nervous. Not because she ever thought Jared would hurt her, but her reaction to him unsettled her. Even though Ian passed over a year ago, she wasn't sure she was ready for anything new. Having an attraction to Jared was one thing, but giving in and starting something would only complicate it while they were still figuring out what they could be to each other.

Maybe coming back to Snowy Springs had been a mistake. Being around Jared again left her confused by her reaction to him. Guilt niggled her, even though it didn't make any sense. Just because she'd taken comfort in a hug and noticed Jared looked good, didn't mean she was betraying Ian.

And even if she did find someone new, Ian wanted her to be happy. So why be upset about a natural, biological response to a good-looking guy?

Savannah's voice rising to a squeak brought Anna Beth out of her own head. Savannah and her father were having an enthusiastic debate about why they should replace the prime rib for Christmas dinner with healthier alternatives. Mike wasn't taking the suggestion well.

"I'm merely offering a few alternatives to red meat. Doctors say that too much red meat isn't good for you and with your health scare—"

Mike held up his hand, cutting off his youngest daughter. "Let me stop you right there, sweetheart. I love you, but I am a meat-eating machine. And if you convince your mother not to fix prime rib, it won't be a merry Christmas for anyone."

Savannah rolled her eyes. "You are so dramatic."

"Maybe, but I'm also dead serious. I need my coffee, meat, and whiskey. That's all there is to it."

Anna Beth laughed, covering her mouth with her napkin. The first time she'd walked into the Jeffries' house, Forrest and Grayson were fighting and Savannah was standing off to the side, screaming, a headless doll clutched in her hand. Isa lay on the couch watching TV and Jared took Anna Beth by the hand and led her back outside, away from the noise.

Although there were no more dolls or wrestling matches, the level of chaos stayed the same, as three-year-old Alanna ran around the dining room screaming, "Ring around the rosy!"

"Can you grab her?" Isa hollered to Gil, who caught his daughter in a bear hug. She squealed as he blew a raspberry on her neck.

Forrest and Grayson were going at it over some sports team, their voices getting deeper and louder. Anna Beth actually winced when Forrest nearly took her ear drum out rattling off stats.

Finally, Karen slapped her palm down on the table and the room fell silent.

"Alright! Since the ladies made dinner, we're going to retire to the living room to get ready to decorate the tree. Mike, you're in charge of eggnog. The rest of you, dishes, table, and countertops."

"What about dessert?" Casey asked.

Mike shot him a stern look. "We just finished eating dinner. Let that settle and we'll talk dessert when the tree is finished."

Casey snapped his mouth closed. Anna Beth's initial impressions of the teenager were not favorable and during dinner, her opinion hadn't changed. There were a few times where he'd actually seemed to warm up, so it could be that he had a hard time letting his guard down, but she was still on the fence about him.

As everyone stood up, heading for their prospective stations, Anna Beth's shoulder collided with Jared's arm as they passed by each other. The contact set her off kilter for a moment and she weaved to the side. When he grabbed her arm to steady her, the heat of his palm burned through the sleeve of her sweater and goose flesh spread along her skin.

This was the second time in the span of an hour that Jared's touch had left her discombobulated. In the bathroom, taking comfort in his hug let her slip back in time. Although he'd filled out since she'd last embraced him, he still smelled the same. The familiar scent of pine and spice eased her sorrow for a split second.

Then reality came crashing back. Jared wasn't her rock, her friend. They were merely acquaintances with a shared past.

"Sorry, I'm still a klutz," she said, subtly moving her arm.

He released her immediately and she noticed his cheeks stained red. She hadn't meant to embarrass him.

"It's my fault. I forget how tiny this dining room is."

A yellow and green sponge hit Jared's cheek with a splat and he yelled, "Ow."

"Chop chop, big brother." Grayson stood by the sink, winding a dish towel up between his hands. "You're washing!"

"Are you okay?" Soap bubbles slid down his cheek as he nodded and giggles chased away her brief dip into depression. "I forgot how crazy this place gets."

"Just another night at the Jeffries' Family Circus. I wish I could say these weren't my clowns, but I claimed them long ago."

Another wave of sadness swept through her. She missed that feeling of belonging. If she hadn't come back to Snowy Springs, she would be all alone for the holidays.

Still am. The Jeffries aren't mine.

"You're lucky to have them."

"I know that." He bent over and picked up the sponge. "I better get over there or he's going to toss a towel next. Or the bristled scrub brush. That one might hurt."

As confusing as her reaction to him was, she still enjoyed Jared's personality. They'd had their awkward moments since their reunion, but the more time she spent with him, the more she craved his good-natured humor. Maybe because he always seemed to be smiling in her memories.

Except that one. If only she could erase it and they could get back to being friends.

"I'll let you get to it then," she said, taking a step around him. "See you in there for the tree decorating."

"Just don't touch the Scooby-Doo ornament. It's mine."

"Yes, sir."

Anna Beth headed into the living room with the rest of the women in Jared's family, and as she stood along the edge of the room, a tight ball formed in her throat. Savannah sat in her father's chair, untangling a strand of beads while Megan worked on the Christmas lights. Isa must have taken Alanna into the other room because she could hear the toddler screaming down the hallway. And Karen had her head in a large box of ornaments, laying them out across the coffee table in single rows. Homemade popsicle stick angels, clothespin reindeer, and painted glass balls told their family story. Anna Beth wondered if the ornaments she made her parents were in a box somewhere at her aunt's place or if they'd been donated to some church function years ago. Anna Beth hadn't thought about them in years, but maybe she'd ask Sarah. What was one more box of memories in her storage unit?

As a child, warm and intimate Christmases were the norm, until she'd moved in with her aunt. The small tree Sarah put in the corner of the room, on top of a high round table had been perfectly adorned with expensive glass ornaments which Anna Beth hadn't been allowed to touch. After she'd married Ian, they'd gone all out for the holidays, including a big Christmas Eve bash with their friends. But when his health deteriorated, they skipped the party. Though their festivities were just the two of them, it was still wonderful.

Over the course of their marriage, Ian and she had collected ornaments from every place they traveled. They held memories of anniversaries, her first passport stamp, and other special moments. She hadn't even brought the box out last year, as they'd spent the night before Thanksgiving until his death in the hospital and he hadn't been aware enough for Anna Beth to decorate his hotel room anyway. Those ornaments were gathering dust in a storage unit in LA because she couldn't even imagine putting them on a tree without Ian by her side.

The air around Anna Beth thickened and she couldn't catch her breath. Karen glance up from her ornament sorting, frowning.

"Anna Beth, are you alright?"

"Yeah, I'm just a little light headed. Excuse me, I'm going to go outside for a minute." Anna Beth rushed to the door and grabbed her coat. "Just need some air."

Before Karen could question her further, Anna Beth stepped out onto the porch. The minute the door closed, she took a deep breath, allowing the crisp air to burn her lungs.

She reached into the pocket of her coat, but her keys were the only thing she found. She'd locked her purse in the car, along with her anxiety medication. She didn't get attacks often, but when she did, they alleviated the symptoms.

The next best thing was to take deep breaths and think about something soothing.

Her breath swirled in front of her face as she exhaled and Anna Beth smiled, even as tears rolled down her cheeks, thinking of the old Claymation cartoons she and Ian watched every year. She should find one on TV tonight. Maybe Sarah would watch it with her and they could make new traditions. Be close.

Give Anna Beth somewhere to come back to next Christmas.

With the porch light off, the bright winter moon cast enough light that she could see all the way out to the street. It was a beautiful night, with patches of clouds above, and inside, a warm, loving family who'd invited her to be a part of their celebration, sat around making new memories. She should be in there with them.

Instead, she stood on the cold, dark porch feeling sorry for herself. Ian would be so disappointed. She could almost hear his voice chiding her.

Anna Banana, why are you out here when the fun's inside? Shake it off, baby, and have a good time.

She needed to go out to the car. Just one pill to take the edge off and she'd go back inside.

But the minute she reached the stairs, something moved to her right.

"Santa Claus is coming to town!"

Anna Beth gasped loudly as the robotic Santa came to life, his blue eyes flashing. Her heart thundered so hard against her chest, she thought it might rupture.

"Geez, you scared me, stupid thing."

It rudely kept singing and dancing, oblivious to her near-death experience.

"I think you're possessed."

"He's creepy, right?"

Anna Beth squealed and spun around to find Jared stepping onto the porch behind her, still shrugging into his jacket.

"Yes, but so are you! Between freaky Santa and your silent tread, I'm about to have a heart attack."

The flashing lights from Santa's eyes illuminated the sheepish expression on his face. "Sorry, I wanted to check on you. I finished my part of the cleanup and mom said you weren't feeling well. You alright?"

"I'm fine. Really. Just got a little overwhelmed." Santa started going off again and Anna Beth waved her hand. "Can you exorcise him?"

Jared chuckled. "I think I know a prayer or two for evil Santa's."

He went around the back of the moving animatronic and she laughed as Santa's hand chopped at him, nearly catching him on the side of his head. He ducked out of the way and after a moment of fiddling around behind Santa, the robot stopped moving. His eyes dimmed slowly and Anna Beth sighed with relief.

"Thank goodness. Fair warning, if I come back to visit your family again, Santa's gonna die."

"Shhh, don't say that too loud or you might upset mom. She loves that awful thing." Jared came up alongside her and leaned his forearms on the porch railing. "So, was it our incessant need to outdo each other or the amount of decorations we have to hang that sent you out here?"

Anna Beth appreciated his light hearted approach to

probing her for information. Jared had always been good about getting to the bottom of what was bothering her without pushing too hard. Funny how time apart hadn't changed that.

"Honestly, I forgot how crazy your family can get, but it really had little to do with them and more what's going on inside my own head."

"I think you're being too nice. You can admit we're nuts and I promise not to hold it against you."

Anna Beth leaned on the railing next to him, their shoulders brushing. "Not, it's...being around your family is great. It just makes me miss having a family of my own."

"I understand that feeling." She looked over at him in the moonlight. He stared off into the dark, lost in the past. "When I first moved in with the Jeffries, I'd never had a festive Christmas before. Traditions, presents, food that didn't come out of a microwave...it was overwhelming. I ran off and hid for hours. Mike finally found me in his shop. He wasn't mad. He just asked if I felt like coming back or if I needed another minute. I took another half an hour and when I came out of his shop, Mike stood there, waiting on me. It's a heady feeling to go from no one giving a shit about you to a huge group."

"You never told me that." Anna Beth rested her hand on his arm.

Jared shrugged. "Guess it just never came up. I know I'm lucky and, given everything you'd lost, I suppose I never thought you'd want to hear how I spent my first Christmas in a shed, instead of with a family who cared about me."

Anna Beth wasn't really sure what to say. Had he really thought she was so self-involved that she wouldn't listen to his worries and fears?

"I always cared about your feelings, Jared."

"I didn't mean it like that. You were a good friend." Anna

Beth's stomach pitched at his use of the past tense, but she couldn't hold it against him. He turned toward her and she could feel his gaze sweep over her face. "What about you, A.B.? How are you feeling now?"

The warm way her old nickname fell from his lips sent her stomach into a fit of somersaults and she nearly told him everything. Her anxiety attack. Feeling lost and alone. Thankfully, the lump in her throat stopped her from spilling her guts. She'd already broken down in front of this man once tonight, she wasn't quite ready to do it again.

"I'm fine." She pushed away from the railing and let out a breath, making a large *O* with her mouth. Anna Beth rubbed her upper arms and changed the subject. "It's awfully cold. Think it will snow?"

Jared pulled out his phone and tapped on the screen for a few seconds. "The weather app on my phone says no, but it's been wrong before. We were supposed to get eight inches last night and nothing."

"Huh, that's interesting."

"Is it?" She caught Jared's grin out of the corner of her eye as he put his phone away. "I always thought the weather was something people talked about when they had nothing to say." He cleared his throat as he stepped closer to her. "Or too much to choose from, in our case."

The Christmas lights cast colorful shadows across his face as he leaned closer, his warm breath whispering across her skin.

"I've missed you, A.B."

His proximity and scent was a heady combo and against her will, her body leaned toward him. More than anything she wanted to let him hold her and chase the clouds away.

But she didn't want to give him the wrong impression, no matter how good it may feel.

Her hands came up to rest on his chest. "Jared…"

"Yeah?"

"I can't do this."

Nine

Jared backed away from Anna Beth, wishing he could take back the last thirty seconds. Damn it. Since she'd been home, he hadn't been able to think straight and telling her he missed her like this? On a dark porch on a cold winter night, just the two of them? No wonder she freaked.

"Sorry," he said. "I didn't mean to come off so intense. I guess being around you again takes me back. Sometimes it seems like we haven't been apart and the next minute, it's awkward as hell. I swear I wasn't coming onto you." Knowing he was going to ramble himself into a hole, he added, "I'll just let you be."

He turned, prepared to head back inside, but her voice stopped him. "I don't want you to go."

He looked over his shoulder at her, his heart racing. "You don't?"

"No, but...I guess I'm anxious." She tucked a stray hair

behind her ear, her gaze avoiding his. "About what it means being back here. I'm only here temporarily, and I don't want to complicate things."

"What does that mean?" he asked.

"I'm not moving back. I'm leaving the day after Christmas."

Disappointment slammed into Jared like a Mack truck, but he hid it under a cheery tone. "Three weeks is a decent visit with your aunt. Maybe even reconnecting with an old friend?"

Anna Beth finally looked at him. "Is that what you want? To be friends again."

"I never wanted to stop." Her eyes widened at his brutally honest admission and he kept talking before he lost his nerve. "I know I should have never put you in the position I did, and I should have apologized sooner but I honestly didn't think you wanted to hear from me. It's been rough imagining you were somewhere, hating me, but I didn't know how to break the ice."

Anna Beth took a step toward him. "I never hated you. I was upset and frustrated, but I know I hurt you, too. I started to call you hundreds of times, but I didn't know what to say either. I figured you'd either hang up on me or avoid my phone call."

"I only hang up on people who tell me the IRS wants me to send $1500 in Target gift cards."

Jared grinned when Anna Beth threw back her head and laughed.

"Look at us, discussing our feelings like healthy adults," he said.

She returned his smile. "Yeah, this whole open communication thing...who knew, right?"

Jared almost reached for her hand, but held himself back.

He didn't want her to misunderstand his intentions again, and crossed his arms over his chest to keep his hands busy. "I'd like it if we could spend time together. Even if you do leave and head back to LA, I don't want us to lose touch again."

Anna Beth cleared her throat. "I'm not going back to LA."

"You're not? Where are you going to live?"

"I'm not sure where I'm headed next. I'm taking things one step at a time, you know?"

No, he had no idea what that was like because he always had a plan. He'd known what he was doing before he graduated. He'd planned for the type of house he wanted to buy. There had been too much uncertainty in his early years to go without structure and security.

The only thing in his life he couldn't plan for? Emotions. Those suckers came out of nowhere and he had a hard time dealing with them, as his past actions support.

"Sounds like you're taking off on an adventure."

"I'm not sure I'd call it that. I need a change, that's all I know." To his surprise, she reached for his hand. "But I'd like to spend time with you while I'm here."

"Good. Me, too."

She dropped his hand and he missed the warmth of her touch immediately. Maybe he'd been lonelier than her thought. He had acquaintances, dates, but not a lot of close friends, besides Vance. And he wasn't exactly the comforting type.

"I'm sorry I overreacted before," she said. "Being back has me a little high-strung. With the holidays, my aunt, Ian's list—"

"List?" he repeated.

Anna Beth's mouth opened and shut several times as she stuttered, "Yeah, I'm…well, you see…it's just...hard to explain."

Now he was intrigued. "I can handle it. Lay it on me."

She sighed. "I know it sounds a little crazy, but Ian had a flair for the dramatic. In his will, he left me a list of things he wanted me to accomplish for him after he passed."

"Wow, that's…like a bucket list?"

"Kind of. By proxy. They are things he wants me to do as a sort of sendoff."

Jared's stomach tightened in knots. This was why she'd come back? Not because she wanted to, but because of Ian? "How many things?"

"There were one hundred and eighty, but I'm down to thirteen. Wait, twelve. I keep forgetting Olive."

He cocked his head, giving her a puzzled look. "Olive was on the list?"

"Sort of. It was *see an old friend*. Not her specifically."

"Do you get extra points for seeing more than one?"

"No, it's not a points thing."

Jared turned his back on the banister, leaning against it. "So what else is on it? Climb Mt. Everest, or something?"

Anna Beth chuckled. "No, simpler tasks. I'm not sure I want to get into it."

Jared nodded, thinking about the letter from Ian sitting in his top drawer at home. He'd asked Jared to help Anna Beth when she came back to town, but the letter was sent two years ago. Why would he want Jared to help Anna Beth with a post-mortem bucket list?

Still, if the list meant spending more time with Anna Beth…

"Well, I'm not trying to pry, but if you need help doing any of them, I'm here for you."

"Thanks, Jared. That's really sweet."

As much as he enjoyed having Anna Beth to himself, the temperature had dropped at least ten degrees in the last few minutes and he was shivering despite his down jacket. "It's getting cold. We should get back inside and help with the tree. It's a lot of fun. Dad is usually pretty liberal with the brandy in the eggnog, so one sip should warm you right up."

Anna Beth hesitated, before taking a step toward the porch steps. "Actually, I think I'm going to go back to my aunt's. Will you thank your mom for me and tell everyone I said good-bye?"

"Yeah, sure. Be careful driving." He stuck out his hand. "Here, give me your phone. I'll put my number in."

"Is it the same one you had in high school?"

"Yeah."

"Then I already have it."

The realization that she hadn't given up on him sent a zing of excitement through Jared's body.

"Text me when you get home."

"I will." To his surprise, Anna Beth walked back to him and wrapped her arms around him in a tight hug. "Thank you for being so understanding."

Jared held her loosely, afraid if he pulled her too close, she'd bolt. He breathed her in slowly, the scent of fresh baked bread and sugar cookie perfume mingling deliciously. She relaxed against him, laying her cheek on his chest and he reached up to stroke her hair.

Finally, she pulled away with an awkward laugh.

"Sorry. I forgot what good hugs you give."

"Well, the first ones free, but I charge five dollars a hug after that."

"Seems pricey."

"I'm a cop. Gotta keep myself in coffee and donuts somehow."

She shook her head as she turned away. Glancing back over

her shoulder, she headed down the porch steps. "I'll be sure to bring my wallet the next time I see you."

"Sounds good. Text me when you get home."

"I said I would. Damn, you still love to mother hen, don't you? Must be what makes you such a good cop. You care about everyone."

Especially you.

He couldn't say that out loud, though. "I'll try to be more of a bad cop."

She stopped at the bottom of the steps, her expression serious. "Don't change. The way you care is an amazing quality."

Jared's cheeks burned at the compliment. "I really couldn't if I wanted to. It's in my nature to worry."

"It's one of the things I lo...like about you." Jared hadn't missed her slip of the tongue, but didn't dwell on it. Slipping back into old habits seemed like an easy feat for both of them. Anna Beth used to tell him all the things she loved about him. She'd caught herself now probably because she didn't want him to get the wrong impression, but she didn't need to worry. Being friends with her was all he wanted.

"Glad to hear you still like me."

Anna Beth's gaze lifted and she whispered, "I never stopped."

The air around them charged as their gazes met and held. Anna Beth was the first one to look away, taking a step down the walkway.

"Goodnight, Jared."

"Night." Jared watched her head down to her car. As Anna Beth cut across the edge of the lawn, the first few snowflakes fell, like white puffs of cotton candy. Jared shook his head. His life was as unpredictable as the weather.

Anna Beth pulled out onto the road just as the door behind him opened and Savannah stepped out. "Brrr, geez, is it finally snowing?" Savannah came up alongside him, her arm brushing his. "Where is Anna Beth?"

"She needed to get home to her aunt."

Savannah gazed out into the night, which was getting whiter by the minute. "Are you sure that was it?"

"That's what she said."

"But what did *you* say to her before she bowed out?"

Jared glared at her. "Why do you think I said something?"

"Because I know you. You have a tendency to put your foot in your mouth with most people. I'm sure it's worse with the woman you love."

Jared sputtered. "I don't love Anna Beth."

Savannah scoffed. "Oh, yeah, okay. Sure."

"What's that supposed to mean?"

She put her hands on her hips, facing off with him. "You don't remember, do you?"

"Remember what?"

"A few weeks after Anna Beth left town, Vance called me. The two of you were too drunk to drive, so I picked you up. After I dropped Vance off, you could barely walk so I had to help you inside. You told me everything."

Jared grimaced. "Shit."

Savannah dropped her hands from her hips and placed a comforting hand on his shoulder. "I know it broke your heart to lose her, but I hope you aren't still butt hurt that she didn't choose you."

"No. We're friends."

Savannah clapped her hands gleefully. "That's wonderful."

"Yeah, except she's leaving the day after Christmas. We'll reconnect just in time for her to move on."

"She might change her mind. Snowy Springs has this magical way of drawing people in."

The way she said it, along with the small smile on her lips, gave him pause.

"Savannah…"

"What?"

"Whatever you're thinking of doing, don't."

"I wasn't plotting anything."

"Aha! Your Freudian slip proves you are up to no good." He crossed his arms over his chest. "I know you. You like playing matchmaker, but I am telling you, I don't feel that way about Anna Beth anymore. I just want to get back what we had before, and if you mess with that by creating one of your big romantic traps, I'm going to tell mom about the time you borrowed her diamond earrings and lost them."

"First of all, they aren't traps, they're well thought out plans." Savannah ticked off her fingers. "Secondly, I replaced the earrings and, third, she already knew, so joke's on you."

Jared grabbed her in a headlock like when they were kids and playfully dragged her toward the front door. "I mean it!"

She squirmed away from him with a huff. "Fine! I won't meddle. But I can't speak for the rest of the Jeffries. Everyone wants to see you happy."

Jared groaned, knowing she was right. If Mom or Isa got wind that he still had feelings for Anna Beth, he'd be doomed.

Ten

Fat, wet snowflakes landed on Anna Beth's windshield as soon as she pulled out onto the road.

Awesome. Just what I need after that emotional rollercoaster.

Anna Beth hated driving in harsh weather, especially when it came down like meteors from space.

She could've made it through the rest of the night with the Jeffries, but talking to Jared about being friends again got her thinking. In less than three weeks she'd be gone again. Rebuilding deep, emotional connections seemed like a way to complicate things rather than an attempt to resolve them.

Especially when those connections might not be as platonic as she'd originally thought.

It could be loneliness. It had been over a year since someone held her, and she'd known Jared a long time. He was kind and funny and good-looking. It was only natural for her to feel attracted to him. She felt safe with him.

Olive's voice flitted through her mind, reminding her of her mutually beneficial relationship with Vance. Anna Beth immediately brushed the idea aside. Even if she was down for a little recreational mattress mambo, it wouldn't be with Jared, not with their history.

He's not in love with you anymore. What's the harm in a little quid pro quo?

She knew the answer before she even finished the thought. Anna Beth wanted Jared back in her life but she didn't want things to get all screwy again.

By the time she reached the edge of town, the snow hammered down on her with a vengeance. She couldn't see anything except swirling flakes and the snow-covered highway. Suddenly, her high beams flashed across a shape in the road. She swerved to miss it; her heart thundering painfully fast.

What the hell was that?

Anna Beth pulled over onto the side of the highway and grabbed the flashlight from under her seat. She rolled her window down and swung the beam of light in the middle of the road at the lump. It slowly turned its head and looked at her. By the shape of the ears, she realized it was a small cat.

Climbing out of the car, Anna Beth didn't stop to consider how dangerous it was to cross into the middle of the highway in a blinding snowstorm. With her car still running on the side of the road, she hustled toward the animal, expecting it to bolt. Snow hit the side of her neck and face, melting against her warm skin and dripping down under her sweater.

The kitten didn't move. It hunkered down when Anna Beth knelt next to it, the snow on the road soaking through the denim of her jeans. The bitter cold stung her skin but she ignored it as she reached out to touch the snow-covered feline. Her hand pressed along its thin back and it shivered. If it was hurt, she feared picking it up and injuring it further, but she needed to get them both out of the road before someone came along. It would be just her luck to get hit trying to be a hero.

Shrugging out of her jacket, she wrapped it around the kitten and picked it up. Tears stung her eyes as the poor thing continued to quiver, but it didn't try to escape. She carried it back to her car and by the time she shut the door on the blowing snow, her body shook with cold.

While the hot air in her car slowly took the bite out of Anna Beth, she flipped on the dome light and pulled back the coat to get a look at the kitten. It meowed weakly, never opening its eyes. She could make out stripes on its forehead and a white mask around its tightly shut eyes. Her heart constricted as she rubbed the slight body through her jacket, simultaneously trying to warm it and let it know it was safe.

"Hey, baby, what were you doing out there in the middle of the road? Are you lost? Or did some A-hole dump you?"

The kitten finally opened its eyes and lifted its head to look at her. It released a raspy meow. Anna Beth hadn't had a cat since before her parents passed, so she wasn't sure if that was normal. Their family cat passed a few months before her parents and when she'd moved in with her aunt, Anna Beth never bothered asking for another pet. Ian had been highly allergic to animals and couldn't be around cats long, but she'd always wanted another pet.

She nestled the kitten onto her passenger seat, still wrapped in her coat. Once her seat belt was clipped in, she pulled the car back out onto the street and headed for her aunt's. Sarah would probably flip out when she saw what Anna Beth brought home, but there was no way she could leave it to die. If she had to, she would find a temporary place for her and the furry baby to stay.

Another weak meow came from her cold passenger and she crooned to the kitten. "It's okay, honey. We're almost there. I'll get you inside and dry you off. Then I'll get you some food."

By the time she pulled into the driveway, the kitten was meowing loudly, and frequently, although it hadn't moved from the safety of her coat. She turned off the car and swiftly picked up the wrapped kitten, before bolting for the front door as quarter size flakes came down around her, sticking to every surface she passed. She carried the cat into the house, mentally preparing herself for the explosion from her aunt. Anna Beth opened the door with one hand, the kitty clutched against her chest and stepped over the threshold.

With the door shut behind her, she leaned back against the wood and breathed a heavy sigh. What a night.

"Anna Beth? You're home earlier than I expected." Her aunt's voice carried from the direction of the kitchen.

Here we go…

"Everyone asked about you today, but I told them you had to get your writing...done." Anna Beth straightened as her aunt came into the entryway, wiping her hands on a dish towel. Her eyes immediately went to the squirming jacket in Anna Beth's arms. "What do you have there?"

Anna Beth pulled the jacket back, revealing the kitten's damp head. It looked around, meowing, its blue-green eyes wide with fear.

"I saw her huddled in the middle of the road, getting snowed on and not moving. I couldn't leave her. If you don't want to have her here, I can ask Olive if we can crash with her, but it's really coming down outside, and I'd rather not go back out in it."

Sarah's expression gave nothing away as she walked over slowly, her low heels clicking on the wood floor. To Anna

Beth's surprise, she *tsked* sympathetically and ran her hand over the kitten's head, stopping to rub one of her ears.

"It's a good thing you found her. Or him." She handed Anna Beth the small towel she'd carried into the room. "Start drying her with that. I'll go get some more towels. Head on into the living room and I'll meet you there."

Still in shock at her aunt's calm reaction, Anna Beth did what she was told and sat down on the couch with the kitten in her arms. She pulled the coat back and rubbed the towel over the damp fur, feeling the bones on its back and sides. She cringed at the obvious neglect the skinny creature had endured and her heart melted as the little body vibrated with a rumbling purr against her hand.

"You're going to be okay, sweetheart."

Sarah came in with two towels and a wide smile on her face. "Here we go. That hand towel is probably soaked by now." Sarah opened the towel on her lap and reached over to take the kitten. She wrapped her up and started rubbing her all over.

"Poor thing doesn't weigh much," Sarah said, holding her inside the towel.

"She doesn't seem to be hurt. Just cold and scared."

Sarah's lips thinned. "And starving. Someone probably dumped her and she was out looking for food when the storm hit." Sarah rubbed the top of the kitten's head until her fur stood on end. "Could you imagine neglecting such a sweet face?"

The high inflection in her aunt's voice was new and a bit unsettling. "I thought you'd be upset. I didn't know you liked cats."

"Actually, I love cats. I used to have two. Sabrina and Linus. Sabrina was my favorite movie growing up and when they remade it with Harrison Ford? Mmmmhmmmm."

Anna Beth blinked. Her aunt had just made a yummy sound about a man. *Holy crap.*

Sarah, oblivious to her disconcertion, continued with her story. "I adopted them not long after I moved into this house and they were good company. Linus passed away at fourteen, but Sabrina lived another five years. After that, I wasn't ready for another pet. When I finally thought about it...well, the grim reality is, there is really no good ending when you have an animal. They die, whether you have them for one year or nineteen, and the pain is still the same. I decided I didn't want to go through that again."

Anna Beth still hadn't adjusted to this softer version of her aunt. She sounded as though she was about to cry.

"I never knew that," Anna Beth said.

"It was before you came to live with me and it hurt to talk about them." Sarah met her gaze and the sadness in her aunt's eyes hit Anna Beth harder than a punch to the gut. "I don't love easily, as you well know, but when I do, it's deep."

Before Anna Beth could form a response, Sarah lifted the towel and the kitten looked between them, her blue-green eyes squinting.

"Let's see what you are so we don't have to keep calling you it." Sarah lifted the kitten's tail and laughed. "Definitely a she." She covered her with the towel and continued drying her. "I bet you're warmer."

Anna Beth was still processing her aunt's moment of vulnerability when Sarah handed the kitten off to Anna Beth. "I'm going to run next door and see if my neighbors have some canned food. I know they have a couple cats, but not sure what they feed them."

"Thank you. I know this isn't what you expected and I appreciate your help."

Sarah stroked the kitten's head and the baby cat leaned into the touch. Sarah smiled.

"I have a feeling she's going to be fine. You're a hero. Not everyone would have stopped in a snowstorm to save a cat." Sarah patted Anna Beth's shoulder. "I'm proud of you."

Sarah's kind words left Anna Beth speechless and as she watched her aunt kick off her high heeled shoes for a pair of snow boots, she wanted to ask Sarah about the changes in her, but she worried if she brought the softness to her aunt's attention, would Sarah clam up again.

When the front door closed behind her, Anna held the kitten against her chest and rubbed her hand along her body, tears blurring her vision. A lump caught in her throat and she tried to swallow past it, but her emotions were too much to slow the tidal wave of sobs. The last thing she wanted was for Sarah to come back and catch her bawling just because she'd said she was proud of her.

Anna Beth used the edge of the towel to dry her face. As if she knew Anna Beth needed it, the kitten stretched up and rubbed her head along Anna Beth's chin.

She laughed wetly. "Well, aren't you sweet." Anna Beth picked her up and held her in front of her face for a moment. "I think she's right. You're going to be fine."

Her phone vibrated in her pocket and she put the kitten back in her lap before she pulled it out with one hand. It was a text from Jared.

`Did you make it home okay?`

She sent a response while the kitten nudged her head against her hands, demanding attention.

`Yes, you'll never believe what happened.`

Anna Beth held the kitten up and took a cheesy selfie. It wasn't noticeable that she'd been crying, so she sent it to him.

`Isn't she cute?`

`I'm more of a dog person, but she's alright. ;)`

He sent back a cheesy picture of him with his Scooby ornament.

Anna Beth laughed and the kitten looked up at her with narrowed eyes, as if she disapproved of the joke. "I think you're more than alright."

She positioned the kitten like a baby against her chest. It was the first time she noticed the kitten's paws were huge and shaped like lobster claws. Or mittens. Her phone vibrated again and she checked the message.

`You're an angel for saving her.`

Her aunt said something similar, and while Sarah's words had rocked her emotionally, the simple compliment from Jared gave her butterflies.

Her aunt burst through the door and walked into the living room, her hair covered by a thin layer of snow. She swiped at it with one hand and frowned at the trail of wet footprints behind her. "I'll have to mop that later."

"I can do it once we get her situated," Anna Beth offered.

"Either way." Sarah pulled two cans from her pocket and held them up with a smile. "I got a couple cans to tide us over until the storm lets up. I'm hoping it stops snowing in the morning, but I got an alert on my cell for a winter storm warning. Just hoping they're wrong. I'm going to put half of this can on a plate and we'll feed her in the kitchen."

Anna Beth took one of the kitten's paws and waved at her aunt with it. "Did you see her feet? They look like lobster claws."

She stood up and walked over to her aunt so she could get a closer look. Sarah picked up the kitten's paws, examining them. "Oh, extra toes. Some cats have them. We'll have to check to make sure none of the nails are growing back into her pad."

"I think we should call her Mittens."

Her aunt patted her hand with a smile. "That's a wonderful name. Let's get some food in her."

Anna Beth followed blindly behind her aunt, her eyes tearing up again. "Sarah?"

She looked up from opening the can. "Yes?"

"Thank you, for everything. I appreciate you."

Maybe it was just a trick of the light, but Anna Beth thought there was a sheen of tears in Sarah's eyes.

"Of course. I appreciate you, too."

For the first time, Anna Beth didn't regret her return to Snowy Springs. Maybe Ian really had been onto something.

Eleven

Jared woke up sputtering as something warm and wet slid across his lips and cheek. His eighty-pound chocolate lab, Rip, hovered over him, panting in his face. When Jared didn't move fast enough, Rip let out a series of ear-splitting, excited barks. Jared groaned.

"I bought you a doggy door so you could let yourself out to pee. Why are you all up in my grill at…" Jared squinted at his clock on his night stand. "Six-twelve in the morning, on a Sunday?"

Rip bounced off the bed and came back with a stuffed duck toy in his mouth. He dropped it, slick with dog drool, on Jared's chest.

Jared grimaced. "I get it. I haven't been home much the last few days and you missed me. Still doesn't mean I want such a rude awakening."

Rip laid down on the bed with a huff, as though he didn't appreciate being lectured.

Jared stretched before climbing to his feet. He stared down at his dog, whose tail thumped rapidly against the comforter as he walked around the end of the bed.

"I'll go get cleaned up and, if you're a good boy, we'll get a pup-cup at Foam Capped Java."

The minute he said pup-cup, Rip released a stream of excited barks and tore out of the room, zooming back a minute later.

"Yeah, you're excited. Now, give me some space. I need to make myself gorgeous."

Jared picked his phone up off his charging station and slid his thumb over the screen. A new text from Anna Beth with an attachment. He clicked on the picture. It was a selfie of her, smiling while the kitten she'd found asleep on her chest.

`I think I'm in love.`

The message was sent after eleven last night, but he'd already passed out by then. After only four hours of sleep yesterday, followed by hours with his family decorating, he'd been dead on his feet and barely remembered the snowy drive home, let alone climbing into bed.

She probably wasn't awake yet. Lord knows, he wouldn't be if not for his pain in the rear dog. He texted her back anyway.

`Very sweet. I like her stripes.`

Jared set his phone on the bathroom counter. He took off his boxers and went through the short hallway into his tile shower. Jared bought the house as a foreclosure last year and worked his ass off remodeling it, especially the destroyed bathroom and kitchen. He'd built his shower as a walk-in with dual shower heads on opposite walls and the deep soaking tub under the window looking out over the trees. He never used it, but maybe he'd meet someone to build a life with who would enjoy it.

He finished washing and rinsing his hair and body and stepped out of the shower. He dried off and wrapped a towel around his waist while he finished his routine.

He turned on his playlist and 90's grunge blared through the room. Rip lifted his head off the bed and his tongue lolled out of his mouth as he watched Jared moonwalk to his dresser. His parents had dogs while he was growing up, but they'd never let them up on the furniture. Jared didn't mind sharing his bed with Rip. His pal could sleep anywhere he wanted.

And if a woman ever had a problem with it, he'd show her the door.

Jared dug inside the top drawer and his hand touched the envelope mixed in with his socks. His heartbeat kicked up a notch as he pulled it out and slid the folded letter from inside. Another envelope dropped onto the hardwood floor, but that one wasn't addressed to him. It had Anna Beth's name on it.

Jared opened his letter, reading it again.

Jared,

This letter probably came as a surprise to you. You may have even forgotten who I am. I'm going to write this letter as though you haven't. I don't know why you and Anna Beth stopped talking, although, I can hazard a guess. She is an amazing woman, but I bet you already realized that.

I don't know when but, at some point, she will go back to Snowy Springs without me and I'd like to make a request of you. Please, look out for her. Help her. She will be hurting. I want someone who knows and cares about her to watch over her.

I might be pushing my luck, but here goes. I've enclosed a letter for Anna Beth. Please, make sure she gets it when her list is finished?

The way Anna Beth talks about you, I know you're a good man. We only met once before the wedding and I wish we'd had a chance to get to know each other. Thank you in advance.

Best,
Ian Crawford

Jared slipped the folded letter back into the envelope and picked Anna Beth's letter off the floor. He stared at it, wondering what Ian had written and why he'd entrusted it to Jared.

None of his questions would be answered until Anna Beth finished her list, so speculating would only drive him crazy. He placed both letters back into the envelope and slid it in the drawer, reaching for a pair of socks. Clad in jeans, a t-shirt, and a hoodie, Jared went downstairs with socks in his hands, Rip tearing past him down the stairs.

"Hey! If you trip me and I break my neck, you don't get whipped cream, bud."

Rip went to the door and sat, his tail slapping impatiently against the wood floor. Jared sat on his leather couch and put on his socks. He'd just slipped on his tennis shoes when he realized he left his phone upstairs.

"If only you were like Lassie and could get my phone."

Rip barked at him as Jared ran back up the stairs. When he picked up his phone, he noticed the blinking light and opened it up to find a message from Anna Beth.

Morning.

Jared grinned at the sleepy emoji she'd tagged on the end of her text. He was feeling the exact same way.

Morning, A.B. How'd you sleep?

Alright. The kitten liked the crook of my neck, so I'm a little stiff. You?

I slept okay until my dog woke me up.

Jared attached a picture of Rip from camping a few months ago.

I guess he didn't get the memo that Sundays are a day of rest.

Awww, he's so handsome.

Yeah, he gets that from me.

Anna Beth sent back a gif of Ryan Reynolds rolling his eyes. Jared countered with Jim Carey's grinning Grinch.

You are still such a goober. I'm heading to Foam Capped to work on my screenplay.

I was going to take Rip there for a pup-cup. Mind if we say hi?

Not at all. I'm leaving now. See you in a few.

Jared whistled the whole way down the stairs and when he jumped the last two, he caught Rip watching him, his head tilted curiously.

"You, my friend, are about to meet someone mighty special."

Saying it aloud sent a little thrill down his spine. Even temporarily having Anna Beth in his life again made his day better and he couldn't wait to see her. Jared grabbed his coat and Rip's leash from the hooks by the door, latching the latter onto Rip's red collar. He didn't bother to lock his front door, his mind preoccupied with Anna Beth and how she felt about them hanging out. She'd instigated the meet up, but was she as excited as Jared?

Jared opened the passenger door and clicked his tongue. "Rip, up."

Rip jumped onto the floorboard then the seat. Jared tossed in his leash and shut the door. Dancing his way around the front of the hood, he realized his face hurt from smiling.

You need to chill. It's one cup of coffee.

"You ready, bud?" he asked as he slid into the driver's seat.

Rip's head bounced, as though nodding. It had been just them for more than two years and, at times, Jared felt sure his dog actually understood him.

Ten minutes later, Jared parked in front of Foam Capped Java next to Anna Beth's car. He helped Rip out of the truck and led him toward the entrance. Anna Beth sat at a table in the corner, her laptop covering half of the surface. Her hair was held piled on top of her head with two black chopsticks. Several curls escaped and hung down along the nape of her neck. Her brow furrowed in concentration and he stopped to study her.

Anna Beth and looked up from her laptop screen and spotted him. A wide smile spread across her face and she waved enthusiastically. It was downright enchanting.

Enchanting? What the fuck, man? You need a guy's night with Vance. What's next? Lifting your pinky when you drink?

Jared waved back and took a step in her direction.

"Hey, Jared!" The owner, Kelly, never batted an eye when Snowy Springs patrons brought their dogs inside as long as they were well behaved. Just another benefit of living in a small town. She stood behind the register, holding up a small white cup. "The usual for Rip?"

Jared faced Kelly, hoping neither woman noticed the burning in his cheeks. "Yeah, thanks, Kel. And I'll take a large white mocha." He held out a twenty, but she shook her head.

"It's been covered."

"It has?"

"Yep." Anna Beth came up alongside him and Kelly winked. "Glad to have you back, Anna Beth. Be just a minute."

Anna Beth leaned on the counter next to him, her vanilla scent swirling around him pleasantly. "What did you get?"

"Large white mocha for me and a pup-cup for Rip. You didn't have to pay for my order."

"I know. But that's what friends do, right? Buy each other coffee?"

"Yeah, but I could have bought yours."

"Next time, if I don't beat you to it."

Jared shook his head. "Did you order something yet?"

"Not yet. I was just getting situated. I'm kind of a freak when I work. Everything has to be just so." Without warning, Anna Beth knelt down and her voice went up two octaves. "You must be Rip. You are gorgeous. Has anyone ever told you that?"

Rip loved everyone he'd ever met, but only a select few got the lap treatment. Rip knocked Anna Beth backward, onto her butt, and Jared reached out to help her, horrified. Before he could pull his dog off her, Anna Beth laughed, wrapping her arms around Rip. The sight of her sitting on the tile floor of the coffee shop with Rip licking her cheek warmed Jared to his core.

"What a love bug. I may have to claim you. How do you feel about cats, though?"

Rip sniffed the front of her shirt in response and then rubbed his cheek against it with a whimper.

"I hate to break it to you, but this fur ball and I are an inseparable pair. If you want him, you get me too." Jared wanted to kick himself as soon as the words tumbled out but, to his surprise, she winked at him.

"I could live with that."

Her words were a gut-punch. He knew it was only good-natured razzing, but he wanted it to be more. After all these years, he was still carrying a torch for Anna Beth Howard.

Son of a bitch.

Twelve

Anna Beth stroked the top of Rip's head, currently nestled in her lap. The dog hadn't left her side since Jared sat down and, when Rip leaned against her, Anna Beth melted. She grinned at Jared from across the coffee shop table.

"Pretty sure I'm his new favorite person," Anna Beth said.

Jared cocked a brow and took a drink of his coffee, his brown eyes filled with amusement. Noticing how his t-shirt hugged his broad shoulders, she silently scolded herself for checking him out. He set his cup down on the table with a gentle tap. "You're still not taking my dog."

Anna Beth sighed dramatically. "Fine, I'll let you keep him." She shot him a sly smile. "For now."

Jared chuckled, a deep rumbling in his chest, and she shivered. Had his voice always been so low and sexy?

Snap out of it. There will be none of that! Friends, remember?

"Why did you name him Rip, anyway?" she asked.

"My favorite character on Yellowstone."

"I haven't seen it."

"What?" Jared's horrified expression sent her into a wave of giggles.

"I don't watch a lot of TV. I like movies."

"But you wrote for television, right?"

"Yes, but catching up on a show is major commitment. Most shows can't hold my interest that long."

"Well this one will. It is an amazing show! Maybe we can schedule a marathon while you're here."

"Sounds fun." She rubbed Rip's velvety ear. "I still want to dog-nap him, but considering my vagabond lifestyle at the moment, I won't be owning any pet for a while. Although, maybe if I could train Mittens to walk on a leash, I could keep her. I've seen videos of cats who accompanied their owners everywhere, even long-distance road trips."

"Are you planning to backpack around the country, sleeping in that car of yours?"

He asked casually, but Anna Beth squirmed in her seat. She knew a lot of people thought she was crazy for not settling in one place, but she needed to find her place. Even in LA, she'd never been at home. "I'm not sure what happens once I'm finished here. I sold my house in LA, so my future plans are up in the air."

Jared shot her a puzzled gaze. "Why did you sell your house?"

"It was Ian's idea. We'd talked about moving out of the area for a while because I never liked living there. The house was big and modern, which I hated, and our next-door neighbor was an evil curmudgeon."

Jared chuckled. "You lived next to a cranky old man, huh?"

"Like Mr. Wilson turned up to one hundred. It's one of

the things I'm really glad Ian asked for on the list, because I'm not sure I would have done it otherwise."

"Why not? If you hated it, why stay?"

Anna Beth thought about all the firsts they'd had in that place. All of the happy times that were now clouded by the fact that Ian wasn't there anymore. "Because it was familiar. But, Ian knew I'd need a fresh start."

"He sounds like a great guy. I'm sorry I never got to know him."

She laughed. "He actually knew quite a bit about you. Almost every story I ever told him about Snowy Springs included you. He asked me once why we never talked anymore, but I didn't have a good answer for him."

"You never told him what I did?"

"No," she admitted, quietly.

"If our roles were reversed, and you'd told me? I would have kicked his ass."

Anna Beth shook her head with a smile. "He wasn't like that. He loved to goof around, but could flip a switch and be logical and level-headed in two seconds flat. He didn't hold grudges."

Jared reached for her hand and squeezed. "If it hurts to talk about him, we don't have to."

His warm, rough palm rubbed across her knuckles and her stomach clenched with awareness. Immediately ashamed, she pulled away. She should not be reacting to Jared's touch while speaking of her dead husband.

"It does hurt, but it's good to talk about him. It's been a year, and he wasn't himself for months before that..."

She trailed off and Rip, as though sensing her sadness, whimpered and rubbed his cheek against her leg. Anna Beth scratched behind his ear and he moaned.

"Are you going to tell me about the reverse bucket list Ian left you?" Jared asked.

"It's really just things he wanted me to accomplish in his memory. Everything you want your loved ones to do after you die."

"Sounds interesting." Jared picked up his coffee and took a drink. "Well, I offered to help. Take advantage of me."

The turn of phrase startled her, especially the images that came along with it. Taking advantage of Jared had been in the forefront of her mind since he held her. It was a bad idea all around, and she'd hoped this crazy attraction to him would go away. After all, he'd said himself he wasn't looking for anything more than friendship.

Suddenly, Jared laughed. "What's that blush about?"

"Nothing," she muttered.

"You sure? A blush like that makes me mighty curious what has you frazzled."

Anna Beth wracked her brain for an appropriate answer and blurted, "The list. One of the things he wants me to do is dress up like The Grinch and deliver Christmas presents to the children's hospital. I'm just embarrassed about it."

"Really? Didn't you ever tell Ian how you nervously puked your way through the Christmas choir concert your sophomore year? Performing is not your strong suit."

"I did, but he enjoyed pushing me out of my comfort zone."

"Gotcha. Well, something tells me we need to build up to that one. What else do you have?"

Anna Beth pulled the journal from her laptop bag, opening it flat against the table. She ran her finger along the page, emotions flooding through her as she read her husband's neat handwriting.

"Cut down my own Christmas tree. Make an ornament.

Dance like no one is watching. Kiss…" Anna Beth hesitated. Would Jared get the wrong impression and think she was hinting?

"Kiss?"

She cleared her throat and forced herself to finish. "Kiss someone under the mistletoe."

"There's no shortage of mistletoe or available men, so that one's easy. Does your aunt have a tree yet?"

"No," Anna Beth answered tersely. Kissing someone else would not be easy for her, even if she was surrounded by thousands of men. She knew he probably skipped over that one for her sake, but sweeping it under the rug like that bugged her.

Did you really think he would offer himself up as tribute? Come on. He is trying to respect boundaries. Don't hold being a good guy against him.

"How about I grab you after work?" Jared said, pulling her from her thoughts.

"What?"

"You need to cut down your own tree, right? Tomorrow morning, we'll head out to Stubb's Christmas Tree Farm. I can teach you how to use a saw and we can grab lunch on the way back."

Anna Beth gave him an evil grin. "You're a brave man for encouraging me to swing a sharp object around."

"Nah, no swinging involved. Just a chainsaw, like Leather Face. If you accidentally maim me, I'll get some time off work during the holidays. Win-win."

"I guess. Maybe I'll grab an old burlap sack and make a mask. Scare the locals."

"Or we could *not* give the good people of Snowy Springs coronaries."

"Fine. I will behave." Realizing the double entendre to

her words, she cleared her throat. "I mean...it sounds like fun. I'm in."

"Fantastic." Jared rapped a knuckle on the table. "We should probably let you get some work done. Come on, Rip."

Rip grunted and nuzzled closer to Anna Beth.

Anna Beth giggled when Jared scowled and ducked his head under the table. "Hey, I bought you a pup-cup. Don't you tell me, 'no.'"

"Actually, I bought him the pup-cup," Anna Beth teased.

Rip made a rumbling whine, backing her up.

Jared sat up straight with a grin. "I guess he told me."

"Sounds like it. If you have some errands to run, I'm happy to keep him with me. I won't run off with him, I swear."

Jared ran a hand through his hair. "I guess I could go to the store and grab a few groceries. Are you sure?"

"Oh, yeah. He's not a bother at all."

"Well, thanks. For the coffee and watching him for me." Jared picked up his knit cap and gloves from the table top and stood. "Be a good boy for Anna Beth and, when I come back, no lip from you."

Rip dropped onto his belly with a huff.

"Am I crazy for thinking he understands me?" Jared asked.

"Not at all. I don't think we give animals enough credit."

"Alright, I'll be right back. Thanks, A.B."

"You're welcome."

Jared headed for the door. Her gaze involuntarily drifted to where his jeans hugged his rear end.

When he turned back to wave, her face caught fire. Had he noticed where she'd been looking? Anna Beth waved awkwardly and when he was safely out the door, she quickly focused at her laptop screen. She needed to concentrate on getting words down instead of how good Jared's butt looked.

She opened her document and read through the last page she wrote, but for some reason, the family drama wasn't calling to her. The characters didn't flow. They fought her at every turn. Other voices had been whispering to her for days, characters far more light hearted and cheery.

Anna Beth stared at the screenplay she'd been working on for months but after ten minutes of typing and erasing the same few sentences, she opened a new file.

Anna Beth closed her eyes, her mind wandering. She prayed to the muses, for some sign of inspiration.

Rip nudged her hand and when she didn't immediately pet him, he flopped onto the ground with a grunt.

She grinned as she peeked under the table at him. "Are you pouting?"

The dog turned his head, his teeth flashing in a smile.

Anna Beth sat back up, chuckling. Animals really were funny creatures and seemed to be the best part of any good movie.

Her eyes closed once more and cheery whispers echoed through her mind. The first scene popped into her head like a tiny projector display. Concentrating, she opened her eyes and typed. Words flew onto the computer screen with ease, something she hadn't experienced with her family drama screenplay, even from the beginning.

The screenplay opened with a woman back in her hometown, suddenly knocked over by a large chocolate lab. She lands on her back in the snow and the cold, white stuff slips into every crevice. She's ready to give the owner a piece of her mind, but when she looks up, she's faced with a very hot guy. Someone she used to know.

Before she knew it, Anna Beth hit return on page five and didn't even look up when Jared dropped into the chair beside her.

"Wow, you're in the zone, huh?"

Anna Beth finished typing the last sentence in the scene and met his gaze with a grin. "Actually, yeah. I have to admit, my writing's been a little slow lately, but today, I feel inspired."

"It's the magic of Snowy Springs, I'm telling you. It's amazing what this place can do for your soul."

"Is that why you never left?" she asked.

Jared shrugged. "That, and my family is here. We might not be bonded by blood, but Karen and Mike mean a lot to me. Besides, I get enough alone time at my place. I live off the beaten path and I enjoy the quiet."

Anna Beth pushed her laptop aside and leaned on the table, lost in her train of thought. "Being around your family makes me miss my parents. Although things with Sarah are better than they were, I still remember how exciting it was, waking up on Christmas morning and finding Mom and Dad on the couch. The fire would be roaring and there were always mountains of presents under the tree." Anna Beth grinned sheepishly as she reached for her coffee cup. "I was a bit spoiled."

"You don't say?" Jared teased.

"Not like the evil brat kind, but I *was* an only child and they tended to go overboard. Mom wrapped them all in different paper, too. She always had the biggest smile when I opened that one gift from Santa. And, after dinner, Dad would bite the leg off a gingerbread man and chase me with it, just to make Mom laugh. I found that happiness again with Ian, but now…"

Her voice trailed off, afraid if she said another word about it she might burst into tears.

Jared slid his chair next to hers and dropped a muscled arm around her shoulders, bringing her against him. He turned her to face him with his other hand on her chin, his gaze holding hers. "You've lost so much, A.B., but I know you'll find that kind of happiness again. You deserve it."

The intensity in Jared's eyes set her skin tingling and her voice came out hoarse. "I hope so."

"I know so." His gentle smile tugged his lips up, crinkling his eyes and she wanted to run her hand along his smooth cheek. Before she could act on the impulse, Jared let her go and climbed to his feet.

"Now, I am going to take my obnoxiously needy dog and get out of your hair. Tomorrow at ten?"

"I can't wait," she said, meaning it.

"Alright." He leaned over and picked up Rip's leash. "Come on, you'll see her tomorrow."

Rip kept looking back at her with dark, soulful eyes and she laughed. As she watched Jared load Rip into the truck, Anna Beth couldn't stop smiling. No matter how confusing her feelings for Jared were, being around him was good for her writing.

Or, maybe he's just good for you?

When she turned back to her screenplay, Anna Beth silently admitted that could be true.

Thirteen

Jared pulled up in front of Sarah's house on Monday morning with two coffees from Foam Capped Java in his cup holder and Rip in the back seat of his truck. Rip eyed the brown bag next to Jared, licking his lips. Jared moved the bag away from his dog and scowled.

"These sandwiches are for humans, not dogs."

Rip let out a series of high-pitched barks and bit the back of the seat.

"Hey! Knock that off and stop arguing. Lately, your attitude sucks. If you were human, I'd call you Casey."

Rip cocked his head with a whine.

"Fine, you're not that bad, but I'm taking these with me in case you get any ideas." Jared picked the bag back up and climbed out. He headed up the walkway, nearly slipping in the fresh layer of powder on the cement.

He couldn't wait to see Anna Beth. Jared stood on the

porch, taking deep, calming breaths. As much as he wanted to play it cool, he'd spent all night at work thinking about today. He knew it was just one old friend helping out another, but catching up with Anna Beth proved to be an addicting pastime for him.

He knocked on the front door with three sharp raps. It opened slowly, revealing Sarah in a lavender dress, looking ready to head out.

"Good morning, Jared."

"Hi, Sarah. Is Anna Beth ready?"

"She's just getting her boots on, but there's a complication."

"Why is that?"

"Come in and see for yourself."

Jared stepped inside and into the living room. Anna Beth sat on the couch tying her boots as a rambunctious gray tabby attacked the laces. Anna Beth kept pushing the wiry fluff ball away, and the cat would simply come back for more. When Anna Beth finally managed to get them secured, the kitten went after her dangling ponytail, biting the top of her head ferociously.

"Dang it, Mitts! You're being a pain." Anna Beth pulled the kitten off her head and held her in front of her face, scowling. "Don't I play with you enough?"

The kitten batted at her face in answer and Anna Beth chuckled, cuddling her close. "You're too cute to be mad at."

"Let me be the judge of that," he said.

Anna Beth looked up as he crossed the room, a broad smile on her face. The gleam in her eyes was so bright, it only encouraged the giddiness bubbling in his stomach. She was as excited for their excursion as he was.

"Look at you right on time."

"I would have been here sooner, but I needed to stop for nourishment." He held out the paper bag to her. "I'll trade you two breakfast sandwiches for one spunky kitten."

"I'm not sure how she is around men,"Anna Beth warned.

"She's fine," Sarah said.

Anna Beth shot her aunt a puzzled glance.

"How do you know?"

Sarah's face flamed. "Look at her. She isn't shying away from him, is she?"

"No, she is not." Anna Beth held Mittens out reluctantly.

He took the kitten from her with one hand while she cradled the bag. The tiny tabby sniffed the front of his shirt and stiffened. She leaned away from him, hissing at his shirt as though it would come alive at any moment.

"Oh, you smell Rip. Not a fan of dogs, huh?" Jared held her against his chest and rubbed her ears and chin until she purred for him. "There, see? I'm not so bad, even if I am a dog person."

"You're just the kind of man it takes a few minutes to warm up to," Sarah said from the doorway. "Or years, in some cases."

Anna Beth laughed.

Jared grinned at Anna Beth's aunt. "I'm offended, Sarah. Are you saying you weren't my number one fan from our first meeting?"

"I think you know the answer to that."

Sarah's tone was teasing, but Jared knew Sarah hadn't liked or understood his friendship with Anna Beth when they were younger. After years of working together at the police station, his relationship with Sarah overcame her initial prejudices and they were on very good terms.

Mittens rubbed her face against his chin and then climbed up onto his shoulder. She sat with her butt next to his cheek and her tail curled over his upper lip.

Anna Beth bent over laughing until Sarah came around to see what was so funny. She covered her mouth and coughed.

"I mustache you a question," Jared said. "Does this cat make me look dashing?"

Anna Beth wheezed, tears spilling from the corner of her eyes.

Sarah, still grinning, closed the distance with her hands out. "Oh my goodness, give me the kitten. You two, get going." Jared lifted the kitten from his shoulder into her waiting hands.

"We will be back this afternoon," Anna Beth said.

"Get us a full tree. Not one of those ugly sparse ones that are all the rage." Sarah set Mittens down on the ground, chuckling as she ran from the room in a grey blur. "I'll pull the ornaments down from the attic while you're gone."

"Are my parent's ornaments up there?" Anna Beth asked, softly. Jared caught her earnest expression and his heart squeezed.

"I think so. I'll get those too."

"I can help when we get back."

Sarah held up a hand. "No, it's fine. I have a friend coming over and he can get them for me."

Anna Beth placed one hand on her hip, her tone teasing. "When am I going to meet this mysterious friend?"

Mittens picked that minute to pounce back into the room and attack Sarah's skirt. A ghost of a smile passed over Sarah's lips as she scooped the pest up, ignoring the kitten's attempts to eat her fingers. "When I'm ready. Now, scoot."

Anna Beth kissed Mittens on the head again as she passed and then bussed her aunt on the cheek. Jared caught Sarah's surprised expression as Anna Beth headed out the door. Jared squeezed Sarah's shoulder.

"I'll bring her back in one piece."

"Of course, you will. If I had any doubts, she wouldn't be leaving with you."

Sarah's light tone belied the warning in her eyes.

"Fair enough. Have a good day, Sarah."

Jared closed the door behind him and caught up to Anna Beth, reaching for the door handle to open it for her.

"You don't have to do that."

"I know. Do you mind?"

"Not at all."

Anna Beth climbed up inside and greeted Rip when Jared closed her door. As he passed the front of the truck, he saw Rip lean over the seat and lick her cheek. Jared grinned when she laughed. Rip taking to Anna Beth as though she'd always been a part of their lives only reinforced Jared's notion that Anna Beth was special.

Jared climbed into the truck and gave Rip a stern look. "Don't be fooled by him. He's buttering you up so he can steal our sandwiches."

"Awww, I'm not stingy. I'll share with him."

"No way. He had breakfast and people food makes him gassy."

Anna Beth sent Rip a sympathetic glance. "Sorry, Rip. Daddy's being mean."

Jared shook his head as he turned the ignition. "I'm not mean. I just don't want to be stuck in a car with his noxious ass."

Anna Beth bent over in her seat, laughing heartily, nearly hitting her head on the dash. Jared smiled as he pulled out of the driveway and onto the road. He'd always loved making Anna Beth happy, no matter how silly it made him look. He'd never been an extrovert, but with Anna Beth, he'd enjoyed breaking from his comfort zone because he trusted her not to make fun of him.

It was easy to slip back into the comfort they'd had as kids, even with everything that happened.

"The coffee closest to you is yours."

"Oh, good. I didn't have a chance to grab a cup before you picked me up."

"Overslept?" Jared noticed Anna Beth hadn't put on makeup and although he thought she looked beautiful, he noticed dark circles under her eyes.

"A little. I was up late, working."

"That's a good thing, right? Got a groove going?"

"Yes, except I started something completely different yesterday and I haven't been able to stop."

The way she laughed struck a chord of genuine curiosity. "What is it?"

"A romantic comedy. It's pretty fun, actually, and so easy. I have to admit, I've been struggling with my original screenplay, but this...well, it doesn't feel like work."

"A rom-com, huh? That's not usually your bag, is it?"

Anna Beth blushed scarlet. "Not usually, but I guess I was inspired."

Jared almost asked *by what?* But he didn't want to seem like he was fishing. And if there was another guy in the picture... Well, he *definitely* didn't want to know.

"I think it's great you can do what you love and still make money at it."

"A lot of people enjoy their careers. Don't you love being a police officer?"

"Yes, and no. I want to help people. Keep them safe. But a lot of the job is enforcing the law, which doesn't necessarily endear you to your community. It's never fun to see a cop."

"If they didn't break the law, then they wouldn't get the cops called or pulled over."

Jared chuckled. "You would think people would understand that, but that's not the way it works."

"That blows. I'm sorry."

He shrugged. "Not your fault. I chose this career, and it's what I want to be doing."

"It must be hard having people rip on you for something they did." Anna Beth handed him his sandwich, which he ate one-handed. He saw Anna Beth slipping a small sliver of bacon back to Rip, but he didn't bust her.

"It's not easy, but luckily, Snowy Springs isn't a high crime area. The most I get are the cranky motorists."

Anna Beth took a sip of her coffee before confessing, "To be honest, if you pulled me over, I'd be cranky."

"I appreciate the warning."

She didn't respond and Jared glanced over at her in the passenger seat, staring out the window as the trees past. He almost asked what struck her so quiet, but he didn't want to be too nosy. He'd already pried information about Ian's list out of her.

"So, Stubbs Farm, huh?" she said, finally turning his way. "It's been a while since I've been there."

"And still haven't made it down Stubb's Sledding Hill."

Anna Beth coughed on a mouthful of sandwich. When she finally stopped, she asked, "Are you crazy? If you couldn't get me on Slaughter Hill at fifteen, you're not dragging me up that mountain at twenty-six."

"You're still a wuss."

"I prefer to think of it as intelligent. If I don't go down a giant hill with a crap ton of trees, I live to write another day."

Jared turned into the entrance of the farm and parked his truck. "First things first, tree cutting. Then, we'll discuss your lack of adventure."

Jared climbed out of his truck with his coffee in hand, downing the now tepid liquid and slipping the empty cup into the door of his truck. He opened the back and grabbed Rip's leash as the lab leaped out of the back seat and onto the ground.

"A.B., you wanna hang onto Rip while I grab the saw?"

"Absolutely."

When she reached for the leash, their hands held for a moment, and he stared into her wide green eyes as lightning bolts shot up his arm from their connection. Her lips parted and a soft sigh escaped between them.

"Do you feel that?" he whispered.

Anna Beth blinked several times. "Yes."

Thank God, it wasn't one sided this time.

"What are we going to do about it?" he asked.

"I'm…I'm not sure."

Jared released her hand, moving to cup her cheek. She swayed toward him when he leaned over and kissed her forehead.

He released her suddenly, before he lost all sense and kissed her somewhere else.

"We'll put a pin in it for now." He grabbed the chainsaw from the back of the truck, his heart still galloping in his chest. "Let's get your tree."

Fourteen

Was it possible to explode from pent up hormones? If so, Anna Beth would be considered combustible.

She stared at Jared's broad shoulders as she followed him through the trees with Rip by her side. When he'd asked her if she felt it too, all the air left her body. She'd barely been able to release that breathy yes. Anna Beth could still feel the warm press of his lips against her forehead and the sensation of his breath on her skin. They were out here among the trees, trying so hard to be the friends they were before, but it was different. He was different.

When they were teens, she'd thought he was cute and sweet. It was a simple, innocent crush. Nothing about the way her body reacted when they touched now was innocent though, and she had no idea what to do about this insane attraction to him. Because, as much as she fought it, the feelings weren't going away.

At least he wasn't pressing her to figure out what she wanted to do about their chemistry yet, because she had no clue how to answer him.

"How big does your aunt want the tree to be?"

Anna Beth picked up her pace to match his, but the minute she sped up, so did Rip. "Ack, slow down, or Imma face plant, Rip."

"You can go ahead and drop the leash," Jared said. "I just didn't want anyone to see him off it and complain. A police officer breaking a leash law. Wouldn't be right."

Anna Beth chuckled, dropping the leash to the ground. "Something tells me you're a rebel with a badge."

"That may be the sweetest thing anyone's ever said to me." In a deep, commanding voice, he called, "Rip, heal."

Rip ran to his master's side, keeping pace with him.

"That's impressive."

"Not really. If you spend time working with a dog, they'll respond to your attention." He stopped, letting her catch up. "Now, you were going to tell me how big you want your conquest to be."

Anna Beth stumbled, catching herself before she fell. "What?"

Jared arched a brow. "The tree?"

"Oh, right." God, she must be beet red. "We're putting it in the living room. With the vaulted ceiling, she thinks seven feet would be perfect."

"Mmmm, we'll have to hike a little farther in then." He turned around and kept moving as though the steady incline in the snow didn't bother him a bit.

Anna Beth sucked in a breath and followed, keeping her breathing as even as possible so he wouldn't realize how out of shape she was.

"Fine by me. You're the one who needs his beauty rest."

Jared smiled over his shoulder. "You think I'm pretty, huh?"

Her face warmed, but she didn't let him completely fluster her. "Actually, I insinuated you need more sleep to be pretty."

"Tsk, tsk, so mean to the guy helping you cut down a tree."

"I was kidding and you know it, drama llama."

"I guess I'll have to take your word for it." Jared yawned and Anna Beth laughed. "Sorry."

"No need to apologize. I know you should be sleeping right now, and I appreciate you staying up for me."

Jared stopped, letting her catch up. "Isn't that what friends do?"

"Of course." She stopped next to him, taking a deep breath. "Hang on a second."

Jared made a guilty face. "Sorry, I have a long stride. My mom is always griping at me when I get ten steps ahead."

"No it's fine, I just need to catch my breath. I don't do a lot of hiking. My work is pretty sedentary, and although I have a walking desk for my treadmill, both are packed away in my storage unit." Taking one last deep breath, she straightened up. "Speaking of work, do you like working nights?"

"Yeah. I can get things done in the morning after I get off work and then crash."

"I'm not much of a night owl. I prefer getting up with the morning sun."

"You mean bedtime?"

"Not for everyone." Anna Beth laughed.

"I know, I'm just teasing." Jared pointed up ahead. "I think I see our Huckleberry. Just a little bit further."

"Great." Anna Beth eyed the chainsaw warily as Jared

made a beeline toward a gorgeous noble fir. "I've never used a chainsaw before."

"I'll show you how to do it. When you cut the tree, you'll need to be on the ground to cut low enough."

Anna Beth looked around the trees they passed. Where there wasn't snow, there was dirt. "On my stomach?"

"Or squat, but it's easier when you lay down. How about this one?"

At least seven-foot-tall, the full tree flared out at the bottom with thick needles. It was beautiful and exactly what her aunt wanted.

Anna Beth followed Jared around the tree as he inspected it. "No holes. You like?"

"I like."

"Then, let's do this." Jared picked up Rip's leash and led the dog off to the side. "Stay." Rip lay down and watched his master walk back.

Jared held the chainsaw out for her to take and Anna Beth hesitated. "Here, I'll come behind you and go through how to get it going together."

When Jared wrapped his arms around her from behind, the front of his body pressed along her back. The contact created instant electricity between them, although he seemed oblivious. While her heart raced, he calmly spoke in her ear, his warm breath tickling the sensitive spot on her neck.

"Is this okay?"

The shiver that shot through her body had nothing to do with the cold. "Mmmmhmm."

"Good. Take the chainsaw from me."

She did what he said and he continued, "Now, we're going to flip it to full choke, here, by pressing this lever up. Then, pull the cord until it starts and dies. After that, flip the lever to half choke like this and pull the cord till the saw starts. Once it's running, flip the choke off and hold the blades against the trunk. When you're ready, pull the trigger."

"What's the trigger?"

"This handle here." He covered her hand with his and moved it over the end. "Feel it?"

The motion brought his body tighter against hers and her breath rushed out. "Yes."

"Then let her rip."

Jared stepped back and to the side to watch her. Anna Beth went through his instructions again, and when the chainsaw came to life, it vibrated all the way down her arms. Her stomach fluttered nervously.

"Do I need safety goggles for this?"

Jared laughed. "You'll be fine. Now, turn it off by flipping the choke lever and get into position. I think you'll have more control on your stomach."

Anna Beth lay down on the ground and crawled under the tree. The scent of moldy earth hit her nose and she wiggled under the lower branches Jared held up for her.

With a deep breath, she went through the steps he'd explained and pressed the rotating blades against the trunk. Her arms vibrated as they sliced through the meat of the tree. A fine shower of sawdust sprayed the ground in the opposite direction as the blade slid through the wood. When the tree disappeared above her, she shut off the chainsaw and stood.

Jared held the tree a few feet away, grinning. "Look at you."

"I did it!"

"You sure did. Next, you can come over and help me split wood for my fireplace."

"Not a chance. My arms feel like they're going to fall off."

"It's like that the first time, but you get used to it." Jared held the tree out for display. "Should we carry it back and get this baby ready for travel?"

"Let's do it. Wait!"

"What's up?"

"Will you take a picture of me with the chainsaw and the tree?"

He smiled. "Come on over here and I will."

Anna Beth took ahold of the tree trunk near the middle as Jared backed up with his cell phone.

"All for the gram, right?"

"Just for me. Proof that I did it."

Jared snapped the picture and walked back over to take the tree from her. "If you ever forget, I'll remind you how awesome you are."

Anna Beth's stomach fluttered again, but her reaction had everything to do with Jared's warm brown eyes staring at her like he wanted to kiss her. Did she want him to? If Jared did, should she drop the chainsaw and hold him or hang onto it? Why was she overthinking this?

Finally, he looked away and hefted the tree off the ground by the trunk and a branch. Relief and disappointment filled her at the same time.

"Rip, heel."

The brown dog came up alongside them and Jared headed back toward the truck.

Anna Beth did a better job keeping up with him on the way back. "Do you want me to take one end and you hold the other?"

"Nope, I'm good."

"I feel weird watching you carry that tree alone."

Jared chuckled. "You shouldn't. You cut down this big mother. Least I can do is get it back to the truck."

"Thank you for helping me do this."

"Happy to. I get to spend time with you and you get to check another item off your list. Good deal for me either way."

Jared's words warmed Anna Beth from the inside out. After she paid, they loaded the tree and chainsaw into the back of the truck, she asked, "What about you? Don't you need a tree?"

"I'm not as tough as you. Usually get my tree pre-cut from Snowy Springs General."

"Sissy," she teased.

"Speaking of sissies..." Jared reached into the back of the truck and pulled out a sled. "You ready?"

Anna Beth's eyes widened. "Hell, no."

"Come on. I'm sure Ian would approve of this being added to the list of things you need to do. Overcome your fear, A.B."

"Not gonna happen."

Jared unclipped Rip's leash. "Come on, buddy. Let's go play."

"Jared, no. I'm not doing this." Jared clucked like a chicken and she laughed. "Very mature."

"I promise you'll be perfectly safe." He held his hand out. "Trust me."

Anna Beth hesitated, ultimately taking it. "If I die, I'm going to haunt you forever."

"Deal."

Jared retrieved an extra pair of gloves from the truck for her and led her toward the hill. She followed behind him through the snow, Rip bouncing along beside them. Off the designated trails, snow flew up past her snow boots and soaked through her jeans, but Jared's hand surrounding hers made the rest of her feel toasty.

"What did you mean by you *usually* get your tree from Snowy Springs General?"

"I decided not to do one this year. Save some money."

"Why?"

"Cause it's just Rip and me. We normally go to my parents for all holiday festivities. Didn't seem practical. Besides, I never put any ornaments on, just lights."

Anna Beth frowned. "Why no ornaments?"

"My mom has all the ones from when I was a kid, and it's not something I'd shop for on my own. I think tree decorating is more of a family or couples thing."

Anna Beth thought about the box of ornaments she'd asked her aunt to find. Most of them were hand made and cutesy. They didn't belong with her aunt's expensive glass ornaments.

Maybe she should buy one of those three-foot-tall ones in a pot and set it up in her room.

It suddenly sounded like a lot of effort and she understood Jared's point.

When they reached the crest of the hill, Anna Beth swallowed, all the elation melting away. The hill was clear for the most part, but towards the bottom, trees sporadically grew with only a few feet between them. Everyone she'd grown up with had gone down Slaughter Hill at least once and lived to tell the tale, but it still scared the hell out of her.

"This is nuts."

"Come on, selfie time," Jared said.

Anna Beth laughed as he pressed his cheek to hers and held the camera up.

"Say, danger!" He snapped the pic and showed it to her. "See? You barely look terrified."

"You are so not funny."

"I'm hilarious." Jared set the sled down and got on the back. He pulled the gloves he'd brought her out of his pocket and held them up to her. "Put these on, sit your ass down, and let's go."

Anna Beth pulled the gloves on and then slowly climbed onto the sled with her feet on either side. Jared's arm wrapped around her waist, pulling her back against him, her butt cradled in his crotch.

"You ready?" he asked.

Heart pounding a terrified tattoo against her breast bone, Anna Beth nodded. "As I'll ever be."

"If I yell, 'bail', roll off."

"Seriously?" she cried.

"Yep. Pick your feet up."

"Oh, God."

"One."

The trees suddenly looked much closer together. "Jared…"

"Two."

"I don't—"

Jared pushed off before three, both his arms going around her body. Anna Beth screamed as the wind whipped her face, snow flying around them as they rushed down the hill. She heard Rip barking, but couldn't see him, the world around her a blur of shapes.

"Lean right," Jared said.

Anna Beth leaned and they glided past a tree. Exhilaration seized her and she squealed with laughter.

"Not so bad, right?"

"Not yet!"

Jared laughed and she reached down, covering his hands at her waist with hers.

"Left."

They leaned together, but the minute they rounded that tree, there was another in their path.

"Bail!"

She didn't have time to react before Jared's arms tightened

around her and they rolled off, into the snow, over and over until they slowed to a stop.

Anna ended up on top of Jared, but snow still covered her back, soaking into her jeans. She pushed up, her gloved hands sinking into the powder.

"Are you alright?"

Jared's beanie was nowhere to be found and a thick layer of snow clung to his hair. He opened his eyes, grinning up at her.

"I'm great. Fun, right?"

Anna Beth returned his smile. "Yes, except I'm soaking wet."

His hands drifted down to her waist and squeezed over her jacket, massaging the muscles of her lower back. "I guess we should get you back to the truck and warm you up."

Her breath caught as his touch burned through her clothes. "What about you? Aren't you cold?"

"Not at the moment."

Anna Beth's gaze drifted to his mouth and her head dropped. Jared leaned up, closing the distance between them.

Suddenly, a brown snout pushed between them and a pink tongue caught Anna Beth right on the lips. She wrinkled her nose and sat back, pushing at Rip as he rained kisses all over her face.

"Damn it, Rip. You have the worst timing," Jared said, maneuvering into a sitting position.

Anna Beth ducked her head against Jared's chest with a laugh, avoiding more dog licks and felt Jared's hand slide down her head to the back of her neck.

She met his gaze, still smiling.

"A.B.?"

"Yeah?"

"I'm going to wait until three this time and then I'm going

to kiss you. If you don't want me to, all you have to do is say so. One..."

Anna Beth blinked, her brain screaming that the dog interrupting them was a sign, that they shouldn't be doing this. That it wasn't good for either of them...

Oh, screw it. Why would you fight something that makes you feel good?

"Two."

Anna Beth didn't let him get to three. She leaned in and pressed her mouth to his.

Jared's fingers tangled in her ponytail and he opened his mouth under hers, giving her access. Anna Beth drew him closer, moaning as their tongues met.

God, it feels so good to be close to him.

His other arm snaked around her waist and she rolled her hips as she straddled his lap, trying to ease the arousal between her legs.

Jared pulled back, breathing hard. "Anna Beth, we need to get out of here. As much as I'm enjoying kissing you, I'm about to develop frostbite on my ass."

"Oh! Crap!" Anna Beth scrambled off his lap and climbed to her feet. Jared laughed, getting up off the ground and scraping snow off his pants.

Once the haze of desire cleared, she realized her legs were stinging in the snow-soaked denim jeans. "I'm freezing too."

Jared tucked a strand of hair behind her ear gently, his gaze locked on hers. "Let's get back to the truck. We can go to my place to warm up."

Anna Beth swallowed, her stomach performing somersaults on the long walk through the snow. How warm was he talking? Getting cozy by the fire or heating things up under the covers? Because one of them, she definitely wasn't ready for.

Before her mind ran away from her, Jared reached back for her hand.

"I suggested my house because it's only a few miles away. You can borrow some clothes and we'll dry yours before I take you home." Jared kissed her hand. "That's it."

Having him say it out loud left her disappointed. "Nothing else?"

He glanced back at her and winked. "Not unless you want to."

Anna Beth knew she wasn't prepared to jump into bed with Jared but they'd already crossed the line. Another a kiss or two couldn't hurt.

Fifteen

Jared held the door for Anna Beth as she stepped inside, Rip hot on her heels. He kicked off his boots and slid them with one foot under the bench behind the door and hung his jacket up on the hooks against the wall.

It took everything he had not to pull her to him and kiss her as she passed. He'd promised to take this at her pace and he'd meant it, so jumping her as soon as she made it inside his house could send her running for the hills.

But it was down right torture to be this close to her and do nothing. The sensation of her lips on his would forever be burned into his mind as the most amazing kiss of his life.

"I'll head upstairs and grab some dry clothes. Feel free to look around. It's my Mona Lisa."

"My aunt said you did all the renovations yourself."

"I had some help from friends and family, but most of it was just me."

"Impressive."

Jared followed her gaze around his living room. His floors were a marbled laminate with accents of gray and red. With the exception of the gray accent wall, the rest of the living room sported walls in a clean eggshell white. His fireplace recessed into the gray wall, while his brown leather couches ran adjacent with each side of the fireplace. Gray and red plaid throw blankets hung over the backs of the couches and in the center sat a dark wood coffee table, with wagon wheel accents on the end.

"I'm surprised you don't have a TV in here," Anna Beth said.

"It's usually just me and I watch in bed, so…"

Why did you mention your bed? Now she's going to think that's what's on your mind.

Not that being intimate with Anna Beth was far from his thoughts, but not what he meant now!

Anna Beth cleared her throat. "I like it."

"Thanks. I'll be right back."

He jogged up the stairs and pulled two pairs of sweatpants, two t-shirts, and a sweatshirt from his drawers and closet. When he got back downstairs, Anna Beth's coat lay over the back of his couch. He found her in his kitchen, looking through his cupboards.

"Whatcha searching for?"

"Hot chocolate. Or tea."

Jared set the clothes down on the island and walked over to the corner by the sink. "I have some K-cups over here in the polar bear cookie jar."

The white chubby bear wore a pink and red hat and a scarf of the same color scheme. "Cute."

Jared rolled his eyes. "Mom got it for me. Said my house was too sterile and needed something colorful."

"I agree. It really brings something to the room."

"Yeah, a place to store my coffee." Jared rummaged through the leftover K-cups from the variety pack he'd bought a few weeks ago and pulled out two of the hot chocolates. "Here we go."

"Got any mini marshmallows?"

"I doubt it, but I'll look. Why don't you go change? I can hear your teeth chattering and it's kind of annoying."

"Rude." Anna Beth stuck her tongue out at him.

"Says the grown-ass woman making faces."

Anna Beth giggled as she picked up half of the clothes and walked out of the kitchen. Jared waited until he heard the bathroom door close before he slid his jeans down. The skin of his legs was an irritated shade of pink from the wet material rubbing on it and he'd love nothing more than to stay only in his boxers, but he didn't want to alarm Anna Beth. Instead, he slipped into a pair of baggy sweatpants, thankful for the soft inside against his chaffed skin.

Jared could just imagine Anna Beth running like a cartoon character through his front door, leaving a human shaped hole in the wood if she caught him in his skivvies.

The bathroom door opened and Anna Beth came back into the kitchen. She slowed in the entryway when she saw him shirtless, wearing only a pair of sweat pants. Jared picked the dry t-shirt off the counter, swiftly sliding it over his head.

To his surprise, she set her wet clothes on the counter and leaned against it with a grin. "There was no hurry. I was enjoying the view."

His cheeks warmed. "Your teasing is gonna get me into trouble."

"Why is that?"

"Because I'm trying to take it slow, and I really don't want to."

This time, she blushed. Instead of razzing her about it, he turned away to open the cabinet. "No marshmallows."

"Where is your dryer? I'll put the clothes in."

Jared pointed. "Through there."

She came around beside him, picking his clothes up off the floor. He reached down to stop her and her head bumped into his chin.

"Shit! Are you okay?" Her hand pressed along the side of his face and he covered it with his own.

"Yeah, I'm good," he said. "I was just going to say, you don't have to dry mine. I'll wash them later."

Her thumb stroked along his cheek. "Alright."

Jared kissed her palm, then nibbled her wrist. "You smell good."

"Jared?"

"Yeah?"

"Can you kiss me, please?"

Her words shot through his body like a bold of electricity. Forgetting all about the hot chocolate and clothes, Jared hooked his other arm around her waist and pulled her against him. His head dipped, but instead of taking her parted lips, his mouth pressed just below her jawline. Her sharp intake of breath told him everything he needed to know and he trailed kisses along Anna Beth's throat until he reached the tender point under her earlobe.

The delicious vanilla scent of her skin drew Jared in and he wanted to kiss every inch of her body, something he'd dreamed of for years.Anna Beth moaned when he took her lobe between his lips and nibbled gently, his cock ramrod straight against the cotton sweats when she rubbed her body against his.

Jared finally took her lips in a hard, hot kiss, losing himself in the taste of her. He'd imagined what it would feel like to have Anna Beth in his arms and now that he'd experienced the reality, he wanted to stay like this forever.

But if he moved to fast, overwhelmed her with his need, she could bolt. Despite every part of him protesting, he broke the kiss, breathing rapidly.

"Sorry."

Anna Beth was panting, her wide green eyes glued on his face. "I'm not."

"Wrong thing to say."

"What do you me—oof!"

Jared picked her up against him, his hands gripping the backs of her thighs as carried her into the living room. Rip barked in circles around them until Jared sat down on the couch, Anna Beth straddling his lap.

Anna Beth giggled as Rip jumped up next to them, going for her face.

"Agh, he doesn't like it when we're too close," she said. "Rip, off."

The lab jumped down with a whimper, still watching them intently. Jared's focus returned to Anna Beth as he held her, his hands slipping under the t-shirt she wore and slid along the bare skin of her back. So soft. Warm. He wanted to dig his fingers into the muscles of her back and bury his face in her chest.

She closed her eyes, her full lips parting as she breathed his name. "Jared."

Anna Beth leaned over, wrapping her arms around his neck. He met her kiss and continued massaging her back, taking in her moans every time their lips met. Jared longed to move his hands around and cup her breasts, but he kept himself in check.

Even if it killed him.

Anna Beth's hands on his chest slid south across his abdomen. Lower. So close. Almost fucking there.

When she stopped moving, he almost howled in frustration, until he heard the distant ringtone.

"Shit, that's my phone." She smiled apologetically. "I'll be right back."

Jared sat there, staring down at his tented erection. Trying to get a handle on himself, he chanted quietly, "Pus. Rotten garbage. Maggots."

It didn't work but worth a shot.

Jared listened to Anna Beth speaking, her voice rising in worried tones and climbed painfully to his feet. He stopped in the doorway and watched her pace, her brow furrowed as she held the cell phone to her ear.

"Is she okay? I'll leave now and meet you at home. No, she's my responsibility, I should be there. Are you sure? Thanks, Sarah."

She removed the cell phone from her ear, holding it at her side limply.

"Everything alright?" he asked.

"Not really." Anna Beth grabbed his sweatshirt and pulled it over her head before answering. "That was Sarah. She's took Mittens to the vet."

"What for?"

"Sarah said she started wheezing when she breathed and Sarah thought she might have a fever. The vet said she has pneumonia, so she needs antibiotics."

Jared moved to her side and ran a hand over her hair. "I am so sorry she is sick, but I think Mittens is tough. She'll be fine."

"I hope so." Anna Beth slipped her arms around him, resting her chin on his chest. "I know we were in the middle of something, but can we pick this up later?"

"Yeah, of course. Let me get my keys and I'll take you home." He dropped a kiss on her forehead and she released him.

"Thanks, Jared."

"Sure. We should get your tree in some water, anyway."

"Right. I almost forgot about that."

Jared grinned. "I'm going to take that as a compliment."

Anna Beth laughed. "You should."

Jared headed upstairs to grab his jacket and two pairs of socks for him and Anna Beth. He hated to cut his time with her short, but maybe it was better this way. A few more minutes of her straddling him, and he'd have forgotten all about going slow and had her flat on her back, his head between her...

Stop thinking about that, for fucks sake!

When he reached into his sock drawer, his hand closed around the letter at the bottom. He didn't want to think about Ian Crawford right now. Making out on his couch with Anna Beth probably wasn't what Ian had in mind by helping her. And with that thought, Jared's erection dissipated.

Should he tell Anna about the letter? Ian's instructions were specific, but would she be pissed at him later for not telling her?

If he was being honest, Jared wasn't ready yet. It might make him a selfish prick, but he wanted a little more time with Anna Beth without Ian hovering between them like a ghost.

He put the letter back, covering it with his folded socks once more.

"Jared? What are you doing?"

"Just grabbing socks. Be right there."

Jared closed the door and took the stairs two at a time. He'd give Anna Beth her letter when she finished her list and hopefully, whatever was inside didn't destroy the blossoming connection they were building.

"Here's some socks."

"Thanks." She held a bundle of damp clothes in her arms. "Is there a bag I can put my wet clothes in?"

Jared grabbed a plastic grocery bag from the top of the fridge. "Here you go. I can dry them and get them back to you."

"No, it's okay. I appreciate the offer though." She shoved the clothes into the bag, then stood up on her tip toes and kissed him. "You're sweet."

"I know, but my willpower can only take so much. Let's get you home and see how Mittens is feeling."

Jared shrugged into his jacket while Anna Beth sat down and put her feet into his socks. Watching her on the couch, wearing his clothes, nothing had ever felt so right. Anna Beth belonged here, with him. He knew it in his gut.

The question was…how would he convince her of that when she was hell bent on leaving?

He took her hand and lifted her to her feet. "You look good in my shirt, by the way."

"Is that your best line, Officer Cross," she teased.

"I was being ardently sincere!"

"Uh huh."

Jared kissed the back of her hand. "I'm wounded." He led her through the front door, shutting it on Rip, who barked with outrage through the thick wood.

"Sorry, buddy. I still love you."

Anna Beth laughed. "It's so funny the way you talk to him."

"He's my only company most of the time. Gotta show him respect."

Jared turned the keys in the ignition and cranked the heat on high.

"Hey," Anna Beth said.

Jared turned in time for her to slide across the seat and kiss him. "Thank you. This is the best day I've had in a long time."

"It won't be the last, A.B. I promise you that."

Jared cupped her cheek, his heart aching like crazy. Before

she'd come to town, he'd been so sure he was over her, but the truth was, he'd never stopped wanting Anna Beth Howard. Now, he had less than three weeks to convince her to stay.

Sixteen

Cycling through several emotions as they made the drive back to her aunt's house, Anna Beth stared out the window trying to make sense of them all. Frustration that they'd been interrupted. Worry over Mittens. Happiness as Jared drove with one hand and held hers with the other.

And below all that, the niggling sense they were making a colossal mistake.

As good as it felt being with him, something could just as easily go wrong and then they'd be right back where they started, only worse. The two of them not talking and Anna Beth missing him like crazy.

Whenever she'd slipped and mentioned Jared to Ian, he'd always urged her to call him to work things out, but Anna Beth could never work up the courage. A few days ago, she'd thought they could rebuild their friendship again, but there was no way they could go back to being platonic even if Anna Beth wanted to.

She'd never be able to forget the way his kiss made her burst into flames.

Jared parked along the street in front of her aunt's house and killed the engine. There was a blue pickup in the driveway next to Anna Beth's car.

"Wonder why Ernie's here," Jared said.

"Ernie? From The Peaks?"

"Yeah, that's his truck."

Anna Beth smiled, the potential of solving the mystery of her aunt's special friend pushing back her deep, emotional dilemma. "Let's go find out."

Jared squeezed her hand. "Should we get the tree first?"

"Absolutely. And I'm helping this time.

Anna Beth let go of his hand and climbed out of the truck. She caught her aunt watching them from the window and wondered if she was upset to see her. Sarah told her on the phone she didn't need to come home, but Anna Beth didn't feel right leaving her aunt alone with a sick kitten. Mittens was her responsibility, but if she'd known Sarah wanted her to stay away because she wasn't ready to introduce Anna Beth to her company, she probably would have stayed at Jared's despite her concern for her kitty. They'd made so much headway in their relationship, Anna Beth didn't want to ruin it by pissing Sarah off now.

Even if she was dying to meet the person who had made Sarah so emphatically happy.

Jared climbed into the back of the truck while Anna Beth took the skinny end of the tree and lifted. A rusty old truck slowed next to them and the passenger rolled down their window. It was Rachel Walsh, Bianca Price, and Linda Richards, three of her aunts sewing circle friends. Anna Beth had a fondness for them, as they tended to be more laid back than the other women Sarah collaborated with.

"Anna Beth, it is so good to see you," Bianca called from the driver's seat. A thin woman in her fifties, Bianca wore her blonde hair in a sleek a-line.

"You too. What are you ladies up to?"

"We are going by the community center to work on stockings for the winter festival. Are you two going?" Rachel asked.

Anna Beth glanced at Jared, who shrugged. "I'm not sure yet."

"We hope to see you there!" Bianca said with a wave. "I must say it's nice to see you two together. I always thought you would make a handsome couple."

Anna Beth blushed. "We aren't a couple. Just friends."

"Oh!" Bianca's expression fell. "I am sorry to assume. Good luck getting that tree inside. Tell Sarah we said hello."

"Will do."

Once they were out of sight, Anna Beth snorted. "Man, people really can't mind their business, can they?"

"Not here."

His tone of voice was cool and clipped.

Anna Beth frowned. "You okay?"

"Yeah, I'm just cold and tired. I want to get this tree set up so I can get home and go to bed."

"Of course. Sorry." Anna Beth's stomach knotted. Where had this shift in mood come from? Five minutes ago, he'd been so sweet and tender. Anna Beth racked her brain all the way up to the house for what could have set Jared off and nothing stood out.

When they reached the door, Anna Beth twisted the knob and pushed her way in. "We're here."

She turned the corner into the living room and found Sarah and Ernie sitting next to each other on the couch. Mittens padded out of the kitchen and meowed at her feet.

"Hey, baby. I'll pick you up in just a minute." She carried the tree further into the living room so Jared could get inside.

Ernie stood up. "Hello, Jared. Anna Beth. Let me help with that."

"We got it," Anna Beth said. "Where we going?"

"Sarah, do you have a bucket for the tree?" Jared asked.

"I put it in the kitchen. It's already filled in the corner."

"Great. We'll be right back, then," Anna Beth said.

Jared led the way into the kitchen, walking all the way to the end of the room so Anna Beth could get all the way through the door. He stuck the bottom of the tree in the bucket of water and Anna Beth let go so he could lean it against the wall. Neither of them said a word for several moments until Jared broke the silence.

"You're going to have to keep this filled."

"I will. Thank you."

"Yeah, of course. I'm just going to say good-bye to your aunt and Ernie before I take off."

Anna Beth frowned as he left the kitchen. Mittens wound her way between her legs and she finally picked up the tabby.

"What do you think is wrong with him?"

Mittens rubbed against her chin in response, her purr a rattling sound in her chest.

"Poor baby. At least you're still in a good mood."

She heard the front door open and rushed into the entryway. Jared was in the doorway with one foot on the porch.

"Hey. Were you going to leave without saying good-bye?"

He shot her a narrowed glance. "No, I was just going to grab your bag of clothes."

Temper pricked Anna Beth as he stood there, looking completely put out with her. She needed to get to the bottom of his attitude. "I'll go with you." She kissed Mittens and set her down on the ground. She waved at Ernie and Sarah. "I'll be right back."

She closed the door behind her, following a silent Jared down the walkway.

"What's up with you?"

"Nothing."

"Nothing? Bullshit. You are being curt towards me."

Jared sighed, running a hand through his hair. "I'm sorry. I'm just thinking."

"About what?"

"I was thinking about today. It was a really good day, one of the best I've had in a while."

Anna Beth softened. "Me, too."

His tone hardened as he added, "But you're going to leave and the more people who see us, the more they'll suspect there's something going on."

"True." Anna Beth didn't like this coldness, not after what they'd shared.

"And I'm not sure I want the attention."

His words landed like a ton of bricks in the pit of her stomach. "Earlier, you didn't seem to care."

"I was caught up in the moment before. Now I've had some clarity. I need to think."

"Think about?"

Jared crossed his arms over his chest. "About whether I'm prepared to keep things casual between you and me. Because that's what we're doing right? If we keep going the way we are, we're together until you leave and that's it."

Anna Beth didn't know what to say. She didn't want to promise him she'd stay because she wasn't sure she wanted to. But she didn't want to just hook up with Jared either.

Maybe she needed time to sort through her feelings, too.

"I don't know what you want me to say? I'm okay if you need a few days, but you were the one who started this. You said three weeks was plenty of time to connect with an old friend."

Jared sighed, dropping his arms from their defensive position. "I know and I'm not trying to send you mixed signals. I don't need you to say anything. I think we both need a day or two to consider what we're doing and the repercussions of our actions."

"I agree," she whispered.

He opened the passenger door and pulled out her bag of clothes, handing it to her. "Thank you. So, just wait and see?"

"Yeah." He squeezed her shoulder gently. "I'll text you in a few days."

A lump formed in Anna Beth's throat as she watched him walk around his truck and climb inside.

She waited until he disappeared around the corner before she trudged back up to the house, tears spilled over onto her cheeks.

When Anna Beth shut the front door behind her, she ducked her head so Sarah and Ernie wouldn't see her crying and peeked around the corner.

"Hey, I'm not feeling so great. I think I'm going to carry Mittens upstairs and take a nap. You two enjoy your visit."

"Anna Beth, are you alright?" her aunt asked.

"Oh yeah." Her voice came out hoarse and she cleared her throat. "It's been a busy day. Just need a little power nap. It was nice seeing you again, Ernie."

"You too."

Anna Beth picked Mittens up and climbed the stairs slowly. When she reached her room, she sat on the bed, stroking the kitten's soft fur. Mittens squirmed away from her to attack a bit of fluff on the floor and Anna Beth lay back on the bed, letting the tears slip along her cheeks and into her hair.

She hated this confusion and hurt. Why couldn't she have gone with her gut and kept her hands to herself?

Because it felt too amazing to ignore.

And now they were back to not talking because a couple of women thought they were a couple?

Put yourself in his shoes and how it might look. Especially if you do leave in less than three weeks.

Anna Beth knew her inner voice had a point, but she didn't have to like it.

A few minutes went by and Mitten's hopped onto the bed, cuddling into the crook of her arm. Anna Beth turned onto her side and snuggled with the kitten, the steady rumble of her purrs soothing her heartache.

She heard the front door open and close. Footfalls on the stairs told her Sarah was coming and she wiped at her face when her aunt rapped softly on her door.

"Come in."

Anna Beth didn't sit up when her aunt poked her head in.

"Hi. Are you alright?"

"Yeah, I'm just tired."

To her surprise, Sarah came into her room and sat on the end of her bed. She placed a hand on Anna Beth's leg and squeezed her calf. "If you need me, I'm here to listen."

Although they'd made leaps and bounds in their relationship the last few days, Anna Beth didn't know how to talk to her aunt about men.

"Thank you. I'm fine," Anna Beth said.

"If you're sure..."

Sarah stood up, preparing to leave and loneliness ripped through Anna Beth, causing her to blurt out, "Ernie seems nice."

Her aunt paused at the door and turned, her lips turning up softly. "He is. I enjoy his company."

"That's important. How did it happen?"

Sarah came back to the bed and sat. "I guess two years ago at the Sweetie Pie Dance. It's the first one I ever went to that I entered a pie into the auction. Ernie won my pie and my company for the night. We'd been acquaintances all our lives, but that night changed something. He asked if he could take me to church on Sunday and after that, we've spent all our free time together."

"That's really romantic."

"I suppose it is."

Silence stretched between them, until Anna Beth laughed. "I guess it's strange for us to be talking about men."

"Well, we've never done it before, but that's my fault. I didn't make it easy for you to talk to me about anything." Sarah stared at the floor, the vulnerable expression on her face making her appear younger. "You looked so much like your mother. It made it hard to be around you at first. Then I'd done so much damage, I didn't know how to repair it. Everything I tried, you threw it back in my face."

Anna Beth couldn't argue. She'd kept her aunt at arm's length after years of rejection and she hadn't trusted any overtures in her part. But here she was, trying again after all these years.

"I'm sorry, Sarah. I know I acted like a brat sometimes."

Sarah dabbed at her eyes and this time, Anna Beth saw the tears rolling down her cheeks. Astonishment swept over Anna Beth as her aunt continued. "I never handled it right when you acted out. My parents weren't the most attentive and when they were, it was usually after too much to drink. It never ended well for me or your mother."

Anna Beth sat up, her hand rubbing her aunt's back. "Mom never said anything."

"Of course she didn't. You were a child. She doted on you and did her best to be the opposite of our parents. I took the other road and chose not to have any children. Too afraid that I would end up losing control if I let my emotions get the best of me."

Anna Beth moved next to Sarah and took her hand. "My mother yelled when she got mad or frustrated, but I never thought for one second that she didn't love me because we had a prior relationship filled with warm, wonderful memories. You and I didn't have that. I thought you hated me."

Her aunt squeezed her hand. "I know that and I'm sorry. Ernie suggested I start seeing a counselor last year and talking through my emotions really helped. As happy as he makes me, I still have a habit of pushing him away when things get hard."

"That's good, though. At least you're trying to change for the better."

"I am just sorry I didn't do it sooner."

"I'm sorry too."

And then, something happened. Her aunt's arms wrapped around her shoulders and they were hugging.

Anna Beth burst into tears, clinging to Sarah as she sobbed.

"Good lord, Anna Beth, whatever is the matter?"

"I'm so confused," Anna Beth cried.

"About what?"

"Everything."

Sarah clucked her tongue. "Did something happen between you and Jared?"

Anna Beth pulled away, wiping at her cheeks. "We kissed. But then he isn't sure he wants to start something if I'm leaving and I'm not sure I should have started something if I don't want to stay. But I couldn't seem to help myself. It just felt right. Does that make sense?"

"You've always been in touch with your emotions. Do you think kissing him was wrong?"

"No, I mean...it didn't feel wrong at all. But he is afraid of what people will say."

Sarah snorted. "Sounds like he needs to care less what other people think and man up."

Anna Beth burst out laughing.

"What did I say?" Sarah asked.

"Never in my life," Anna Beth gasped, "did I ever expect to hear the words *man up* come out of your mouth."

Sarah's cheeks flushed. "It's something Ernie says. Not to me, but to his kids and grandkids."

"You've met his family?"

"Yes."

"How was that?" Anna Beth asked in awe.

"Overwhelming at first, but we've grown close. They are all very kind adults. And the children are sweet."

Anna Beth couldn't believe this conversation. She never could have imagined Sarah being close to anyone and now, she knew how it felt to be jealous of a bunch of strangers. Ernie's kids got to meet the aunt she'd always wanted.

Suck it up, buttercup. You can't change the past, but you can move onto a brighter future.

"I wish relationships weren't so hard."

Sarah patted her knee. "Nothing ever comes too easy, I'm told. Everything worth having takes work."

"I'll keep that in mind."

Seventeen

A shrill ring woke Jared out of a sound sleep Wednesday morning and he reached blindly for his phone. When he turned it over, Snowy Springs High School flashed across the screen.

Son of a bitch, Casey, what did you do now?

"This is Jared Cross."

"Hello, Officer Cross, this is Principal Gayle Hastings at Snowy Springs High School."

Jared chuckled softly. "I know who you are, Ma'am. I went to your school."

He didn't mention that Principal Hastings had thrown him under the bus numerous times. If something went missing. When he'd been tormented by his classmates. Her stance on bullying nonexistent, when it should have been zero tolerance. He'd been thrilled to graduate from that hell hole.

"Yes, I forget sometimes," she said dryly. "I'm calling

because I'm afraid Casey has been suspended and I can't get ahold of your parents. You being the emergency contact, I was hoping you could come pick him up."

"Sure, I can grab him. May I ask what he did?"

"He stole a laptop from the computer lab."

Jared sat up, his heart racing. What had the kid been thinking? If they pressed charges, that would mean time in a juvenile center for Casey. Karen and Mike would be wrecked when they found out.

"You caught him with the laptop?"

"No, it hasn't been recovered yet, but a witness came forward who saw him take the laptop."

Shit, this is bad.

"I'll be right there."

"Thank you. Good-bye."

Jared lay there for several minutes, thinking about the downhill slope his week took since he left Anna Beth on Monday. He hadn't meant to be so cold to her, but being seen together by some of the biggest gossips in town sent him into a panic. People would speculate about what was going on between them. The looks. The whispers. Jared hated being the center of attention, especially if the gossip could potentially end with Anna Beth leaving town and him broken hearted.

It was bad enough to have his mother and her church friends discussing his dating life, but the whole town?

He got dressed, silently switched gears to griping to himself about Casey.

Maybe the kid's just rotten. Who would be stupid enough to steal a laptop from their school, especially during the day when anyone could see?

After the fifteen-minute drive to the high school, Jared came through the front door, thinking of what he'd say to

Casey. The front desk clerk buzzed him into the office area and she told him to head on back.

Principal Hastings stood when he walked into the room, her graying blonde hair still in the same severe French braid she'd worn when he was a student.

"Officer Cross, thank you for coming."

He took her outstretched and squeezed it firmly. "Hello, Principal Hastings. Please explain to me what happened."

She looked sternly at Casey, even as she spoke to Jared. "As I said on the phone, there was a witness who saw Casey walk out of the computer lab with the laptop, but by the time we pulled him out of class, he'd hidden it somewhere."

"So, it wasn't in his locker or backpack?"

"No. But the student didn't come forward for at least an hour."

Jared turned toward Casey, whose brown eyes were wide with fear.

Suddenly, he pictured himself in Casey's place, waiting for Karen to show up and lay into him, to not even give him a chance to explain and take everyone else's word for it. And the relief he'd experienced when she'd believed him.

They might not get along, but Casey was family. And family deserved support. The benefit of the doubt. Someone had to be in his corner and this was Jared's chance to repay all the good Karen and Mike did for him.

He sat next to Casey and put his hand on his shoulder. "What happened, Casey?"

Principal Hasting spluttered, "Officer Cross, I already told you what happened."

Jared shot the principal a hard look. "I listened to your version of the events and now I want to hear Casey's. You pulled him in here with no proof besides the word of another student. Who is it? A faculty member's child?"

Her affronted expression didn't fool him. She'd always had favorites and everyone knew who they were.

"Of course not!" she swore.

"Another prominent town figure's spawn?"

Principal Hasting's back stiffened. "I'm sorry, but we have a strict confidential reporting system. It is in place so students will come to us without fear of reprisal from their fellow classmates, and I do not appreciate your insinuation that I would let a student's family influence me."

Jared stood and squared off with her, his arms crossed over his chest. "I don't appreciate Casey being dragged out of class and threatened without a shred of evidence. My brother suspended for theft based on another student's word, and he doesn't even get to face his accuser? Does that seem fair?"

"This is a school, Officer Cross. Not a courtroom."

"You're right. And Casey is one of your students. Did you ask Casey if he did it?"

"Yes, I did, and he denied it. Something he'd do if he took the laptop as well."

"Sound logic. Especially since he's a troubled kid, right?" He didn't give her a chance to respond, focusing on his stunned brother. "Casey, tell me what happened."

Casey swallowed hard before he spoke, everything coming in a rush. "I swear, Jared, I was in class the whole time. I didn't steal anything. I was sitting in history when Carol, the office aid, came and got me."

Jared pushed back the doubt and did what he knew his mother would do. He advocated for Casey. "I believe you." He turned his attention back to the Principal, scowling. "Principal Hastings, when you didn't find the laptop in Casey's backpack or locker, did you do a school-wide locker search?"

"No."

"What about the student who accused my brother? You said that he admitted to waiting an hour to report the theft. Wouldn't it make sense that he might have hid the laptop and then accused Casey to throw off suspicion?"

She scoffed. "I'm *sure* this student didn't steal the laptop."

"Really? How sure? Would you bank your job on it? Because the minute I leave here with Casey, I'm going to be on the phone telling the school board, the paper, the mayor…everyone who will listen that you suspended a student without physical evidence he committed the crime. I think they'll have questions as to why, don't you?"

Principal Hasting's mouth flopped open and closed like a fish for several seconds, before she stuttered, "I su-suppose we co-could verify the student's lo-locker is clear."

"Excellent idea."

When the Principal left the room, Jared turned in his chair. "Are you okay?"

"You really believe me?"

The look on Casey's face hit him like a sock in the gut, so filled with hope, and any lingering doubt of his innocence washed away. "I know you, kid. If you did it, you'd be acting like a little turd right now. Besides, this isn't my first run in with Hastings. She likes to use the easy scapegoats. Do you know who accused you?"

"Not for sure, but I would bet my Xbox it was Lane Shipman."

"Shipman…as in Shipman Construction?"

Casey nodded. "He's had it out for me since I got transferred. Karen tried to set up mediation with his parents, but they wouldn't go for it. He lies about everything and all the faculty believe him. He's just a dick."

Like his old man.

Hank Shipman hadn't appreciated Jared pulling him over for doing seventy-five in a forty-five several months ago and complained to Jared's chief about Jared violating his rights. Thank God for dash-cam footage and the fact that Hank was abrasive as hell. No one could stand him or believed Jared overstepped.

Jared ruffled the kid's hair. "I believe you, and I wasn't lying about going to bat for you, Case. We're family, and I'll do everything I can to make sure they don't pin this on you, but you need to be as smart as Mom thinks you are. No more juvenile shit. Get me?"

"Yeah. I thought they were going to call the real cops and not just you."

Jared smiled wryly. "Thanks, bro."

Five minutes later, Principal Hastings came in and held her hand out to him.

"Officer Cross, I am deeply sorry for disturbing you. Casey is free to go back to class."

Jared took her hand slowly. "Let me guess, your search turned up one lost laptop?"

Principal Hastings lips thinned. "Yes, your hunch was right."

"Then I think you owe Casey an apology. Don't you?"

"Absolutely." She appeared constipated as she held her hand out to Casey with a strained smile. "I'm sorry for accusing you, Casey."

Casey opened his mouth, but Jared shot him a warning look. Whatever he was about to say, he thought better of it and took her hand with a nod.

"Casey, wait in the hallway for me. I'll be there in a moment."

Once Casey was out of earshot, Jared faced Principal Hastings.

"I understand that Casey has had some problems since my father was diagnosed with cancer, but that does not give you the right to terrorize him with this flimsy charge."

"Officer Cross, I am very sorry for the misunderstanding, but I assure you, I had good reason to believe the student in question."

"What reason? Because he's a Shipman?" The principal's eyes widened. "Yeah, I know who accused my brother. You made a mistake, fine. That doesn't change the fact that Casey is a good kid going through a hard time and instead of understanding that, all you saw was a troubled, foster kid and an easy target." Jared shook his head. "You're just lucky you got me instead of my mom or things could have been a lot worse. Have a nice day, ma'am."

Jared walked out and saw a sullen, dark haired kid sitting in a chair outside the office. Casey stood behind the kid in the glass hallway pointing and mouthing, *That's him*!

Jared stopped alongside him. "You're Lane?"

Lane looked up with a belligerent expression on his pudgy face. "Yeah? Who are you?"

"I'm Casey's brother, Officer Cross, with Snowy Springs PD."

"Okay. And?"

"Stealing a school laptop? That's a felony. Hope they don't press charges. Good luck."

The kid paled and Jared pushed through the doors, grinning.

"What did you say to him?"

"I wished him luck."

Eighteen

On Thursday, Anna Beth sat at the kitchen table, staring at her laptop while Mitten's slept on her shoulder. She'd barely written a sentence in the past two days. If something didn't come to her soon, her laptop may end up soaring across the room.

All because a certain peace officer didn't know how to use a freaking phone!

Not that she cared anymore. Things were crazy busy and she had lots of things to do. Give Mittens her medicine. Hang with her aunt. Write her screenplay — that wasn't going so well — but she'd bought all the ingredients to check another item off Ian's list. Bake and donate five dozen Christmas cookies, which worked out great because the holiday festival could use more sugary treats. She could bake the cookies Friday, then donate them for snacks at the tree lighting ceremony Saturday. She didn't need to give Jared Cross a second thought.

The only crimp in her plan were the couples who would no doubt be enjoying the activities at the festival. Sharing hot chocolate, Christmas lights and kisses beneath the mistletoe. Up until this morning, she'd held out hope Jared would ask her to go with him, even if they kept things platonic.

That didn't look like it was going to happen. Jared had only sent her a few short texts over the last few days, which hurt more than she cared to admit. She'd really thought they were connecting, and she'd let herself get caught up in it, despite her brain repeatedly telling her to keep her lips to herself.

Smart brain. Dumb lips.

"I see you're getting a lot done today."

Sarah's statement startled Anna Beth so badly, she knocked over the iced coffee she'd made, which scared Mittens who took off down her back, digging sharp claws into her skin.

"Ow! Shit."

"I'm so sorry! Did she hurt you?"

Anna Beth quickly picked up her laptop and moved it to the counter before the drifting rivers of mocha reached it. "I'm fine, really. I'm just having a hard time concentrating."

After cleaning up the spilled coffee, she pulled down the back of her shirt and turned. "Any blood?"

"Not that I can see. Want me to clean them anyway?"

Anna Beth shook her head. "Nah, I'm okay."

"Do you want to come with me and Ernie to the farmer's market this morning? Some fresh air might do you good."

The last few days, her aunt and Ernie had gone out of their way to include her in all of their plans, even a movie night watching White Christmas. Although it dropped her Christmas movie list down to twenty-three, catching her aunt's boyfriend nuzzling her neck had been ninety-shades of awkward.

"As much as I like Ernie, I'd feel like a third wheel and besides, I need to work. I haven't written anything in days."

"I think what you need is a day to get out of your head and blow off some steam. Why don't you call Olive and do something fun? A little female companionship cures the mopes like nothing else."

"I'm not moping," Anna Beth grumbled.

"Yes, I can see you're the picture of happiness. My mistake."

"You know this cheery, smart ass you've become? I'm not sure I'm loving her." When Sarah's face fell, Anna Beth apologized immediately. "I'm just kidding. I'm not in the frame of mind to be funny. Sorry, I'm being a grouch."

Sarah bounced back with a sympathetic frown. "I understand. Just don't sit around all day staring at that screen. You are a brilliant writer, but you have to go out amongst people to get real experiences."

"I promise not to be a hermit. Now, go have fun. I need to find Mittens and see how traumatized she is."

"She'll get over it." Her aunt leaned over and kissed her cheek. "Have a good day, my dear."

"You too," Anna Beth said softly. Every time Sarah showed her any kind of warmth or affection, she got choked up.

She needed to get a handle on her emotions, before she lost it in front of the wrong person.

The front door closed behind Sarah and Anna Beth went in search of Mittens, who had her face buried in her kibble. "I guess you're alright."

Music blared from her cell phone in the other room and Anna Beth raced to answer it before it stopped ringing.

"Hello?"

"It's your favorite person in the whole world," Olive said.

"You don't sound like Reece Witherspoon."

"Very funny. What are you doing today?"

She glanced at her computer, knowing the words weren't coming. "Absolutely nothing, why?"

"Wanna go to Tammy's and get glammed up for a girl's night out?"

Did Sarah call her? Were the two of them conspiring?

"We're having a girl's night? Where?"

"Fire and Ice Pub has karaoke on Thursdays and free cover if you have boobies!"

Anna Beth groaned. "Karaoke?"

"No, you said it wrong. Your voice is supposed to go up three octaves with a clear inflection of excitement in your tone. Karaoke!"

Anna Beth did not sing in public, but maybe going shopping would get her out of her funk. "I tell you what, I'll meet you at Tammy's and we'll see where it goes from there. Deal?"

"Sounds fair, but just know, the karaoke is going to get you."

"See you soon, goob."

Anna Beth showered and threw on a sweater with a pair of distressed jeans. Mittens curled up in a ball on her bed, one giant foot covering her face, a spot of pink from her antibiotics stuck to the fur on her paw. Anna Beth bent over and kissed the kitten's soft belly, smiling when she heard the low rumble of her purr.

"Alright, baby, I'll be back a little later. Behave."

Mittens didn't even open her eyes as Anna Beth left the room. She sat in her car for ten minutes, waiting for it to warm up and checked her phone. The last text she'd received from Jared at six in the morning featured a bear, poking his head out of a dumpster while "*good morning, brunch?*" flashed across the screen. She hadn't bothered to respond. If he couldn't shoot her a personal message, he could stay on *read*.

What the heck did he expect? It had been a long time since she'd been with another man, but she didn't remember dating being quite this hard. Then again, her best friend preferred to hook up with someone she loathed rather than have a meaningful relationship, so maybe Anna Beth was the crazy one.

Fifteen minutes later, she walked into Tammy's shop and found Olive holding up two sheer baby doll negligees, one in green and the other in red.

"I really think I like the green one," Olive said.

Tammy stood in front of her with her hands on her hips, her sassy mohawk shimmering with silver glitter. She wore a black top with the word "CHEERS" in sequins and her pants were black with silver paint splatters all over them.

"I wouldn't lie to you, baby girl. Buy the red one. His tongue will fall out of his head when he sees you in it."

Tammy caught sight of Anna Beth and waved her forward. "Anna Beth, back me up. Red over green, don't you agree?"

Olive turned her way and waved the two nighties at her. "Seriously, which one?"

Anna Beth looked between the two and smiled sheepishly. "I like the red."

"Whoo hoo!" Tammy crowed.

"Damn it!" Olive said. "I know it's hot but the green is so pretty."

"Why don't you get them both?" Anna Beth asked. "Let whoever you're wearing them for decide."

Tammy tapped one of her perfectly manicured nails to her lip thoughtfully. "I like it." Tammy held out her arms. "Bring it in, you!"

Anna Beth laughed and hugged the other woman. She loved Tammy's warm, exuberant nature.

"Now, what can I do for you?" Tammy asked.

"We're doing a girl's night tonight and Anna Beth needs something sexy." Olive did a little shimmy for emphasis.

Anna Beth rolled her eyes. "I really don't."

"Why not?" Tammy asked.

"Why not, what?"

"Why don't you need something sexy? It's alright to dress up and embrace your sexuality. Let me ask you something, do your bra and panties match?"

Anna Beth sputtered. "I…well, I'm wearing…"

Tammy looked up toward the ceiling, as though praying for strength. "I don't even know why I asked. I can tell by your uni-boob you're wearing a sports bra and, girl, no man wants to take off your shirt and see that underneath."

"I'm not showing *any* man my bra," Anna Beth huffed.

Olive set her lingerie down on the counter. "Do you see what I'm dealing with?" Tammy nodded sympathetically and Olive took Anna Beth's shoulders in her hands. "My friend, you are in desperate need of fun."

"I have fun," Anna Beth grumbled.

"No. You have work. When is the last time you cut loose?"

Anna Beth bit her lip, wracking her brain for an answer that wouldn't make her look pathetic.

"That's what I thought," Olive said.

Tammy nodded. "When you are getting dressed, you need to beautify yourself from the inside out. Lotion, lingerie that makes you feel confident, and don't forget to shave your legs. No man wants to snuggle up to a polar bear."

Anna Beth laughed. Her legs were stubbly with several days growth and her underwear did not match. She'd fail Tammy's confidence test for sure.

"I can tell by your expression you need me desperately." Tammy took Anna Beth by the arm and led her to the fitting rooms, unlocking one of the doors for her. "Go inside and I'll bring you some bras. 36D?"

"Man, you are good."

"It's my job, dear. Just think of me as your fairy godmother, but with better style. I'm going to bibbity bobbity boo you to fab town."

Tammy closed the door and Anna Beth sat down on the leather bench, releasing a heavy sigh. She took off her shoes, trying to get in the mood for a fashion montage. It probably wouldn't be a bad idea to buy some new bras and panties. Most of her panties came from a multi-pack.

She was standing in her bra and undies when Tammy knocked.

"I've got some things for you, Anna Beth."

Anna Beth opened the door a few inches, but the stack of items Tammy held was too large to fit through. She opened it wider and Tammy looked down, gasping.

"What are those?"

"My underwear?"

"Oh, honey, women who wear that underwear either hate sex, or are experiencing that time of the month." She shook her head in disappointment, the spiky mohawk unflinchingly stiff. "This is worse than I thought. I'm going to look through our special section and pick out some styles to go with the bras I brought you. Let the beautification commence."

When she closed the door again, Anna Beth stood there for several moments. Olive came back to check on her, knocking. "You alright in there?"

Anna Beth poked her head out with a scowl. "Tammy made fun of my underwear."

"Are you wearing granny panties?"

"They're briefs!"

"You deserve it." Olive rolled her eyes. "Come on, A.B., stop being stubborn and try some things on. You'll feel better, I promise."

Anna Beth shut the door, silently grumbling as she tried on one of the lacy bras in electric blue and gray. She had to admit, her boobs looked amazing in it. Not that anyone else would admire them, but still, it was a pretty bra.

She slid on a black dress that hugged her body like a second skin. The cowl neck drooped low, showing off hints of cleavage when she moved.

"Anna Beth? You got something to show us?"

When she stepped out of the room, Tammy, Olive, and a few other ladies stared, awestruck, as she walked toward them.

"Is it too tight?"

Tammy's hands flew to her mouth dramatically. "Oh my Graceland. You look fantastic. I have two more dresses you need to try and several tops." Tammy flew to a rack, tossing several items over one arm with super speed. "If I'd known what you were hiding under that blue sweater, I'd have been better prepared."

Olive stood off to the side, grinning. "You look beautiful, A.B. How do you feel?"

Anna Beth looked in the mirror, turning to the left and right.

"Better, actually. Much better."

"Good," Olive said. "This is just what you need to put Jared Cross out of your mind."

"What about Jared Cross?" Tammy asked as she hung the items she'd chosen inside Anna Beth's dressing room.

Anna Beth shot Olive a desperate look, but she either didn't see or ignored it because she kept talking. "He blew Anna Beth off because they were getting too close."

Tammy clucked sympathetically. "I'm sorry, honey. Apparently, that's his M.O., though."

This piqued her interest. "What do you mean?"

"Just that his boots go under a lot of beds. Doesn't date the same girl for long and usually gives him the old it's not you, it's me." Tammy came out of the room with a grin. "Don't get me wrong, I adore the man and he is charming as all get out, but...he's kind of a tramp."

Olive burst out laughing, but Anna Beth bit her lip. She couldn't believe Jared would play with her after everything they talked about. He wasn't a jerk. *Was he?*

Her phone dinged with a new text message and she ducked inside the dressing room to read it.

`Hey A.B. I've been thinking a lot about us. Wanna meet for lunch tomorrow and talk?`

Olive poked her head in. "Is it him?"

"He's asking me to lunch tomorrow."

"Eff that with a toilet brush. He needs to sweat for a bit. Leave him on read. It will drive him crazy."

Anna Beth wavered for a moment before setting her phone down. "You're right. This is girl time. He can wait."

Nineteen

Jared walked into Fire and Ice Pub on Thursday night ready to kick off his three-day weekend. Vance was already inside, getting the first round of drinks while Jared parked the car. He took a second to check his phone again while he headed for the front door. He'd sent Anna Beth a message, asking her if she was free for lunch tomorrow, but she hadn't responded.

Can you blame her? You pulled away and have avoided a real conversation for days. Face it, jackass, you fucked up.

The music blared the instrumental intro to Jingle Bell Rock just before a woman belted an off-key rendition of the classic song. Karaoke could be entertaining, especially when people didn't care how they looked or sounded doing it, and alcohol always helped with the not caring part.

Usually, Jared enjoyed hanging with Vance at the pub, but tonight, he'd rather be home with Rip, vegging out. But he couldn't be alone with his thoughts, especially since they'd been berating him for days. He could have gone with the flow and seen how things with Anna Beth went, but oh no, the man with the plan had to overthink everything. And once again, he'd blown it.

Vance waved at him from the bar and Jared headed that way, weaving through the crowd. When he reached Vance's side, his friend clapped him on the back.

"I ordered two whiskeys, so we can drink like real men."

"Thanks, buddy. I've got the next round."

"I think I'm going to need it," Vance said, staring at something past Jared's shoulder.

Jared followed Vance's gaze to the dance floor and saw Olive in a slinky white dress, her hands in the air, shaking her hips to a Mariah Carey song being slaughtered by another tone deaf patron.

Jared shook his head. "Man, if you like Olive, why don't you just tell her?"

"I don't like Olive. We're just having fun. Just friends. She looks good though, right?"

Jared rolled his eyes. Vance could deny his feelings, but Jared knew he had a major thing for Olive. But he definitely shouldn't be the one to give anyone advice on relationships right now.

"Alright, guys," Cade Brighten said from behind them. "Two whiskeys. Enjoy."

Jared grinned. "Thanks."

"Speaking of friends, is that Anna Beth dancing with Olive?" Vance asked.

Jared searched the dance floor again. When he caught sight of her, Jared stopped breathing for a beat.

Anna Beth's blonde hair swung around her shoulders in golden waves as she danced, her breasts bouncing beneath the red halter dress she wore. She had her hands in the air, waving them back and forth. Her joyful expression made the area around her light up too and Jared took a step toward her.

Vance caught his arm. "Whoa, where are you off to?"

"I was just going over to say hello."

"That is not a '*hi*' expression on your face. That is an '*I just saw something I want and I need to claim it*' look and that never goes over well with the ladies." Vance dropped his arm and picked up the whiskey glass. "I thought you weren't talking to Anna Beth anymore."

"What makes you say that?"

Vance cocked his left brow. "Because it's been days since you mentioned her?"

"I don't tell you everything going on with me."

Vance clutched his chest. "That hurts, man. However, I'm going to let it go and give you some advice. She is not here with you. You need to hang back and out of her space unless she gives you an all clear signal to approach."

Considering how bad he'd messed things up, he should've listened. He should've nurse his whiskey slowly and silently, along with his frustrations. Instead, he downed it.

"Ready for the round two, I see."

Jared flagged Cade down again and Vance nudged him. "Exactly what happened between you and Anna Beth."

"She's only here for three weeks, and all I could think about was what happens when she leaves. I got spooked."

"I hear you and I get it," Vance said in a soothing voice.

"Oh, geez."

"But seriously, what if this time around, you two form something great and she stays?"

"Pretty sure I blew it on that one. She's not even responding to my texts."

"What did you send?"

"A cute bear gif inviting her to brunch."

Vance blinked at him before running a hand down his face. "You're so dumb."

Jared scowled. "Thanks."

The song ended and Anna Beth and Olive hugged each other, laughing.

"Maybe all isn't lost,"Vance said.

Anna Beth came his way with Olive close behind. Jared stood still, waiting for her to notice him.

Olive saw him first and gave him a smart salute.

"Officer Cross. Off duty, I see."

Anna Beth's gaze jerked up at the mention of his name, her green eyes narrowing. His mouth went dry and he nervously struggled for something clever to say.

"Jared."

"Anna Beth."

Olive looked between them and rubbed her arms. "Brrr, chilly. Glad I'm not you."

Anna Beth glared at her. "Let's get a drink."

She stepped around Jared and leaned over the bar, the red material of her dress tightening across her ass.

"Sorry, man, but you're screwed."

"Not comforting, Vance."

Anna Beth waved at the bartender emphatically. "Hey, Cade, we need drinks!"

Cade grinned from down the bar and winked. Anna Beth turned around, leaning back against the bar. The stance pushed her tits out, but Jared didn't think she realized how seductive she looked. She smiled at something Olive said, her eyes heavily made up and not at all like her.

Jared glanced around, his jaw clenching when he realized every male within ten feet ogled her, including Vance.

Anna Beth finally met his gaze with an arch look. "You got something to say?"

"Just wondering, how much have you had to drink?"

"Three lemon drops, if you must know, Officer Nosy. But don't worry, I'm not driving."

"Officer Nosy," Olive snickered. "I like it."

Vance patted his shoulder. "Come on, man. Let's go where the welcome's warmer."

Anna Beth snorted. "From what I hear, it's always warm for Jared."

"What does that mean?"

"Word around town is that the ladies love you. Maybe I should call you Officer Friendly."

Jared shook his head. "Anna Beth…"

"That's my name," she slurred

Cade tapped her shoulder. "Hey, beautiful, another lemon drop?"

Anna Beth turned away from Jared, but he saw her run her finger along Cade's hand. The bartender took her hand and kissed the back of it. Under normal circumstances, Jared liked Cade, but right now, he wanted to slam his nose into the bar counter.

"Two, please," she said.

Cade winked. "Coming right up."

When Anna Beth turned back around, her smile slid into a frown. "What's your problem?"

"I don't have one."

"Then stop glaring at me. I haven't done jack to you. I'm just here to have a good time with my bestie." Anna Beth wrapped an arm around Olive's shoulders. "Right?"

"Right!" Olive kissed Anna Beth's cheek.

"Hey, Anna Beth, mind if I steal your bestie for a dance," Vance asked.

Anna Beth shot him a stern look."It's up to her, but if you bring her back to me unhappy, I'm coming for you."

"Understood. Olive?"

Vance held out his hand and Olive took it, but her expression flicked back and forth between Jared and Anna Beth. "You sure you'll be okay?"

"Sure, but I can't guarantee your drink will be here waiting for you. Go, have fun."

Jared stared at her until she finally met his gaze. "What?"

"Nothing. You just look different. Where did you get the dress?"

"Tammy's. It's called a bodycon dress."

"It's nice." He took a step closer, swallowing nervously. "Anna Beth, can we go somewhere quiet and talk?"

Cade came back with the two lemon drops. "That'll be ten for both."

Anna Beth turned away from Jared to face Cade, her voice taking on a flirty tone. "Last time, it was fourteen."

Cade grinned. "You get a discount for making me smile."

Before Anna Beth could pay, Jared held out a twenty. "Keep the change."

"Thanks, Jared." He cocked his head to the side. "See you around, Anna Beth."

Anna Beth stood there with two drinks in her hands, looking fit to be tied. "Why'd you do that? I can buy my own drinks. Now he thinks we're together and we are so not."

"I didn't like the way he was looking at you."

"You have no business caring about the way anyone looks at me," she hissed.

Jared realized she was tipsier than he'd originally assumed and tried to reason with her. "I know you're angry at me, but—"

"If you know I'm angry with you, then why are you here with your chiseled face and hot body, pissing me off more?"

Before Jared could process that outburst, she downed the first drink, then the other, before pushing past him with a huff. She set the glasses down on a nearby table, startling the couple sitting there. She hit the dance floor and he paused, watching from a distance as she closed her eyes and moved.

Jared went back to the bar, giving her space. He waved Cade down.

"What can I get you?"

"Two whiskeys."

"You got it." Cade grabbed the bottle from the shelf on the wall and set two glasses down on the counter. "Hey, sorry man."

"For what?"

"Stepping on your toes with Anna Beth. I didn't know you were a thing."

"We're not. We're just friends. Or I guess enemies, depending on the day."

Cade laughed as he passed the two glasses across the counter top to Jared. "I should have made these a double, then. I don't know how you can be just friends with someone like her."

Jared lost his smile. Right now, he couldn't imagine either.

He paid Cade for the drinks and searched the crowd for Vance.

The song ended and he emerged from the dancing bodies and took the glass from Jared. "Thanks, how did you know?"

"Because I needed one."

"Things didn't go well with Anna Beth."

The karaoke DJ called Anna Beth's name and Olive squealed. Several loud "whoo hoos" echoed through the crowd as she took the mic.

"You could say that," Jared grumbled.

Anna Beth smiled, but when she spoke, her voice trembled. "Thank you. This is really embarrassing, but here goes nothing."

The jaunty tune from *Santa Baby* came out of the speakers and Anna Beth started off hesitantly. As the cheers grew louder, Anna relaxed. She sang along in a husky voice, her hips swaying as she danced, acting out the lyrics with her body while the crowd urged her on. She glided down the steps of the stage, singing about Tiffany's and the people on the dance floor tightened around her. Anna Beth emerged from the mass of people and Jared watched her run her hand across one man's chest. Jared's shoulders stiffened when she twisted her finger around another's tie, using it to drag him down until their faces were only inches apart.

Jared downed his second shot, his breath hissing between his teeth. "I'm getting some air."

Vance called his name, but he kept going. He stepped into the cold, closing his eyes as tiny snowflakes fell against his skin.

The door opened behind him and Anna Beth stood in her tight red dress. His living dream and nightmare all wrapped up in one gorgeous package.

"Didn't like my song?"

Jared released a bitter laugh. "Not as much as the rest of the crowd did."

Anna Beth shrugged. "Just another item checked off my list."

"Good for you."

"Hey, you don't get to be mad at me." She jabbed a finger into his shoulder. "You practically ghosted me for two days, then send me some stupid gif about brunch."

"I'm not doing this with you. Not like this."

Jared walked down the sidewalk, but Anna Beth kept

up. "Oh, what? You think there's some big mystery to your behavior? You got scared."

He whirled around to face her. "You're damn right I got scared. You keep telling me you're only here temporarily. If we get involved and you leave, I'll still be here getting over you. Again."

Anna Beth stared at him, speechless.

"It's easier for me to stay away from you than it is to be around you and pretend I don't want to strip you naked and kiss every inch of your body. Do you understand that? I thought I was over you and then you came back here and it turns out I'm not. And now that I've tasted you, I'm going crazy not being with you."

Her eyes flashed under the streetlamp. "So what? You decide to bail before you get too attached? Too bad for me, I was already there. Your bailing made me feel ten inches tall. I kept telling myself not to cross that line with you, but you made me feel alive again. It's thrilling and wonderful and scary, but I let my guard down. I trusted you and you pulled away from me. But somehow, I'm the bad guy responsible for your insecurities? Screw that, and screw you, Jared."

Anna Beth stomped back toward the bar but he caught her arm and pressed her back into the side of the building. She put her hands up against his chest when he caged her in with his arms on either side.

"I'm an idiot," he said.

Anna Beth stopped pushing against him and glared up at him. "No shit."

"I'm sorry."

Her chin jutted out belligerently. "For what, specifically?"

"For running scared. For not talking to you. For putting my insecurities on you."

After several beats, she whispered, "Keep going."

Jared chuckled, leaning his forehead against hers. "A.B., you make me so freaking nuts. You always have."

"You were already crazy; I just exacerbate the symptoms."

"Fair enough." He rubbed his nose against hers. "Still mad at me?"

"Yes."

"Anything I can do to make it up to you?"

"Tell me you like my dress."

"I fucking love your dress."

Anna Beth chuckled. "Tammy said it would make men go wild."

"I like that part less."

Anna Beth slid her hands under his coat and around his waist, resting her palms at the small of his back. "You're jealous."

"Somewhat."

"You can fix that?"

"How?"

"Stop running away from me."

Jared cradled her cheeks between his hands. His lips covered hers and his hands slid back, his fingers tangling in her hair. She tasted like lemons and sugar. He never wanted to stop kissing her.

Suddenly she pushed away from him. "I'm sorry."

"For what?"

Before she could respond, she vomited all over his shoes.

Twenty

The morning light peeked through the windows and rained warmth over Anna Beth's face, something she would have appreciated if she wasn't sporting a nasty hangover. She groaned as she rolled over, afraid to open her eyes and putting her back to the obnoxious rays of sunshine. How did she ever think mornings were a good thing?

Anna Beth heard Christmas music playing downstairs followed by male laughter. She managed to squint one eye open and realized she was in her own bed.

So, who was the guy downstairs?

Moving at a snail's pace, Anna Beth climbed out of bed and caught a look at herself in the mirror above her dresser. Her hair stood up everywhere and eye makeup drifted across her cheeks, making her look like a sad clown. She wracked her brain, trying to remember last night's events in some semblance of sequence but things were a jumble.

Her dry mouth tasted nasty and she decided her first order of business needed to be a long appointment with her toothbrush. Ten minutes later, her head still pounded, but her eyes were clean. She dumped two Tylenol in her hand and tossed them back before dipping her head to drink from the faucet.

Finally, Anna Beth headed downstairs, wincing at her sore feet. She noticed the heels she'd worn last night kicked off by the front door as she passed. She froze at the entrance of the kitchen. Jared stood in front of her stove, shaking his hips to Run Run Rudolph. Rip sat right next to him, watching his master's hands intently as Jared flipped a pancake on the griddle.

"Hi," Anna Beth said loudly.

Rip took a few steps in Anna Beth's direction, but ultimately decided the possibility of food scraps trumped his affection for her.

Jared, on the other hand, turned the music off and walked over to kiss her cheek. "Hey, A.B. You feeling better?"

"I have a splitting headache, but something tells me that's on me and not you. Also, where is Sarah? Does she know Rip is here? And Mittens?" She glanced around the kitchen. "Rip didn't eat her, did he?"

"No, he's been a perfect gentleman when Mittens was brave enough to venture from hiding. Although, she does puff up and spit at him." He slipped a couple of pancakes onto an empty plate and held it out to her. "And your aunt left for the station an hour ago. She said if Rip broke anything, she'd stuff him."

"That sounds about right." She slid the plate onto the counter and leaned against it with one hand. Anna Beth winced at a particularly sharp pain in her temple. "I feel like a train wreck."

"You look beautiful to me."

"Are you buttering me up? Am I mad at you for something? Because for the life of me, I can't remember what it might be."

"You were pretty irritated with me last night, but we worked it out."

"I'm not irritated with you anymore?"

"I hope not, seeing as I'm making you breakfast."

Anna Beth wracked her brain and some hazy memories surfaced. Singing karaoke. Dancing. Following Jared out of the bar. Screaming at him.

Oh God.

"Did I really puke on your shoes?"

He grinned as he poured more batter on the griddle. "Yeah, but it's okay. I never liked those shoes anyway."

"I'm so sorry."

Jared set his spatula down and took her hands in his. "A.B. we're fine. Honestly, I had it coming."

"You did?"

"A little bit. You were pretty heated about me running scared the last few days." He took her hands and slid them up over his shoulders. "I believe there were even a few curse words."

"Oh yeah. I remember you apologizing."

"I did."

"And then kissing me against the wall."

Jared brushed her mouth with his. "That too."

Tingles scattered across her lips. "Did we decide what all this kissing meant?"

"Not officially but I meant what I said about it being hard to do casual with you. That said, being with you for a short time is better than never being with you at all."

Anna Beth's hands cupped the back of his head. "Maybe we just take it one day at a time? Just be happy in the moment?"

"I'll give it my best." Jared kissed her forehead briefly before pulling back to flip his well-done pancakes. "Well, shit. Go ahead and eat yours. I'll save these for Rip."

Anna Beth buttered her pancakes and pulled the syrup from the cupboard.

"I already warmed some up in the microwave," he said.

"You thought of everything." Anna Beth cut up her pancakes and leaned back against the counter. "Can I ask you something?"

"Yeah?"

"Were you jealous last night?"

Jared arched his brow. "You were mad at me, wearing a flaming red dress and dancing around the bar singing *Santa Baby* with every guy in there drooling...nah, I wasn't bothered at all."

Anna Beth came up behind him and curled her arms around his waist. "Not even a little bit?"

"Maybe a very, very small amount."

"Hmmmm." She kissed his back and let him go, taking another bite of her pancakes. "Well, if you keep feeding me like this, I may forgive you anything."

"I'll remember that." He put the burnt pancakes on another plate and poured more batter onto the griddle. "What do you want to do today?"

"You don't have to work tonight?"

"Nope. I have two more days off."

"I was going to bake cookies to donate to the Christmas festival tomorrow."

Jared gave her a skeptical look. "Do you know how to bake?"

"I've dabbled." Anna Beth caught sight of Mittens in the doorway, watching Rip with her tail twitching. His ears perked up when he saw her and his tail thumped against the tile floor. "I don't think Mittens is enamored of Rip."

"She'll get used to him." He flipped his pancakes and a few moments later, loaded them onto a plate. "After breakfast, let's turn the Christmas music back on and get to work on those cookies."

"Sounds fun. I also need to watch twenty-three more Christmas movies before the twenty-fifth. Maybe we could watch one between batches."

He kissed her mouth, tasting like syrup and butter. She licked her lips.

"Whatever you want to do," he said.

"It's not all about me, you know. I want to do things you want too."

Jared stopped chewing the pancake in his mouth and waggled his brows.

"Oh my God, you perv. I was talking about activities."

"So was I."

Anna grabbed one of the burnt pancakes and threw it at him. It hit him square in the face and Rip caught it before it hit the floor. Jared slowly gazed into her eyes, grinning.

"Really? You're starting a food fight with me?"

"No, no!" she squealed as she took off running through the house. She barely made it into the living room before he lifted her from behind and dragged her back toward the kitchen. "Don't do it!"

"Oh, I'm going to get you so good. Maybe a little syrup on your neck."

Anna Beth couldn't stop giggling as he reached for the tiny pitcher of syrup and she grabbed for his arm. "You're going to make me all sticky."

"You say that like it's a bad thing."

She went limp, slipping out of his arms and onto the floor. When he lay down next to her, she gazed up into his eyes, her laughter dying. Her chest rose and fell hard against his.

"Maybe before we start the cookies, we can get some kissing in?" Jared suggested.

Anna Beth hugged him to her. "I'd love a few kisses."

Jared's mouth covered hers and her exhaustion and headache melted away as she got lost in the sweet taste of his lips.

Something shattered next to them and they broke the kiss. Rip stood over Anna Beth's broken plate, looking so guilty they both burst out laughing.

"I'll tell Sarah I broke the plate," Anna Beth said.

"A woman who would protect my dog from her aunt's wrath? Now, that's hot."

"Mmmm, you think I'm hot, huh?"

"Absolutely. Why don't we get started on the cookies and then retire to the living room?"

"Deal."

Twenty-One

Jared sprawled out on the couch with Anna Beth's back to his front, watching *Home Alone* and trying not to press his lips to the bare skin of her neck. They'd finished rolling out and cookie cutting the dough an hour ago and spent the down time cuddling as batches baked. They had two cookie sheets left to pop into the oven, which was only big enough for one.

They'd shared a few chaste kisses, but Anna Beth's "*Officer Friendly*" comment from last night floated at the back of his mind. He didn't want her thinking he only wanted one thing. Yes, making love to Anna Beth would be amazing, but he wanted more with her. He wanted the playful wrestling and baking together. He wanted to take her sledding again and build a snowman, to watch Christmas movies under a blanket while eating popcorn and M&Ms. He wanted to wake up to her drooling on her pillow and listen to her complain about his snoring.

Jared wanted a life with Anna Beth, and that meant taking his time.

The oven went off and Anna Beth stood, stretching onto her tiptoes. "Pause it for me, please?"

"Sure." He grabbed the remote from the coffee table and hit the button without taking his eyes off her.

Her arms clasped over her head, her breasts thrust against the t-shirt she wore, making him swallow hard. Her fleece leggings molded over the curve of her hips and ass as she walked away from him and disappeared around the corner.

Jared flopped against the back on the couch, staring at the ceiling, thinking of anything else but his hands all over Anna Beth's body.

The oven door opened with a squeak and he heard her crow, "Woo, these are beautiful. I'm slipping the next batch in."

"Great."

"After the last sheet cools, we can decorate them." She skipped back into the room and curled up next to him once more. "I haven't decorated Christmas cookies since I was ten."

"Yeah?" Jared gritted his teeth when she wiggled her butt against his crotch in an attempt to get more comfortable.

She looked at him over her shoulder. "You okay? You sound like you're in pain."

"Nah, I'm good. Ready to resume the movie?"

She reached out and pressed play, then leaned back once more. He hugged her waist with one arm, and watched the movie, keeping his body still. She wiggled her butt against him, the contact such delicious torture he bit back a groan.

"Do you have any plans tomorrow night?" she asked.

"Just the festival. Why?"

"Do you want to go together? As friends, if you want. No making out in the town square."

Jared kissed the back of her head. "I would, but Olive roped me into being Santa Claus. Our other Saint Nick got a case of strep and she caught me in a moment of weakness last night."

"A moment of weakness?"

"I wanted to take you home last night and she negotiated. I made sure you got home safe, and she found her Santa Claus."

"How did you get me home last night?"

"I called Bill at the station to pick us up in his squad car."

Anna Beth groaned. "Oh, my aunt must have loved that."

"I'm pretty sure the lecture I got was meant for both of us and I was supposed to pass on the message."

"Fun. What did you do after you dropped me?"

"Bill took me back to the bar to pick up my car and Vance, but he decided to go home with Olive. So, I sobered up, drove them home before disinfecting my back seat."

"Why would you…no! They did not have sex in your car."

"I wasn't looking, but with the amount of noise they made, I wasn't taking any chances."

Anna Beth broke into a fit of giggles. "Oh my God, that's horrible."

"In their defense, they kept drinking after we left, so they were pretty hammered. I texted Vance and told him he could have my car detailed for Christmas."

"Hey, at least they aren't constantly at each other's throats anymore," Anna Beth said. "So, Santa, do you have to perform the whole time?"

"Just for the two hours before the tree lighting." Jared shook his head. "I still can't believe I'm going to be a bench for a hundred rugrats telling me their hearts' desires."

"I think it's sweet."

"If you got peed on, you wouldn't be so excited."

"Seriously?"

"Oh, yeah. Our other Santa's tell horror stories. It's why replacement ones are so hard to find." He cleared his throat. "On the track of asking you something, the mayor throws a Christmas party every year. Would you like to go with me tonight?"

Anna Beth rolled over so they were facing each other, her arm moving over his waist. "You mean like a real date?"

"Yes, like a date."

She kissed the tip of his nose. "I'd love to."

"Good, because our dispatcher gets a little handsy when she drinks."

Anna Beth snorted. "I'm your buffer?"

"You're the Costner to my Houston, baby."

"Stop being so irresistible and the ladies won't chase you."

"Please. You can't turn all this off."

Anna Beth shoved his shoulder playfully. "I heard all about it at Tammy's. All the ladies love them some Jared Cross."

"Any and *all* rumors about me have been exaggerated. I swear."

Anna Beth nuzzled his neck. "I don't care about your dating history, I really don't."

"You seemed a little put out about my dating history last night. *Officer Friendly* ringing any bells?"

"It seems you aren't the only one with insecurities. When the ladies told me about your track record, I thought you might have been blowing me off like you do everyone else."

"Despite the scarlet brush I've been painted with, I wasn't being a player. If I went out with a girl and we didn't click, I let her know. I never seemed to click with anyone…except you."

Anna Beth ducked her head and he took her chin in his hand, listing her gaze back to his. "Hey, what's up?"

"I feel guilty you never experienced a long term relationship with anyone else, while I—"

"Don't. I'm not keeping score. I'm not bitter that you married Ian. Well, not anymore, at least. I never had you in the first place and even if we'd started dating then, who knows if we'd be together now. Everything happens for a reason and in the right time. You needed Ian and I needed to find myself. Our pasts shape us and I just want to enjoy where we are right now."

Anna Beth slid her hand around his neck, pressing her lips to his. She kissed him hard, and he opened his mouth, his tongue playing with hers as his hands gripped her hips, his fingertips pressing into her butt.

When they came up for air, both gasping, Jared whispered, "What was that?"

"I'm enjoying the moment."

Jared smiled, dropping his head down to lay his forehead against hers. "Me, too."

Anna Beth moved her hands from the back of his neck down to his chest, making her way over his stomach to the edge of his shirt. She slowly inched it up, every graze of her fingers against his abdomen making him crazy.

Jared sat up and helped her by pulling the shirt up and over his head, tossing it to the floor. She knelt on the floor between his legs, her fingertips running lightly over his pecs, tracing a circle around his nipple. He let her explore his body, groaning when she placed her mouth in the center of his chest and left a series of kisses down over his stomach. He cradled the back of her head, his eyes closing as her warm breath reached the skin above his jeans. When her fingers unbuttoned the denim, Jared's heart kicked up ten notches and his cock pressed painfully against his zipper.

Suddenly, the front door opened and a chorus of women's voices erupted in the entryway. Rip, who'd been sleeping on the rug in front of the TV, jumped up and ran into the other room, his whole-body wiggling. Jared lifted Anna Beth by her arms back onto the couch. He didn't bother buttoning his jeans, but grabbed his t-shirt off the ground and slipped it back on.

Sarah and several of her friends came around the corner, stopping when they saw them.

"Well, what are you two doing?" her aunt asked.

Anna Beth reached out and paused the movie. "Just watching *Home Alone* and baking cookies. What are you guys doing here?"

"The heat went out at the community center and they had to call someone to come fix it, so we thought we'd set up a folding table in the kitchen and work here."

Jared stood, smiling. "I guess I should grab Rip and clear out then. Let you have some girl time."

Anna Beth climbed to her feet and glanced from their audience to him. "Thank you for breakfast and helping with the cookies."

"Anytime. Text me later?"

"Yes. Let me walk you out."

Sarah waved her friends into the kitchen. "Why don't you get started and Anna Beth and I will join you in a moment."

The ladies left the room, chatting amongst themselves. Jared shrugged into his coat and hooked Rip's leash onto his collar.

"Jared," Sarah whispered.

"Yeah?"

"You might want to button your pants before you go anywhere else."

Anna Beth covered her mouth and Jared's cheeks burned. He'd hoped no one would notice.

Sarah's lips twitched. "I'll let you say your good-byes."

When she left the room, Anna Beth buried her face in his chest.

"Oh my God, I'm going to die."

Jared chuckled, holding her in his arms. "I'm right behind you."

Twenty-Two

The town square of Snowy Springs glittered with fresh snow that morning and twinkling lights hung above and along the buildings. Small tents lined the edge of the square and each one held a different activity for the citizens attending the festival to enjoy. The blue spruce in the center had to be forty-five feet tall and at least twenty feet wide. Every year, the mayor flipped the switch and the multicolored LED lights wrapped around the branches came to life.

Anna Beth carried three large containers of cookies over to the sweet treat station, smiling at Rachel and her husband Dave. "Hi, Rachel. I have the goodies to contribute before this shindig kicks off."

Rachel stood up and took the containers from her, setting them on the table. Anna Beth, Sarah, Rachel, and the rest of her aunt's friends decorated the cookies she'd made with Jared yesterday. Unfortunately, the ladies had to leave before the frosting hardened, so, Anna Beth and Sarah finished slipping each cookie into a plastic bag and tying it with a cute cookie ribbon Anna Beth bought.

"You're cutting it close," Rachel scolded.

"I know, I just got caught up with writing today. I was on a roll." She turned to Rachel's husband, who looked less than ecstatic to be there. "Hey, Dave. Long time no see. How is the leg?"

Dave smiled below his full, silver mustache. Despite his gruff nature, he'd always been kind to her. "About tired of it, actually. How are you doing, little bit? Been a long time."

"Yeah, I got back into town last week. It's been great."

"Glad to hear it. I wish more young people came home to visit their parents."

Rachel huffed. "He's talking about our oldest boy, Edward. He opened a Bed and Breakfast in Florida, right on the beach. Keeps trying to get us to go down there, but Dave's being stubborn."

"I hate Florida."

"Oh, you hate everything!"

The couple glared at each other and Anna Beth cleared her throat. "You haven't seen Jared, have you?"

Rachel broke the stare-down with her husband and pointed down the row of tents to a red shed at the end. "I saw him head that way to Santa's Shack. Don't know how they're going to make someone so young and handsome look like Santa."

"Honestly, I can't wait to see it," Anna Beth said.

Dave, who sat in a chair with his cast covered leg propped up on a crate, reached out to steal a cookie from the container closest to him. Rachel smacked his hand without looking away from Anna Beth.

"Woman, I'm not a child. Give me a cookie."

"Doctor told you to lay off the sweets, Dave."

Dave folded his arms with a huff. "I think you like having me laid up. You have me right where you want me."

"Oh yeah, I love waiting on you and listening to you gripe. I'm trying to keep you out of an early grave, but if you want the cookies, fine!" She set one of the containers on his lap. "Have at it, ya old grump!"

Dave scowled down at the wrapped cookies, before transferring that expression to his wife. "You drive me crazy, Rachel," Dave grumbled, putting the container on the table.

His wife leaned over and kissed him, dropping a cookie into his hands. "I love you, too." Rachel turned back to Anna Beth with a wink. "I don't really deny him anything, but I can't have word getting around I spoil him."

"I don't think you can spoil a husband with love, but I'll never tell your secret," Anna Beth said with a smile.

"Appreciate that, darlin'. Thank you for bringing these by. Have fun."

"Thanks. Take care, Dave."

"I'll do my best, if she doesn't kill me first."

Anna Beth chuckled as she walked away, the sound of their bickering fading. She passed by an ornament creation station, a family selling handmade home décor, picture frame making, and the beverage distribution tent. When she rounded the town tree, she got a good look at Santa's Shack. The red building had colorful wood candies all over it, making it look like a life size gingerbread house complete with gumdrops on the roof and candy canes along the doorframe. She headed up the ramp and knocked on the closed green door.

It swung open, revealing Olive in full elf costume.

"Well hello, little girl," Olive said in a high, squeaky voice. "Are you here to see Santa?"

Anna Beth made a face. "That's creepy."

"Just getting into character." Olive laughed. "He's finished with his make-up."

"Make-up?" Anna Beth stepped inside and in the corner sat Jared on Santa's chair, but he looked nothing like himself. His nose was bulbous and the white mustache and beard matched perfectly with his white, bushy eyebrows.

"What the heck?"

Jared turned her way and she could barely see his smile through the thick hair around his mouth. "Ho-ho-ho. Still think I'm sexy?"

"Ew, gross," Olive said behind them. "I'm going to get a cookie and coffee. Be back in a few. Behave, you two."

Olive closed the door behind her, leaving them alone in the shack. It looked like a real room with an electric fireplace off to the side, walls painted with fake windows and views of snowy hills complete with reindeer playing. A beautifully decorated Christmas tree graced the corner. A table with paper angels, pencils, and coloring crayons was beside the door.

"This is pretty swanky. I thought Santa had to sit outside during the festival."

"Guess they finally realized poor Santa was freezing his ass off."

Anna Beth laughed and crossed the room to stand in front of him. "Whoever did your face is very talented."

"Believe it or not, it was Tammy. She used to be a makeup artist and theater major before she married her husband." He placed his Santa hat on his head and fluffed the long white curls attached to it. "Think I'll fool the kiddos?"

"Hmm, I need to hear your Santa voice again. I'm not sure you can embody the jolly quality Saint Nick has."

Jared took a deep breath and said, "Why, hello, Anna Beth.

Come and sit on Santa's lap and tell me what a good girl you've been."

He waggled his eyebrows and Anna Beth groaned. "You're going to give me nightmares about pervy-Santa."

Jared patted his red velvet knee. "Come on. Don't be shy."

She walked over and sat on his knee, poking at his giant stomach. Her finger sank into the padding. "Is this fat suit?"

"Yeah, someone made it with memory foam and fabric. Weird, right?"

"Very."

Jared's hand rubbed her back, his brown eyes meeting hers. "I'm glad you stopped by."

"Aw, did you miss me today?"

"I actually did. Is that too much?"

Anna Beth placed her arms around his shoulders, which were also soft and cushiony. "No, it's perfect because I missed you too. I wanted to see you earlier, but I was on a roll in my screenplay and couldn't stop."

"I know. It gave me a chance to get a lot of stuff done. However, I could use a kiss."

"I don't know. Seems a little naughty."

"I like naughty."

Anna Beth leaned over and kissed him, turning her head so she didn't mess up his nose. When Jared deepened the kiss, Jared's Santa beard tickled her face. She didn't care and lost herself in him.

Suddenly, the door burst open behind them and an excited young voice screamed, "Santa! Santa! Santa?"

Anna Beth jumped off Jared's lap and turned to find a little girl about six-years-old staring wide eyed at them. A woman in her thirties ran in and took her hand.

"Carly, I told you we had to wait."

Carly ignored her mother and scowled at Anna Beth. She raised a pink gloved hand and pointed. "Mommy, that woman was sitting on Santa's lap and they were kissing!"

Anna Beth wished she could melt into the floor. Thankfully, Jared stood up and walked over to the child. He knelt down on one knee in front of Carly, almost to her eye level.

"Shh, don't tell but this pretty lady is Mrs. Claus, in disguise."

Carly's eyes widened. "She is?"

"Yes. You see, Mrs. Claus likes to travel around the world bringing gifts too, but she can't do it looking like herself."

Carly looked from Jared to Anna Beth, then up at her mother. "Do you think that's true, Mommy?"

"If Santa says so, then it must be. Now, let's go back outside and wait to be called."

Once Carly and her mother left, Anna Beth groaned. "Well, that was embarrassing."

"Nah, Carly's fine. We didn't traumatize her and now, she can run around and tell all the other kids she met Mrs. Claus too. She's going to be a celebrity with the elementary school crowd, I guarantee it."

Olive came through the door, an amused expression on her face. "A concerned mother warned me that Santa and Mrs. Claus were inside and needed their privacy."

"On that note, I am out of here. I'm going to meet my aunt at the wreath construction booth."

Jared caught her hand and squeezed. "When I finish here, I'll come find you."

"Should I look for Santa, or will you be back to yourself?"

"As long as Tammy can get this all off, I'll turn back after seven."

"See you then." She let go of his hand and headed out

the door. Anna Beth passed by a line of kids and heard a loud whisper, "That's Mrs. Claus."

She rolled her eyes. Little Carly won the gossip-in-training award.

When Anna Beth got all the way to the other end of the tents, she found her aunt speaking to Karen Jeffries. Sarah held two bags and they had their heads close together, as though conspiring.

"Hey, there. What's up?" Anna Beth asked.

"Nothing, dear." Sarah held out her bag. "Your wreath supplies."

"Thanks. How are you, Karen?"

Karen smiled. "I'm good, Anna Beth. Did you go by and see Jared?"

"Yeah, he looks great. Tammy did an awesome job making him look the part. Are you going to make a wreath?"

"I am." She held up the paper sack she was carrying. "It's for Jared. The Christmas décor at his house is incredibly lacking."

Anna Beth laughed. "The cookie jar you got him is adorable."

"Oh, you've been to his place?" Karen asked.

"Yeah, I went over there after we went sledding. Jared let me borrow some clothes because mine were wet."

"Interesting. Well, it looks like they're ready for us to go in and start creating. You can tell me more about what's going on with you and Jared while we make our projects."

Anna Beth followed behind her aunt and Karen into the tent. A long table was set up with metal wreath frames. They walked around to the other side and sat down. Anna Beth realized they flanked her on either side.

She pulled out her supplies, putting it in piles to better organize it.

"Hi, Mrs. Claus!"

Anna Beth looked up to see Carly waving at her enthusiastically. She waved back and Carly, obviously satisfied, dragged her mom out of sight.

"Mrs. Claus?" Sarah asked.

She closed her eyes. "I'll explain later."

"Does it have anything to do with our new Santa?" Karen prodded.

Anna Beth's cheeks warmed.

Karen grinned and started wrapping a green ribbon around her frame. "Interesting. Very interesting."

Twenty-Three

Jared kept moving different muscles in his face as he walked out of Santa's Shack and headed towards the tents. The heavy prosthetic nose and beard made his face sore and itchy and although it had been removed, his face hadn't fully recovered.

The tree lighting ceremony kicked off in fifteen minutes and then everyone headed over to the community center for the stocking raffle and dinner. He pulled out his phone and shot Anna Beth a text.

`Where are you?`

It didn't take long for her to respond.

`At the Ornament Creation Station.`

`I'll be right there.`

Jared wove his way through throngs of people, most of them heading in the opposite direction toward the tree to get the best spot. He stepped into the ornament tent, surprised to find his mother sitting next to Anna Beth and Sarah. He wanted to head straight for Anna Beth and give her a kiss, but wasn't sure if public displays were on or off the table. He settled for laying a hand on her shoulder and giving her a squeeze.

"Hey," he said.

Anna Beth leaned her head back to look at him, smiling. "Hi."

"How is it going?"

"Great. We're about finished."

"Hello, Jared," Sarah said.

"Evening, Sarah. Mom? You going to say hi or are you too busy for your favorite."

His mom didn't even look his way, too busy concentrating on her ornament. "Hi, honey. Did you have fun at the North Pole?"

"Not as much as you three," he said, noting several full bags around each of their chairs. "Did you hit every craft hut?"

"We did," Anna Beth said. "I can go with you if you want to do one."

"No, it's fine. It's almost time for the tree lighting ceremony, anyway."

"I made you something," his mom said. She set her ornament down and reached under the table, revealing a large Santa tote bag. From inside the bag, she pulled out a burlap ribbon wreath with holly berries, pine cones, and a little wood cabin. On the porch of the tiny structure was a figurine of a couple embracing and a brown dog sitting at their feet.

The woman had blonde hair.

Jared gave his mother an exasperated look. She'd made no

secret she wanted to see Jared and Anna Beth together, but she didn't need to make it so obvious.

"It's nice, Mom. Do you have an extra bag for me to take it home in?"

"Of course I do." She handed him one with green cactuses wearing Santa hats. "I want my bag back though."

Jared slid the wreath into the bag and away from Anna Beth's gaze. She'd been too busy finishing her ornament to see what his mother created. Hopefully when she did see it, she'd be flattered.

Bells rang, indicating the tree lighting would commence in five minutes. Anna Beth set her ornament down and grabbed a white box from the center of the table. She placed the ornament inside, but he didn't see what it was before it disappeared.

Sarah stood up on the other side of Anna Beth, gathering up her bags. "Ernie is going to meet us for the ceremony by the drink tent."

"I'm ready," Anna Beth said.

Karen grabbed a box and placed her ornament inside. "Me, too."

"Can I help you with your bags, ladies?" Jared asked.

"That's okay, sweetheart," Karen said with a smile. "I'm going to find Mike and Casey. They've been delivering the wooden snowmen and reindeer all afternoon, so I don't know if your dad is going to feel up to going to the raffle. Anna Beth, Sarah, thank you for letting me tag along with you."

"Thank you for joining us," Sarah said.

"Absolutely." Anna Beth hugged his mom. "It was so much fun."

Jared held his arms out and his mom came in for a hug. She stood up on her tiptoes and whispered, "I love this girl."

"I know you do."

His mom winked at him and walked out into the crowd. Jared reached down and grabbed Anna Beth's bags.

"I can carry those."

"I know you can, but I want to. Is that okay?"

Sarah huffed. "Anna Beth, stop arguing with the man and let him carry your bags."

Anna Beth grinned sheepishly. "My aunt says I shouldn't argue."

"You should listen to your elders."

"I was on your side, until you called me old," Sarah deadpanned. "I'll see you at home, Anna Beth."

"I didn't call you old!" Jared called after her, but she didn't turn around. Jared looked down at Anna Beth. "I think I upset your aunt."

"No, she was teasing you. She does that now. It's slightly unnerving." Anna Beth looped her arm through Jared's. "Should we go?"

"Sure."

They gathered at the back of the crowd just as the mayor stepped up to the podium. "Citizens of Snowy Springs! Thank you for joining us tonight for our annual Christmas Festival and Tree Lighting Ceremony! It's you, our citizens, who make this town a wonderful place to raise a family. I'm proud to be a part of this community and I hope everyone here feels the same way. Without further ado, let there be light!"

The mayor flipped the switch and colorful sequence lights lit up the tree, flashing different patterns. The silver star on top sparkled and the crowd erupted into thunderous applause.

"Thank you to Cortez Electric for volunteering their time to make this tree shine. Now, please join us across the street at the community center for dinner and our stocking raffle!"

Jared held up the bags. "Should we put these in the trunk of your car and head over?"

"Yes, please. I don't think either one of us want to carry them around all night."

Anna Beth took his arm again and leaned her head against his shoulder, her sweet scent surrounding him. He kissed the top of her head.

"I had so much fun tonight," she gushed. "Being back here is so different."

Stay.

The word tickled the tip of his tongue, but he didn't want to ruin their night by bringing up her future plans. They'd agreed to one day at a time.

"I'm glad you're happy."

"Are you happy?" she asked.

"Yes. This is the happiest I've ever been."

Anna Beth kissed his shoulder. They arrived at her car and when she unlocked it, Jared placed the bags in the trunk.

Jared took Anna Beth's hand and brought her in for a kiss. Her arms looped around his shoulders and he pressed his hands into the small of her back. Jared slipped his tongue inside her mouth, kissing her deeper.

"Mrs. Claus?" A chorus of voices cried behind him.

They broke the kiss, spinning to find three families with small children standing behind them, little Carly in front. Her tiny hands were fisted on her hips, a scowl twisting her cute as a button features.

"I'm telling Santa you kissed Officer Cross! You're going to be on the naughty list for life."

The other children nodded in agreement while their parents snickered.

Anna Beth buried her face in Jared's jacket. He shook his

head. "Sorry kids. It was all my fault. Mrs. Claus is too cute. I'll apologize to Santa."

"You better," Carly said.

Jared arched a brow at Carly's mother. "That's a live one you got there."

"Come on, kids. Let's get some food." The mother mouthed, *I'm sorry* as they passed.

Jared hugged Anna Beth hard. "How does it feel to have officially ruined Christmas?"

"Shut up." She laughed into his chest.

He rubbed her coat covered shoulders. "Come on, A.B. Let's get inside."

Warm air rushed from the community center when he opened the door, hitting his cold cheeks. Inside was brightly lit with red and green garland roped across the ceiling. Several people stood behind a table with a gold tablecloth, two of them handling the cash boxes while the rest handed out raffle tickets. Jared took in the giant display fireplace in the middle of the room, red stockings nearly covering the massive prop. A fake fire with floating cloths of red, orange and yellow danced inside.

"Welcome, Jared! Do you already have your meal tickets?" Margo asked.

"Yes, there should be two under Cross."

Margo flipped through her list and grabbed a highlighter. "Got you. Do you want to buy more raffle tickets?"

"I would," Anna Beth piped in.

They each bought fifty extra tickets for twenty-five cents a piece. Margo passed them over with table number fifteen written on the bottom of the stub. White table clothes adorned the surface of the large, round tables and at the center sat beautiful red poinsettias. The place settings were white with gold trim and several baskets of rolls were placed between each seat.

When they reached table fifteen, Vance sat with his back to them at an otherwise empty table.

Jared released Anna Beth's hand and squeezed Vance's shoulders. "What's up?"

Vance held his hand up above him and Jared took it in a firm shake. "Hey buddy. You ready for this?"

"Yep, going to get some food and win some stockings." Jared held the chair for Anna Beth and took the one on the other side of her. "You here alone?"

"Yeah. I asked Olive if she wanted to come, but she had a date."

Vance seemed nonchalant about his bed-buddy being there with someone else, so Jared didn't question it.

"I'm glad we ended up at the same table."

Vance held his fist out. "I took care of it, my broski. Told Margo I needed to be with you, because you give me luck."

"Do you two want to sit next to each other? I feel like I'm the Yoko factor in this bromance," Anna Beth asked.

Jared slid his arm around the back of her chair with a laugh. "Nah, we're good."

Their table filled up with other adults their age as servers came around with salads followed by the main course dishes. By the time they finished dessert, the MC started the raffle.

"Make sure to have all your tickets out. Stocking number one…"

Everyone looked at their tickets, but an excited cry from the other side of the room echoed.

Anna Beth's fork darted over and snaked a bite of his chocolate cake.

"Hey! You chose the cheesecake."

"I just wanted to try a bite." She picked up a piece of her dessert with her fork and held it out to him. "Wanna try?"

Jared took the morsel and licked his lips. "Yum."

"You two make me want to gag,"Vance said.

Jared ran his palm across Anna Beth's cheek, turning her face toward his. He didn't actually plan on kissing her, Jared just wanted to tease Vance, but when her lips parted, her gaze caressing his mouth, he couldn't help himself. He forgot all about public displays or who may be watching, and kissed Anna Beth like they were the only two people in the room.

Vance's less than subtle coughing finally broke them apart, their gazes holding for several moments until they were both smiling.

"I regret sitting next to you two, now, so thanks,"Vance said.

The MC called out the ticket numbers for stocking number two and Anna Beth jumped up in her seat. "I won!"

Jared, Vance, and the rest of their table clapped as she stood up and weaved through the tables to claim her prize.

Vance leaned closer. "Things seem to be going well."

"So far."

"Have you asked her to stay yet?"

"No. I'm going to wait a little longer. We've already had one hiccup this week. I need to show her this is what I want."

"Just don't wait too long."

Anna Beth came back to the table and pulled an envelope from the stocking. "I got a shopping spree at Tammy's!" She did a little dance in her seat and Jared laughed.

Jared's hands were still empty when the MC called out his number for stocking sixteen. Anna Beth hugged him and he walked to the center of the room to collect. He didn't look inside until he got to his seat and pulled out the envelope.

"What did you get?" Anna Beth asked.

"A two-night hotel stay for New Year's weekend at that swanky new hotel outside of town."

"Wow, that's great."

Jared left it at that because the last thing he wanted to do was ask her to join him with a table full of people watching. He slipped the envelope back into the stocking.

If he couldn't convince Anna Beth to go, it would make a nice gift for his parents.

After the last stocking was claimed, Vance grunted beside him. "I got skunked again."

"I'm going to the ladies' room. Make sure Vance stays away from my gift certificate."

"Oh, I'm taking it! I need me a new pair of satin chonies."

She laughed. Once she was out of earshot, Vance picked up Jared's stocking and looked inside.

"This is great. Gives you a reason to jump the gun and ask her."

"She already saw and didn't say anything."

Vance nudged him with his shoulder. "Maybe because she knows you're unsure and she's afraid of spooking you again."

"I don't know."

"Look, I've been on the other side of her all night and she is into you. And not just for a late-night booty call. Keep that prize your back pocket. I think things are going to work out for you this time."

Jared caught sight of Anna Beth coming back and his heart squeezed.

"I really hope so, man."

Twenty-Four

On Thursday afternoon, Anna Beth stood in the middle of Tammy's shop, decked out in an ugly Christmas sweater and Santa hat over the green, fuzzy costume she had on. Tammy spent two hours applying prosthetics and green makeup to her face and neck. Tammy giggled as she took a picture. "Eat your heart out, Jim Carey. There's a new Grinch in town."

Anna Beth turned and looked at herself in the mirror. The prosthetics made her nose non-existent, and her voice nasally.

"Jared is going to die," Anna Beth said.

"If you don't mind me asking, how are the two of you?"

"We're good."

They were, although she hadn't seen much of him the last few days because he'd been sleeping during the day while she'd been helping her aunt. After he went back to work Sunday night, they'd done a lot of texting and phone calls in the morning and late afternoon, but she missed his face. His kisses. Pretty much, everything.

Tammy grabbed a few items from a clothing rack and walked around, putting them away, talking as she worked. "I know it's hard to move on when you lose someone. I closed myself off when my first husband died."

"I'm so sorry."

"Thanks." Tammy leaned against the front counter, her eyes taking on a faraway look. "It was twenty years ago. We were high school sweethearts. Married at eighteen and madly in love. We were twenty-two when he went for a ride on his motorcycle and a truck took a blind corner too wide. It hit him head on."

"How horrible."

"It was. Even years after, I didn't want anything to do with men or relationships, no matter how many times my mom tried to set me up. I left town for a while, went to school and got a job as a makeup artist in New York. I finally came back here and the first thing I did was get stuck in the snow and need to be rescued by a cantankerous tow truck driver."

Anna Beth smiled, already knowing what happened next.

"What's funny is, I fell in love with him and we have two beautiful boys. Life puts you where you need to be when the time is right. You just have to watch for the signs."

The bells above Tammy's door jingled. Tammy glanced over Anna Beth's shoulder; her eyes wide. Then she burst out laughing.

Anna Beth turned to see what had her in stitches and she covered her mouth in shock. Jared stood in the doorway in a dog costume, a single antler horn tied atop his head.

"I'm Max from How the Grinch Stole Christmas," Jared said. "I thought the kids would love it."

Tammy still couldn't catch her breath from laughing too hard.

"Well, you got Tammy rolling. I think you look great."

His brown eyes sparkled as he looked Anna Beth up and down. "You too, Grinchy."

She spun around. "Right. Tammy is amazing."

Tammy finally came up for air, wheezing, "I'm sorry. That just caught me off guard. You two are going to slay them. Anna Beth, come by afterwards and I'll get that stuff off you and you can pick up that thing."

"What thing?" Jared asked.

"The none-of-your-business thing," Anna Beth said.

Jared threw his hands up and backed away playfully.

Anna Beth chuckled. "I'm teasing. It's for your party on Saturday at The Peaks."

"It's not green and fuzzy, is it?" he teased.

"Maybe."

Jared wrapped her up in a tight hug. "You could show up looking like Freddy Kreuger and I'd still be smitten." He leaned down to kiss her but stopped a few inches away. "I don't want to mess up your make-up."

"Just keep track of all the times you want to kiss me and we'll take care of that before you go to work."

"I like the way you think."

Anna Beth laughed and caught Tammy watching them, a sly grin on her face. "You two are so cute."

Jared grinned. "Thanks, Tammy." He took Anna Beth's green gloved hand. "We should probably go."

"Yeah. Thank you, Tammy."

"Absolutely, sweetie. Anytime!"

They left the store and Jared helped Anna Beth climb up into the truck. She looked in the backseat at the gifts Jared picked up from her aunt's house. There were thirteen kids in the hospital right now, but she'd wrapped a few more just in case.

Jared climbed into the driver's seat and cranked up the heat. "So, how's Mittens feeling?"

"Better. She's a terror. I thought Sarah's head would explode the other day when she took a skein of yarn out of Sarah's knitting basket and dragged yarn all over the living room. It looked like a giant yellow spider web. I took a picture. I'll show you when you aren't driving."

"Probably a good idea. I take it the kitten lived?"

"Yeah, I cleaned it up and helped her untangle it. Plus, Mittens has a way of buttering you up until you forget why you were irritated in the first place. How is Rip? I've actually missed the lug."

"I'm sure he missed you, too, especially since he hates when I work long hours. The four-threes are great, except he hates being alone for ten hours at a time, four days in a row."

"I wrote all day at Foam Capped Java. When I got home, Mitten's wouldn't leave my side. I feel bad that I've been glued to my computer so much, but I finished the first draft of my screenplay this morning. It's definitely a rough draft, but I have a good feeling about it."

"That's great, A.B. Does the hero happen to be a tall, handsome stranger with an adorable lab?"

"Maybe."

"I like it already."

"Well, I might let you read the second draft."

The hospital sat tucked back off the highway, partially hidden by large pine trees. Jared parked on the back side and they both grabbed a large black trash bag and filled it up with gifts.

"Do you have your Grinch voice down?" Jared asked.

She cleared her throat and talked out of the side of her mouth. "Hello...children."

Jared chuckled. "That's hot. You may have to do that for just me, later."

Anna Beth's cheeks flushed beneath the makeup. Although they'd made out, their intimacy hadn't gone beyond kissing and light petting. But Jared's comment made her think about the red plaid bustier she'd bought to wear under her black dress on Saturday. It came with matching cheeky undies and Tammy convinced her it would drive him crazy.

Although she'd thought about being in bed with Jared, Anna Beth didn't know how ready she was to take that step. What if they were awkward together?

They passed through the front doors to the information desk. As the staff caught sight of them, everyone smiled.

"The Grinch," the receptionist said.

"Yes, what do you want?" Anna Beth said, already in character. When the group laughed, a giddy sensation spread through her.

"They are here to see the kids," a guy in blue scrubs said.

"Sure, just sign here and Kayla, the one in the pink, will take you down."

After they showed their IDs, they were handed visitors passes and followed Kayla down the hallway to the elevators. Sweat coated Anna Beth's skin beneath the green fur suit and she resisted the urge to wipe her forehead.

"The kids know they are getting a special guest, but we didn't give them any other details. They are going to be really surprised. Props to whoever did your makeup, by the way."

"Thanks," Anna Beth said.

They stepped out of the elevator and passed through a

doorway lit by a string of green garland dotted with tiny red bows. Kayla waved at a short woman in business casual attire.

"Oh my gosh. I'm Janet, the Peds Director. I want to thank you both for doing this. Officer Cross, you make an adorable Max."

Jared barked and Anna Beth laughed.

"And you must be Anna Beth." Janet took her hand and squeezed it. "Welcome. I'll take you around to each room. We'll start with little Hunter. He's four."

"Can we set the bags somewhere and take the individual presents around?" Anna Beth asked.

"Absolutely. Right through here to my office."

Once the bags were stashed away, Anna Beth followed behind Janet into Hunter's hospital room. The little boy sat up in bed in a blue hospital gown, watching cartoons. His mother looked up from her book when they entered, her face brightening.

"Hunter, there is someone here to see you," Janet said.

Hunter turned big hazel eyes their way, his short brown hair mussed.

His face split into an excited smile. "The Grinch!"

The IV tube in his arm moved as he crawled closer to the edge of the bed.

"Hello, Hunter. What are you in for?"

"I puked blood. They thought I might have torn my 'softgus, but I didn't."

Anna Beth's stomach turned. "Well, that's worse than running out of hot garbage. Are you feeling better now?"

"Yes, I stayed the night here. I get to go home today. They gave me pancakes with extra syrup."

"Hey, hey, what about The Grinch? Let's get me some pancakes, huh?" Anna Beth took the package from Jared and held it out to Hunter. "Now that my heart is ten times its normal size, I wanted to bring you something to make you feel better."

Hunter ripped into the package excitedly. "Wow, a Scooby Doo Lego set."

"What do you say?" his mother prodded.

"Thank you!"

Anna Beth bowed. "You're welcome, Hunter. And a Merry Christmas to you."

"Merry Christmas," Hunter and his mom chorused.

When they made it out of the room, Jared gave Anna Beth a big hug.

"What was that for?"

"I'm proud of you, that's all. You made that kid's day."

"You really did," Janet said.

Anna Beth coughed, trying to fight the urge to cry. "Who's next?"

They visited with three kids who were being treated for dehydration, and secondary infections, all under the age of ten. They were so excited to see them and open their gifts.

The next stop on their tour was the room of a teenager whose appendix ruptured. They walked in to find a chubby, dark haired boy, his gaze glued to the TV.

Jared coughed behind her and Anna Beth glanced back at him, frowning.

"Lane, you have visitors," Janet said.

The sullen boy looked at them and scoffed. "Dressing up in a costume? What a loser."

Anna Beth's eyes narrowed. "Loohoo-zeher? At least I can keep a hold of both my appendices."

Lane rolled his eyes. "I don't need to be cheered up, or your lame gift. I'm going home tomorrow."

Janet shook her head. "We'll let you rest."

Anna Beth set the gift she'd brought down on the couch in the corner. "I'll leave this here."

"Just take it. I don't care."

Once they were back in Janet's office, she said, "I'm sorry about that."

"It's no problem," Jared said. "I know that kid. He's got problems."

Janet's gaze shifted away. "I cannot discuss our patients, but Lane has spent most of his time with us alone. I was hoping he'd like a little company."

Anna Beth picked up another present, but watched Jared. He kept looking back at Lane's room and, while she was in with a three-year-old with pneumonia, he disappeared.

After she delivered the last gift, Anna Beth and Janet checked around. Anna Beth heard his voice and stopped outside the door to Lane's room.

Jared sat next to Lane's bed; the *Game of Thrones* Monopoly Anna Beth bought Lane set up on his tray.

"I couldn't get past the fourth season," Jared said.

Lane made a noise of disbelief. "You have to keep watching. It's such an epic show. Especially when they battle the White Walkers."

Jared shrugged. "I'll give it another shot, but no promises."

Anna Beth backed out of the doorway and motioned with her head at Janet. "Let's give them some more time."

When Jared walked into Janet's office forty-five minutes later, he shot her a puzzled look. "Hey, you ready to go?"

"Whenever you are. It looked like you were having fun." Anna Beth stood and held her hand out to Janet. "Thank you again. There are some additional gifts in that bag, in case you get any more kids that need a little Christmas cheer. There is a list with what each box contains."

"Thank you both."

Anna Beth followed Jared down the hall and into the elevator. While they stood waiting, Anna Beth nudged Jared.

"Who was that kid?"

"He goes to school with Casey. Lane tried to get him suspended."

"Wait, what? Then why were you being so friendly to him."

The elevator dinged and the doors opened. As they stepped inside, Jared said, "I know the kid's dad and he is a jerk. The way Janet said he's been alone really got to me. He might act like a turd, but maybe it's because he's miserable. I wanted to give him a chance to show me another side and he did. I just had to find a common ground."

Anna Beth's heart swelled and her eyes filled with tears. "You are so sweet."

She didn't even give him a chance to respond before she kissed him, forgetting all about her makeup and green beard. When the elevator stopped, she pulled away.

"What was that for?"

"Because you still tried to help someone who hurt your family. Because you are an amazing man. Because…"

I love you.

The doors opened and Kayla stood on the other side, waiting. She glanced between them, smirking. When they stepped off, Kayla called out, "Hey, Max, you got a little green on your mouth."

Jared chuckled, but Anna Beth didn't react, still reeling from her realization. She'd fallen in love with Jared.

What the heck did she do now?

Twenty-Five

Jared stepped up onto the porch Saturday night to pick Anna Beth up and knocked on the door. He adjusted his tie, wishing he could just toss it into the bushes, but the party was supposed to be professional attire. The mayor put it on to thank government employees every year and this would be his first time attending with a date.

The door opened and Anna Beth stood there, one hand on the open door and the other on her hip. She wore an off-the-shoulder dress that hugged her curves until it hit her hips and flared out, transitioning from black to silver sequins. Her blonde curls were gathered on top of her head with a few pieces trailing down the side of her face and neck. She smiled, her lips the same red as her car.

"Hey."

He swallowed, hard. "You look amazing."

"Thank you. Sarah did my hair."

"She did a great job."

"Come in out of the cold while I grab my coat."

She stepped back and let him pass by. He stopped in front of her and cupped the side of her face. "I don't want to mess up your lipstick, but I really want to kiss you."

Anna Beth stretched up onto her tip toes and slipped her arms around his neck. "It doesn't come off. But you're welcome to try."

"Good to know." He pressed his lips to hers, his arms wrapping around her waist to bring her body flush against his. Jared wanted to stay right there, forever, lost in her kiss, in the sweet way she opened her mouth under his. Her hands gripping his biceps as though she'd melt to the floor if he let her go.

Jared broke the kiss, breathing hard. "Do we really have to go to this thing?"

Anna Beth chuckled. "It's your party. You tell me?"

Jared pretended to think about it. "Two hours, tops."

"Can't wait to have me all to yourself?"

His hands slid down her back, stopping just above her butt. "I want you so bad, I can't see straight."

She released a breathy laugh. "In that case, maybe I should drive."

Jared dropped his forehead to hers and took a deep, shaky breath. "I'll be good."

"Only during the party, I hope."

When he caught her meaning, Jared's jaw dropped. "Are you teasing me?"

Her smile widened as she gave him a one-shoulder shrug. "Little bit."

Jared kissed her again, his teeth grazing her bottom lip. "Keep this up and we won't even make it an hour."

"You say that like it's a bad thing."

He kissed the side of her neck and whispered, "I think little Carly was right. You definitely belong on the naughty list."

"You should join me. It's fun."

Jared smacked her butt playfully. "I don't know what's gotten into you and don't get me wrong, I love it, but I need to make an appearance at this thing."

"I know. I'm just messing with you."

"Don't say that. I was hoping after the party we could go back to my place and enjoy a fire, maybe a glass of eggnog, some *Die Hard*."

Anna Beth huffed and pulled away. "It doesn't matter how many times you argue, *Die Hard* is not a Christmas movie, and it doesn't count on my list."

"That's just un-American."

Mittens came trotting out of the living room, meowing rapidly.

"Awww, baby." Anna Beth picked her up and held her against her chest. "I'll be back soon."

Jared watched in amusement as the tabby kneaded Anna Beth's chest with her tiny paws, loud purrs emitting from the kitten.

"Lucky kitty," Jared teased.

Anna Beth rolled her eyes. "Hush. Come on, Mitts. Let's see if you're hungry."

She disappeared into the kitchen and Jared called after her, "By the way, where is your aunt tonight?"

"She's at Ernie's son's house. Did you know his grandkids call her Nona?" Anna Beth laughed. "She never wanted me to used *Aunt Sarah* and now she's a Nona."

"Are you okay with that?"

Anna Beth came back into the room without the kitten,

nodding her head. "Yeah. I realize that Sarah isn't perfect, but thinking back and knowing what I know now about her, she did the best she could at the time. She tried to show me that she cared by helping me with my car and teaching me to sew and taking me with her to all those meetings with her friends. Everyone deserves to find love. So, yeah, I'm happy for her."

Her words struck a chord in him, but Jared bit his tongue. Watching her with those kids yesterday, completely out of her comfort zone, left him totally awed. Even if she was just following a list, her kindness shone through with every interaction. But it wasn't just yesterday. Forgiving her aunt and opening her heart again, giving him another chance. She could have completely shut herself off after she lost her family and her husband, but Anna Beth had too much heart to hide.

And he'd fallen in love with her all over again because of it. In all honesty, Jared never stopped, but like him, his feelings had matured.

Now, he needed to find the right time to tell her.

"Okay," she said, shrugging into her black peacoat. "I'm ready."

"Are you wearing snow boots under that dress?"

"No, heels."

Jared arched his brown. "You're going to walk around on snow and ice in heels?"

"The sidewalks and parking lots are clear and salted. I'll be fine."

"Whatever you say."

Anna Beth slipped her arm through his. "Let's party."

They stepped outside and Jared slowed to keep pace with her. The minute she stepped onto the concrete, she slid. Luckily, Jared's reflexes were fast enough to catch her.

"Whoa, maybe I can't walk in heels."

"Guess you need a little help after all."

Jared swept her up in his arms and carried her the rest of the way. She opened the truck door for him and when he set her on the seat of the truck, she kissed him.

"I've never been carried before. It's fun. I may have to wear the wrong shoes more often."

"I've created a monster," Jared said. "If it's too hot, feel free to turn the heater down."

"Oh, I don't need your permission to mess with any of your dials."

"Smart ass."

He shut the door on her laughter, grinning as he rounded the front of the truck. He climbed up next to her and put the truck in reverse. Jared backed up and straightened, heading toward the hotel. Anna Beth reached across the console and took his hand.

"This is going to be fun."

When they pulled into The Peaks parking lot, he grabbed two small red bags from the back.

"What are those?" she asked.

"Ornaments. They're doing a White Elephant ornament exchange. Couples are supposed to bring one funny ornament and one classic ornament."

"And what did we choose?"

Jared pulled out the red and white swirled bulb with white glitter dusted over the top.

"Oh, that's cute. I'm going for that one."

He laughed and took out the other. It was a Gingerbread man with his mouth open and a bite taken out of his head.

"You are disturbed."

"It reminded me of that story you told me about your dad

chasing you with the half eaten gingerbread man. I thought it was funny." Jared hopped out and went around to get her.

The minute she opened the door, she pressed her lips to his in a hard, fast kiss.

"What was that for?"

Anna Beth's cheeks flushed. "For thinking of me."

Jared grinned. He brushed his mouth far back on her cheek, near her ear and whispered, "Can't help myself."

Anna Beth smiled, but when he reached for her, she held her hands out. "You don't have to carry me again. I can make it."

Jared lifted her out and kicked the door shut with his shoe. "Yeah, but I feel manly when I carry you. Plus, it makes it easier to do this."

He leaned down and kissed her lightly, playfully.

"Mmmm, so it's for your benefit. I guess I'm okay with that."

The chief and his wife got to the front door first and held it open for them.

"Honey, why don't you carry me across the parking lot?" his wife asked.

The chief leveled Jared with a hard stare. "Lord, look what you started, Cross."

"Sorry, sir."

The chief clapped him on the back as went inside. "Have a good time tonight."

"You, too."

They trailed behind the older couple and followed the signs to a large great room with a full buffet against the wall. The fireplace blazed and a ten-foot-tall Christmas tree sat in the corner. Underneath were small packages with numbers on them.

"Wanna eat and run?" he asked.

"I told you, this is your night, but I think we should play the White Elephant game. I want my ornament."

Jared laughed as Anna Beth took the presents over and set them under the tree. When she came back to his side, she stood up on her tiptoes and kissed him.

"Checking one more thing off my list." She looked up and he followed her gaze to the mistletoe over his head.

"I feel used."

"You shouldn't. I love kissing you. Now let's eat."

"At least my lips rated before your stomach."

Three hours later, Jared laughed again when they ended up back in the truck with not one, but both of their original ornaments.

"I can't believe the chief's wife stole my glass fox and I ended up with this." She held up the maimed Gingerbread man.

"Stop, you're hurting his feelings. Don't you think he's been through enough?"

"I suppose." Anna Beth put the ornament back in the bag. "Why is it snowing again?"

"This is Montana in December, A.B."

"I know, but still."

"Just be glad you aren't driving and buckle up."

Anna Beth pushed the middle console up and slid across the seat next to him. She clipped her seatbelt and leaned her head against his shoulder.

"Take me home, officer."

Jared turned the ignition and after he backed up, placed his hand over her knee. "Your home or…"

"You promised me a fire, eggnog, and a Christmas movie. I plan to collect."

"Yes, ma'am."

She turned toward him and placed a hand on his chest. "Mmmm, I kind of like it when you call me *ma'am.*"

Jared scoffed. "If you're referring to our run in at the market, you caught me off guard."

"I figured, but it was still funny."

"For you, maybe. I felt like an idiot."

Anna Beth slid her hand down over his stomach. "I never thought you were an idiot."

"Really?" he said, glancing down at her with one eyebrow arched. "Never?"

"Okay, maybe a time or two you tested my opinion."

"That's just a sweet way of calling me—shit!"

Jared swerved to avoid the massive bull elk on his side of the road. His heart thundered as he passed it in the left lane.

"Are you alright?" he asked.

"I'm fine, but damn, that was close." She retracted her nails from the front of his shirt. "Did I hurt you?"

"Nah, you're fine," Jared said. "But that elk took ten years off my life."

"Maybe I should keep my hands to myself until we get to your place."

"Probably best. You are too distracting for your own good."

Twenty-Six

Anna Beth stood in Jared's bathroom, staring at herself in the mirror as her stomach fluttered nervously. The sequins on the sides of her dress had rubbed the under skin of her biceps nearly raw and she couldn't wait to get out of it. A stack of Jared's clothes were folded on the bathroom counter for her to change into for their movie night, but she needed him to unzip the dress. And once he unzipped it, he'd see the bustier she wore beneath it.

Which was the whole point in wearing it, but she hadn't been with a man in over two years. What if she sucked in bed? She'd only ever been with Ian, while Jared had experience with multiple girls.

Stop freaking out. This is Jared. You want this. You are over-thinking it and it's making you anxious.

Jared knocked on his bedroom door. "Anna Beth? You okay?"

"Yeah, I'm just thinking."

"Can I come in?"

Anna Beth took a deep, shaky breath. "Yes, come in."

The door opened with a creak and Jared came around the corner into the bathroom, looking completely at ease. He'd lost his jacket, shoes, socks, and tie the minute he walked in the door and, while Anna Beth liked fancy Jared, she preferred the relaxed, rumpled version.

"What's up? Are you ready to watch the movie?"

Anna Beth swallowed. "Yes, but can you unzip me? I can't reach it with these sleeves."

Jared cleared his throat. "Uh, yeah. Sure."

He sounded nervous too, and she relaxed as he stepped up behind her. Not that she wanted him to be scared of being with her, but for some reason, his uncertainty made her more confident. Jared's presence at her back made her skin tingle along her neck and shoulders. His fingers skimmed along her back softly, feather light touches leaving a trail to the top of her dress. The *rrrrrft* of the zipper was the only sound besides their deep breathing. She held the front of the dress against her chest when it would have slid down. He kissed her shoulder tenderly, lingering.

"Done," he whispered.

Anna Beth shivered, the breath she'd been holding rushing out.

"Thank you."

"You're welcome. I'll see you downstairs."

This was the moment. She loved him. She wanted him. All she needed to do was be brave.

Just as he rounded the corner, she called out, "Jared!"

He stopped, his hand gripping the doorway. He turned around, his hands loose by his side.

"Yeah?"

Before she chickened out, she dropped the dress to the floor. Standing before him in nothing but the red plaid bustier and matching cheeky panties, she barely restrained herself from grabbing the dress off the floor and covering herself.

Jared's eyes widened as he took her in, his surprised gaze traveling from her bare feet all the way up to her face. Smoldering. The word fit his expression to a tee and her heart flipped over in her chest as he took a step towards her, then another until they were less than a foot apart.

"You realize you look like Christmas wrapping to me."

Anna Beth released a breathy laugh. "Are you calling me a gift?"

His hand cupped her cheek. "Yes, Anna Beth. The best damn gift I've ever received."

Jared cradled her face between his palms and she opened her mouth as he covered her lips with his own. Shocks of electricity shot through her body, leaving echos of heat as Jared sweetly slid his tongue inside.

Pleasure like she'd never know filled her up, losing herself in his touch as his hands ran over her shoulders and her arms until his fingers laced with hers. Jared broke the kiss, backing up with her toward the bed and Anna Beth kept her eyes glued to his face. When Jared reached the mattress he stopped, his hands still holding hers.

"If you're not ready, tell me and we can just snuggle up and watch TV."

His reassurance and care for her feelings melted her as nothing else could and she slid her arms around him, her cheek pressed against his chest. "I want this. I want you."

Jared lifted her chin with one hand and kissed her again. Anna Beth didn't expect him to fall back onto the bed, bringing her with him with one arm around her waist. Anna Beth never imagined watching him unzip her bustier, without breaking their connection, would leave her panting with need.

And when he rained soft kisses over her collar bone. Her chest. Finally, taking her nipple into his mouth…

It was like being kissed by sunshine.

Anna Beth's shyness dissolved as desire raced through her, and her hands traveled between them to the belt of Jared pants. She's never been great at unbuckling belts, but Jared let her take her time, continuing with his loving administrations. When he took her nipple into his mouth again, licking it with quick flicks of his tongue, she forgot about the belt and her hands fell to the bed, her back arching.

Jared's deep chuckle tickled her chest as he pushed himself up onto his hands, hovering over her. "You are so adorably distractible."

Anna Beth's cheeks warmed. "It's hard to concentrate when you do that thing with your tongue."

Jared kissed her again. "I'll remember that."

When Jared pushed himself up off the bed, she thought he was stopping and protested lightly.

"I'm just helping you out, A.B," he said, finishing what she started with his belt. After shucking his pants and boxers, he crawled up the bed until he lay on his side next to her. "Now, where was I?"

When Jared's mouth covered her nipple again, she moaned, cradling the back of his head in her hands.

Anna Beth's body hummed as Jared kissed his way over her stomach, his hands sliding her underwear off one leg and then the other. His head dipped between her legs and tears stung her eyes as he gently brought her closer to orgasm, taking his time with her. The slow, steady pressure of Jared's mouth and hands on her clit lifted her higher until she was soaring, calling out his name in total abandon.

Anna Beth's eyes fluttered open when she heard a drawer opening and closing and the sound of a wrapper ripping. Jared came back over her, his hard body pressing into hers, and she looped her arms around his waist, cradling his hips with her thighs.

As Jared sank into her, Anna Beth tangled her legs with his, closing her eyes when he filled her. Her mind drifted as he moved inside her to their first kiss in the snow, the joy as she'd lost herself in him, forgetting everything but the way he made her feel. Loving Jared was more than an all-consuming passion and need. Feeling treasured. Protected. Loved.

Anna Beth opened her eyes, her gaze locking with Jared's and she saw it. Love. Jared loved her.

When his rhythm picked up, she held on, burying her face in his shoulder, whispering, "*yes*," in a husky chant as she came again. Jared joined her moments later, the sound of her name on his lips like a little prayer and she almost told him.

I love you, Jared Cross.

Instead, she curled up against his side, her hand splayed over his abdomen, watching his chest rise and fall rapidly at first before slowing to deep, even breaths.

"So..." she said.

"Yes?"

"That was amazing."

Jared laughed, his lips brushing her forehead. "I knew it would be."

"How?" Anna Beth asked, her eyes lids heavy.

"Because it's you."

Anna Beth's eyes drifted closed, a small smile on her face. "That's really sweet, Jared."

"Are you falling asleep on me, A.B.?"

"Mmmmm. A little bit."

Jared tightened his arms around her and she snuggled close.

"Go ahead and rest, sweetheart. We got all the time in the world."

Twenty-Seven

After fifteen minutes of watching her sleep, Jared extracted himself from Anna Beth and went to the bathroom to clean up. He disposed of the condom in the waste basket and took a quick shower, whistling while he lathered and rinsed his body.

Being with the woman you loved was a completely different experience than having sex just to get off. Every look they shared, every moan of pleasure or shiver of release flowed like a song. Something he wanted to replay over and over.

Jared shut off the water and wrapped a towel around his waist, thinking about what came next. Talking to her about staying in Snowy Springs. Finishing her list. Ian's letter. There were only a few more things she needed to accomplish and after that, he'd have to give her Ian's letter. Nervous didn't begin to cover it, but he wouldn't let a ghost come between them. She'd loved Ian, but Jared was here. He loved her and would do anything to make her happy.

That had to count for something.

He came back into the room to find her propped up on one elbow, the sheet pulled over her chest. Her blonde hair fell around her shoulders, onto the sheets, and despite her claim of color stay lipstick, her lips were no longer red.

"All cleaned up?" she said.

"Yeah. I would have asked you to join me, but you seemed to be tuckered out."

Anna Beth yawned. "I didn't mean to be, but it's the good kind."

Jared leaned over the bed, his lips brushing hers. "That's what a guy loves to hear. Do you feel like watching a movie now? Clothing optional?"

Anna Beth giggled. "Hmmm, naked Netflix and chill? Sounds fun, but can I at least borrow some socks. My feet are like ice cubes."

"Sure. I think I have a pair of sock slippers my mom got me last year. They have big foot on them."

"Let me guess, because you have big feet?"

"Exactly." Jared opened his sock drawer and while he dug through the folded pairs, Ian's letter dropped over the side and onto the floor.

Anna Beth, now sitting on the edge of the bed in the sheet, went for it. "I'll get it."

Time stilled as Jared moved to beat her to the envelope. "No, don't."

Anna Beth shot him a puzzled look as he tried to snatch the envelope out of her hand. "I was just going to hand it to you. What's your prob…" Her voice trailed off as she looked at front of the envelope. "Problem."

Jared watched the emotions shift across her face as her gaze flicked from him to the white rectangle in her hand. "What is this?"

There was no easing into this one, not when she looked tense enough to snap. "It's a letter from Ian."

"But why is it addressed to you?"

"I don't know why. He sent it two years ago—"

"Two years?" she said, shrilly. "Why? What does it say?"

Her green eyes were wild and he knew she must be thinking the worst. "He wanted me to give it to you when you were finished."

"With what?"

"I don't know. The list?"

Anna Beth's eyes narrowed. "Wait, you knew all along about the list?"

"No, well, he mentioned a list, but not what it entailed. He just asked me to help you when you came back to town." Jared waved his hand toward her. "You can read it. There's a letter for you inside as well."

Anna Beth pulled out his letter, scanning the page. Jared's stomach lurched as he tried to decipher what thoughts may be rushing through her mind.

"What the…I…I don't even know what I want to say right now." She looked up at him, tears pooling in her eyes. "And why were you hiding it from me?"

"Anna Beth, I wasn't hiding it."

"It was in your sock drawer, Jared, like a dirty little secret." Anna Beth started gathering up her clothes. "I can't believe you kept this from me."

"Anna Beth, I didn't do this to hurt you. I was respecting his wishes."

Anna Beth laughed bitterly. "You didn't even know him."

"That's true, but he entrusted me with it."

"And what about us? He sent this to you when we weren't even speaking and you didn't think to mention it when we started talking again?"

Jared took a calm, even breath. "Honestly, it's not as though we were conspiring to harm you. He wanted me to hold the letter for you until the time was right. I was going to give it to you. Despite whatever you're thinking, I would never intentionally hurt you."

Anna Beth drew a deep, shaky breath. "I know that. Deep down, I do, but...I am too upset to do this."

"Do what? Talk? Let me explain myself?"

"Yes!" She dashed at her cheeks. "Can you please leave so I can get dressed?"

"Anna Beth, please…"

"Jared, I can't think clearly when I'm around you. I thought we were creating something special, but...I need to process everything. And I can't do that here with you."

Jared's shoulders sank like a thousand-pound sack dropped on them from the sky and he turned to go but stopped and faced her once more.

"Honestly, maybe some part of me wanted to follow his wishes because I was afraid if I gave you the letter, I'd lose you to him again. It's not pretty or right, but it's the truth. I did what he wanted because I love you and I didn't want this to end. Guess I called that one, huh?"

She didn't respond, just continued to gather her clothes and he released a shaky breath. "I'll give you some space and drive you home."

"Thank you."

Jared collected some clothes from his drawers and closed the door behind him. The sound of Anna Beth's sobs tore through him, ripping his heart to shreds. He took the stairs slowly, his knees weak. When he finished dressing in the living room, he sank onto the couch, his eyes stinging with tears. Jared sniffed, trying to hold his emotions at bay as Rip trotted over and put his head in Jared's lap.

"Sorry, buddy. Guess I blew it again."

Rip whined, pushing his nose into Jared's hand. Anna Beth came down a few minutes later, wearing the sequin dress.

"You don't have to leave in that. You can borrow some clothes."

"I'm fine. It's just a ten-minute ride."

Jared got off the couch and slipped on his boots. He had his hand on the door knob, when he spun around. "Anna Beth, I really think we need to work this out."

Her shuttered expression remained unmoving. "Jared, I don't like secrets, no matter what the intentions behind them may be. So please give me some space."

Jared didn't have to be a relationship expert to know *space* was the kiss of death.

Twenty-Eight

Anna Beth sat at the kitchen table, Ian's journal closed in front of her. The clock on the oven read five in the morning, but she'd never gone to bed. She'd been drinking coffee and wracking her brain for what Ian could had been thinking.

The letter Ian placed on the back cover of the journal lay on the table beside the envelope Ian sent Jared. She'd read Ian's letter to Jared several times and she still didn't understand.

Why had Ian singled out Jared? She'd talked about him over the years, but Ian knew they weren't close anymore. It didn't make sense for him to entrust a letter for her to someone she wasn't in contact with. He could have picked Sarah or Olive. Why Jared?

"Anna Beth? What are you doing up?"

She glanced over her shoulder at Sarah, then back to the letters. "Pondering the intricate workings of the male mind."

Sarah stopped next to her, dropping a hand on Anna Beth's shoulder. "Have you been down here all-night?"

She nodded. "So far, nothing makes sense."

"That's pretty common. I think men feel the same way about us."

"I am not complicated. I don't hide things from someone I care about because some rando asks me to."

"I see." Sarah padded over and took her green floral teapot off of the stove and filled it in the sink. "Maybe you should tell me why men are so mysterious."

Anna Beth held up the letter to Jared. "Ian sent this to Jared two years ago, with a letter entrusted to him for me. But this," she held up the letter from the journal, "is a letter he left in the back of his journal. First off, why would he send this to Jared, who I wasn't close to for years? And why do I need two final letters?"

"I guess it never occurred to you to read them and find out?"

"I'm supposed to wait until I finish my list," Anna Beth grumbled.

"Do you really think Ian left you the list to make you miserable. What if it was a way to help you heal?" Sarah set the teapot on the burner and turned it on high. "How many items do you have left."

"I need to watch a few more Christmas movies."

Sarah sat down across from Anna Beth and covered her hand with her own.

"Anna Beth, I think Ian would be okay with you opening the letters."

"But which one?"

"I'd do the one he left in the journal. If you and Jared hadn't reconnected, you might never have known about it."

Anna Beth picked up the letter and slipped her thumb

under the seam to open it. When she unfolded it, her eyes traveled over Ian's familiar handwriting, and filled with tears.

Anna Banana,

If you're reading this, I've been gone awhile. I know at times my lists for you might have seemed silly, but I did it for you. If I hadn't gotten you up and moving, you'd be sitting in our "sterile house" (your words), probably alone. I was hoping to time each one perfectly so you would have a year to find yourself again. You spent years living for me and, in a morbid way, I wanted my death to be about your life. I didn't want you spending years grieving. I lived. I created. I explored. I loved.

I hope you went back to Snowy Springs. When you talked about your childhood, it wasn't all bad. I think you feel that way because you're too close to it. I suspect your aunt was hurting as much as you, and I hope you were able to reconcile with her. I pray Olive drags you out and you two tear up that sleepy little town. Most of all, I want you find someone new. You were made to be loved and have a family. Don't shut yourself off from that.

My last wish for you is to be happy, whatever that looks like and to thank you. Being with you was the greatest gift I ever received.

I love you.
Ian

Anna Beth wiped at her eyes, but the tears were falling too fast to stop them.

"What did he say?" Sarah asked.

She passed her aunt the letter and got up to grab the box of tissues from the living room. Mittens woke up on the couch and stretched, her tiny mouth opening wide, before hopping off the couch and following behind Anna Beth, meowing.

Sarah folded the letter and set it in the middle of the table. "I suppose I was an item on that list of his."

"Yes."

"I'm not sure how I feel about that. I will say that I agree with him. I think it's a good thing you returned."

"I do too," Anna Beth said. "And the request may have come from him, but the glass? The chats? That's all you and me."

Sarah smiled, transforming her face, making her look ten years younger. "True."

Mitten's jumped into Anna Beth's lap and curled into a ball, purring loudly. Anna Beth ran her hand over the short, silky fur, comforted by the affection.

Finally, she picked up the other letter. "Guess I should get it over with, huh?"

"Probably best."

Anna Beth opened the second letter.

Anna Banana,

Since you have my letter, I can only assume Jared either mailed it or he gave it to you when you went to visit your aunt. Or the two of you finally took the plunge.

Anna Beth paused, her cheeks burning.

I know the reason the two of you stopped talking

is because you married me. I don't know the particulars, but from what you told me, he's not a bad guy. Not as good as me, of course, but he sounds alright.

She laughed through her tears and Sarah reached for her empty hand, squeezing it.

I want to be clear; I've never been jealous of Jared. Whatever happened between the two of you, I know you loved me. But I could see it in your face, you loved him too. You chose me, but that didn't mean you forgot him.

When you love, you do so with your whole heart and I know it's big enough for more than one person. He may be your first, but I am so grateful I got to be your number one for a time. Now, he can be your last.

I need you to be good with letting him in. I know you. You'll fight it, pretend it's nothing. But real love doesn't come around as often as people think. This is your chance to be lucky twice.

And if it doesn't work out, I know you'll find someone who will love you as much as I do. Don't hide from it.

Shine, my love.
Ian

"My God, Anna Beth, what did he say? You're going to choke if you don't stop crying!"

Anna Beth grabbed two more tissues and buried her face in them, sobbing harder.

Sarah stood up, coming up behind her. With one hand on Anna Beth's shoulder, Sarah picked up the second letter with the other. Her hand squeezed Anna Beth's shoulder and once she laid it back on the table, she wrapped her arms around Anna Beth, resting her cheek against the top of her head.

"I am sorry I didn't visit you more. He seems like a wonderful man."

"He was, damn him."

"What are you going to do?"

"First, I need to blow my nose."

Sarah let her go and picked up her whistling tea kettle. "And then?"

"I'm not sure."

"And what about Jared? I can't imagine you handled it well when you found the letter."

"What makes you say that?"

"Because your mother and I, and you, share the same temper."

Anna Beth ran her hands through her hair. "He is never going to forgive me."

"Horse shit."

Anna Beth gasped. "Sarah!"

Her aunt's cheeks burned crimson, but she lifted her chin. "I've seen you two. Jared Cross loves you. When a man really loves a woman, there is always a chance."

"You think?"

"Ernie didn't give up on me, and I gave him plenty of reasons. All you can do is go to Jared and apologize. The rest is up to him."

Sarah poured her tea and sat down across from her once more. Anna Beth swallowed nervously.

"Sarah, how would you feel about me staying a little longer?"

"Anna Beth. I'd be very happy if you stayed."

"Because, I could find my own place if it's a problem—"

"If it's all the same, I'd rather you live here. This is your home and we're family." Anna Beth burst into tears again and

Sarah cleared her throat. "Stop crying, or I may change my mind."

Anna Beth didn't believe her for a second.

"I love you, Aunt Sarah."

Sarah wiped at her eye discreetly. "I love you too. Now stop with all this. Let's get some sleep."

Anna Beth stood up, heading for the door.

"And Anna Beth?"

She stopped.

"Your screenplay?" Anna Beth held her breath. She'd given it to her aunt to read yesterday and hadn't said anything since, afraid of what she would say about it.

"Yes?"

"It's really good. You're very talented, sweetheart, and I'm so proud of you." Anna Beth's eyes welled up again and her aunt waved her hands, "Nope, that's it. Shoooo! Go to bed."

Twenty-Nine

Jared sat in his cruiser off the side of the highway, watching the commuters go by Monday morning. His shift was almost finished and couldn't wait to get home and sleep. He hadn't done much of that since he'd taken Anna Beth home Saturday night.

He leaned his head back against the headrest, hating how much her walking away hurt. Part of him held out hope she'd read Ian's letter and realized he really did have the best of intentions. But not a word.

She should have believed you. After everything you two have been to one another?

Well, Jared knew what she'd been to him, but he still had no idea if she felt the same. He doubted she had any intention of staying, especially now.

Jared checked the time and reached for his radio to let dispatch know he was heading back, when a red car flew past him.

Anna Beth's Chrysler.

Let it go. You don't want to be that guy.

But she was breaking the law by about fifteen miles per hour.

Before he thought better of it, Jared flipped on his lights and tore after her. By the time he turned the corner heading into town, she was already pulled over, waiting for him. Anna Beth leaned against the back of her car in jeans and her black peacoat, her hair loose around her shoulder.

He stepped out of his car and walked toward her, his heart galloping.

"You know, I believe I told you I hate being pulled over."

"Do you know how fast you were going back there?"

She crossed her arms over her chest. "Sixty-five?"

Jared thought he saw a hint of a smile on her lips and frowned. "That's about right. Why?"

"I wanted to get your attention."

Jared stared at here, trying to keep a rein on his emotions. "You could have picked up a phone and called. Sent a text. Like a sane person."

"I did call *and* text. You didn't answer."

"I don't have my personal cell phone on at work."

"Then my plan seems logical, especially if you weren't getting my messages. I couldn't risk that you'd ignore me."

What the hell? She'd been the one to leave him and now she wanted his attention?

He'd thought he wanted to talk, but he was too tired to process this now.

"Well, I'm about to clock off and go to bed, so if it can wait..."

"It can't." She pushed off the back of her car and shoved her hands in her coat pocket. "You frustrate me."

Jared's eyebrows shot up. "What?"

"You frustrate me! I mean, why do you have to make this," she waved her finger between them, "so complicated?"

The cars passing made it hard to hear, but he caught the gist of it. "Are you on something? How have I made our relationship more difficult?"

"You should have just told me about the letters. Yes, I broke down emotionally, but you should have told me when we started getting close."

"Like I said, I was honoring his wishes."

"And being selfish. You said that too."

Jared sighed, running a hand over his face. "I can't tell if you're apologizing or you want me to. Again."

"No, this is all me. I acted like a jerk about the letter instead of sitting down and listening calmly, letting you explain."

"Alright." What the hell else could he say? Everything she said was true.

"I want you, Jared. I want this."

Jared stood there, hearing her say all the things he's always wanted...but her abandonment was still too fresh in his mind. He wanted her to call, apologize, ask him to work it out, but the reality was, his insecurities were very real when it came to Anna Beth. Her reaction to the letters went immediately to her distrusting him and his intentions, when he'd never given her a reason to think his feelings weren't genuine.

"I appreciate your candor and you've given me a lot to think about."

"Wait, that's it?" she asked.

"For now, yeah."

"I don't understand."

"You had a day and a half to cool down and figure out what you wanted to say to me. I'm sure you can appreciate I might want some time, too." Her face fell and it took everything in him not to reach out and drag her into his arms. "The thing is, I feel like I've been very clear about the way I feel. I've been worried from the start about you not being in this with me. You were so quick to accuse me of betraying you. I just need more time to process."

"It was a fight, Jared. Couples fight. They have misunderstandings and they overcome. That's how relationships work."

"I've never been in a relationship that lasted, so I don't have anything to compare this to. All I know is your accusations broke my fucking heart. You walking away, and not wanting to discuss this as a couple, hurt."

"I'm so sorry." She took a step toward him, but he backed away.

"I know, but..." He couldn't come up with a single thing to make either of them feel better. "We'll talk soon. And slow down."

The weight of his shoes increased with every step away from her, but he needed to do this.

When he left the station half an hour later, he turned his cell phone on when he got in his truck. The whole way home, his phone chimed. Whoever was blowing up his phone, was going to get a piece of his mind.

Jared parked in his driveway, he grabbed his phone and started scrolling. Dozens of text messages from his mom, his sisters, his brothers, and Anna Beth. Anna Beth's texts to tell him she was sorry and she missed him. His mother wanting to know what was going on with him and Anna Beth. His sisters telling him they saw Anna Beth buying coffee. Grayson wanting to borrow money, again. Forrest, telling him to call Mom.

Jared turned his phone on silent and walked up to his front door. Rip jumped up and down excitedly when he walked into his house.

"Hey, buddy." Rip had something in his mouth that was flapping in the air. He pried his dog's mouth open and pulled out a scrap of fabric.

Anna Beth's underwear.

"Not you too."

Rip spun around, his tongue hanging from his mouth.

Jared shut the front door and threw the panties in the hamper in his room, wondering why the universe continued to torture him. He needed a full eight hours of shut eye and then maybe he could muddle through the mess they'd made of their relationship. Once he reached the top of the stairs, Jared's energy faded and he barely remembered to lock his service gun in the safe before flopping face first onto the bed, still in his pants and t-shirt.

Rip let out a series of excited barks, waking him from a dead sleep.

"Jared!"

Jared bolted upright, squinting at the clock. He'd only been asleep for forty-five minutes.

Son of a bitch.

He got up and jogged down the stairs to find his mother standing in his living room, looking fit to be tied.

"What's wrong?"

"Why aren't you answering your phone?" she asked.

Jared rolled his eyes. "Because I worked all night and I needed to get some sleep."

"Olive said a bunch of people saw you and Anna Beth arguing on the side of the road."

"We weren't arguing. She apologized, and I accepted it. She wanted to jump back in, but I need some time. No arguing. Just statements about what the other thinks and wants. That's it."

"What was she apologizing for?"

"Mom…Do you know what it means to have a personal life? It means things are private and nobody's business except the two parties involved."

"I just want to make sure you're not scared of your feelings and blowing things out of proportion. You do that."

"No I don't," he said through gritted teeth.

"I don't want to argue. I guess you are going to just have to figure out what you want now that she's staying."

"Staying?"

"Oh yeah, Sarah told me yesterday at church. Anna Beth is going to be living in Snowy Springs." His mom headed for the door and before she shut it, called out, "Sweet dreams, honey."

Jared kicked the side of his couch. Why were the women in his life hell bent on driving him crazy?

Thirty

Anna Beth banged on Olive's front door, her body tense with frustration. Not to mention humiliation. She's laid out her emotions and Jared practically told her "*thanks, but no.*"

No, he'd said he needed time. Again.

Isn't that what you asked for just two days ago?

Anna Beth cursed the little voice and pounded on the wood again.

"Olive? Hey, I really need to talk."

Finally, she heard feet slapping against the floor inside and the door opened. Olive leaned against it, out of breath.

"Hey, what's up?"

"Can I come in?"

"Yeah sure, it's just...I'm not alone."

Anna Beth shrugged. "Is it Vance?"

"Yeah."

"That's fine, maybe he can weigh in."

Olive stepped back and let her pass. "Let me guess. Officer Cross screwed the pooch?"

"No, well a little, but I'm the one who really messed up and he needs time to process. Again."

"What did you do?"

"Jared's had a letter from Ian in his drawer for two years."

"Whoa, wait. This sounds intense. I'm going to need coffee. Want some?"

"Sure, thanks."

"Vance? You want coffee?" Olive yelled loudly.

"Yes. Hi, Anna Beth," he hollered back.

"Hi, Vance. Your friend is making me nuts."

"Okay."

Anna Beth shook her head as she trailed behind Olive into the kitchen. "I just couldn't believe it, you know? I sat there, wondering what they'd been saying, how long were they corresponding...I guess I lost my mind a little."

"What did it say?"

"To help me when I came back to Snowy Springs in any way he could."

Olive snickered as she pressed the button on the one cup coffee machine. "I bet he didn't mean to help you right into bed."

"Can we not joke about this? I haven't even gotten to the craziest part."

"Go on."

"There was another letter for me with Jared's. It wasn't opened, so I know he didn't read it, but it was basically Ian giving me his blessing to be with Jared."

Olive clapped her hands, stalling when Anna Beth grimaced. "That's good, right? I know you were a little nervous about moving on and I know you loved Ian, but you can love more than one person."

"That's what Ian said. He thought my falling out with Jared had to do with him and that I'd always loved Jared."

"Whoa, that is some heavy intuition."

"But it's not…"

"Don't lie to yourself. You love-loved Jared since we were kids. It might not have been fully fleshed out, but can you say you didn't have feelings for him?"

"No, I can't," Anna Beth grudgingly admitted.

"So, you found letters, you read them, and then…"

"I went off on him for keeping secrets and told him I needed time to process."

"Wait, you pulled a Jared?"

Anna Beth made a face. "Shut up."

"Ian sending a letter and Jared hanging onto it doesn't seem so bad."

"I think I may have been running on some pretty heavy emotions, since we'd just slept together."

"Girl, you let him sneak in them jeans and you didn't tell me?" Olive squealed.

Anna Beth's cheeks burned. "Because I found the letter right after. God, Olive, it was so bad. He drove me home in complete silence."

"So, you acted like a douche. Just tell him you're sorry, give him a happy, and all good."

"No, not all good. I caught Jared while he was at work and apologized, but he said he needed time to think."

"Oh, come on. Clearly you were just overly emotional and jealous."

"What? No. Why would I be jealous?"

"You were jealous because your dead husband sent a letter to someone you cared about but were afraid to face. He took the step for you and you feel manipulated."

Anna Beth frowned. Olive wasn't wrong. "I wouldn't call it jealousy. I just didn't like that he kept this from me."

"Would it have changed anything if he'd told you sooner? From what it sounds like, he was just doing what Ian asked. If he'd told you about the letters sooner, would it have brought you closer to Jared? Or maybe pushed you further away?"

"I don't know. I think it would have been fine."

"Really? You would have let yourself fall for Jared if you got a letter from Ian not just telling you he knew you always had feelings for Jared, but that he was okay with you being together? That wouldn't have freaked you out and send you running out of Snowy Springs for good?"

Anna Beth considered Olive's opinion. In the beginning, she'd tried fighting against her attraction to Jared. There had definitely been guilt attached to it. But if she'd read Ian's letter before, it would have felt...weird to date Jared.

"Fine, my husband hand picking my next boyfriend may have sent me running the other way. But that's not the point. I know I want Jared. How can I get him to forgive me?"

Olive pulled three cups from the cupboard and set them on the counter. "Vance, coffee's ready."

"Can you bring it to me?"

"I'm not your mother, nor your girlfriend. Get your ass out here and get it yourself."

Vance came around the corner in a pair of jeans and no shirt, looking rumpled.

"I was just asking," he grumbled.

She poured him a cup and handed it to him. "Black, like your soul. Now that you're here, how does Anna Beth get back into Jared's good graces?"

"Nope." He tried to leave the room, but Olive grabbed

him by the back of the jeans. When they dipped low, Anna Beth covered her eyes before she got a flash of Vance's butt.

"Hey, hey, hey, what are you doing?" he shouted.

"Get back here and help us brainstorm."

"Jared is my friend."

"And I do that thing you like, so sit."

Vance mumbled something about evil, but sat next to Anna Beth. "What did you do?" he asked.

"Questioned his integrity."

"Ouch."

Olive set Anna Beth's coffee mug in front of her and the half-and-half in the center of the table.

"What you need is something that shows him how you really feel," Vance said sarcastically.

"I told him how I felt."

"Yes, but men are very visual," Olive said. "What would be something you could do to prove to Jared you care?"

"I'll think about it," Anna Beth said.

"Oh, before I forget," Olive said to Vance, "I need you to help me get my Christmas ornaments out of the attic before you leave."

"I'm not your boyfriend or your father," Vance said.

Olive smiled sweetly at him, then took her fist, making a suggestive motion toward her mouth. "Please."

Anna Beth thought about her box of childhood ornaments. She hadn't opened the box yet, but...

Suddenly, she jumped to her feet. "I have it!"

"You have what?" Olive asked.

"I know how to show Jared I care. But I need help."

Vance started to get up again and Olive grabbed his arm. "No." He sat. "What kind of help?"

"Ornaments. Specific ornaments. And a Christmas tree."

"By when?"

"Christmas Eve."

"All the trees at the market are sold,"Vance said.

"That's okay. I know how to work a chainsaw."

Thirty-One

Jared sat on the couch at his parent's house on Christmas Eve, watching the twinkling lights of the tree and wishing he'd gone into work. He wasn't exactly feeling the holiday cheer at the moment. His brothers and sisters were laughing in the other room as they finished dinner. Jared hadn't eaten much, his stomach tied in knots. He definitely didn't feel like visiting.

"Hey." Karen nudged him with her foot. "What are you doing? You've been a grump all night."

"I'm just tired."

Karen sat down next to him, patting his knee. "Why don't we do presents so you can go home and rest?"

"But we haven't cleaned up or had dessert yet."

"It's Christmas. The dinner mess can wait. We'll mix things up this year." She leaned away from him and hollered, "Everyone get in here for the gifts."

The Jeffries filed in, taking seats around the room. To his surprise, Isa waddled straight for the tree and picked up a small square box wrapped in white paper and tied together with a shiny red ribbon. She held it out to him.

"Usually mom picks the gifts," Jared said.

Karen smiled. "That's okay, just open it."

He read the tag. *To Jared. Love, Santa.*

Jared didn't recognize the handwriting. Carefully, he slid off the ribbon and tore the paper. He pulled up the lid on the little white box and inside was an ornament, wrapped in red tissue. Jared picked it up by the hook, noting how heavy it was. The wooden base was a sled. White, glittery puff paint covered the bottom like snow and holly leaves and berries decorated the front. When he held it up to get a better look, he saw that someone had glued a small, red photo frame on top of the sled. Inside was the selfie he'd taken with Anna Beth on top of Slaughter Hill.

"This is from Anna Beth?" he whispered.

"Yes, and there's something else inside."

Jared pulled out a piece of white paper tucked to one side. He unfolded it slowly, his breath catching.

Jared,

Since I've almost finished my list, I thought maybe I should make one for the new year. Let me know what you think…

1. *Convince Jared to forgive me.*
2. *Kiss Jared five times a day.*
3. *Try to control my temper.*
4. *Take a vacation with Jared.*
5. *Slow dance with Jared.*

6. *Take a cooking class.*
7. *Ask Sarah to teach me to knit.*
8. *Knit Jared beanies for next winter.*
9. *Make sure Mittens and Rip become best friends.*
10. *Tell Jared I love him every minute of every day until he believes me.*

Jared sucked in a breath. Anna Beth loved him?

"Was it something good?" Forrest asked.

"Yes." Jared held up the ornament and his sisters all complimented it.

Savannah stood and leaned over the coffee table. "What did the letter say?"

"None of your business," he answered.

Grayson went for the tree. "I'm next."

"Get your butt back," Dad growled. "Only your mom says who is next."

Several arguments broke out between the siblings, but Jared wasn't really listening as he stared down at the picture of him and Anna Beth smiling. Anna Beth loved him. She'd gifted him a picture of the two of them as though they were together. Even though he'd been keeping his distance, she still went out on a limb to show him how she felt.

"If you're not feeling great, honey, why don't you go home and rest?" his mom said.

"Are you sure?"

"I insist, but I want you back here bright and early with your smile in place."

Jared rolled his eyes. "Yes, ma'am."

He got up and said his goodbyes. Once he'd slipped into his coat, he went out onto the porch and took his phone from his pocket. There were no missed calls from Anna Beth.

The door opened behind him and he stopped, expecting his mother to lure him back inside. But, when he turned around, he found Casey, his hands shoved in his pockets, shifting from foot to foot nervously.

"I just wanted to say, I ran into Lane. He told me that you visited and what a nice guy you were. I wanted to say thanks. He was really cool to me and I know it's because of you."

Jared nodded. "You're welcome, Case. I'll see you tomorrow." Jared held out his arms. "Hug?"

"Yeah, right." Casey laughed, ducking back inside.

Jared chuckled. Someday the kid would come around.

When he climbed into his truck, Jared pulled out his phone. Why would Anna Beth go to the trouble of giving him a gift, but not call? He ran his thumb over her contact picture. Maybe he'd just wish her a Merry Christmas. That wouldn't be weird. Get a conversation going, mention he loved her too.

Jared hit the button and dialed Anna Beth, putting it on speaker phone. After two rings, it went to voicemail. She'd sent him there, but he left a message anyway.

"Hey, Anna Beth, it's Jared. I wanted to thank you for the gift and wish you a Merry Christmas. And..." *I miss you? I love you? I'm stubborn? Forgive me?*

Jared didn't want his second time telling her he loved her to happen over the phone.

"That's it. Bye."

Lame, man. Very lame.

Jared backed out of his parent's driveway, thinking about Anna Beth's list. It had taken a lot of balls for her to give his mother that gift. To have him open it in front of his family.

He made the turn towards town instead of home. There was no way he'd sleep tonight without talking to her.

Jared parked in front of her aunt's house, sitting there for a moment with his engine running. He didn't see her car. Just Ernie's truck was in the driveway, but maybe she'd parked in the garage next to Sarah's car.

He turned off the truck, determination guiding his stride as he loped up the walkway. When he reached the top of the porch, he rapped his knuckles on the door loudly.

Sarah answered in a red plaid dress with Ernie right behind her. Both smiled broadly at him.

"Hello, Jared."

"Hi, Sarah. Is Anna Beth home?"

"No, she isn't. I believe, she's at Olive's." Sarah picked up a gift from the table in the entryway. "She left this for you."

Jared took the box, shooting Sarah a questioning glance. That smile never wavered and Jared looked to Ernie for help.

The older man held up his hands. "Don't ask me. I am out of this loop."

Sarah cleared her throat and to his surprise, she moved to close the door.

"Merry Christmas, Jared."

"Merry Christmas to you both."

The door clicked shut. Jared walked back to his truck, holding the package in one hand as he climbed inside.

He tore open the festive wrapping and found another ornament nestled in tissue. Two coffee cups sitting on a couch holding hands, smiling. *You're the cream... To my Coffee* was written in red across the base. Jared held the cheesy ornament carefully, the urgent need to see Anna Beth intensifying.

He pulled out his phone and shot Vance a text.

`You with Olive?`

`Yeah. Why?`

`Trying to find Anna Beth.`

`She's at Fire and Ice. Come by.`

But when Jared walked into the pub, there was no sign of Anna Beth. Olive and Vance waved at him, sitting at a table along the edge of the dancefloor.

"Hey, I thought you said she was here?"

"You just missed her,"Vance said.

"She left you these though." Olive handed him two gift-wrapped boxes.

Jared took the boxes, glancing between them as excitement and frustration bubbled up his throat in a low growl. "What the hell is going on?"

"Open them and find out," Olive said.

Jared lifted the lid on the first one and found a chocolate lab ornament, wearing a Santa hat and chewing a candy cane.

"Hey, look, it's a festive Rip,"Vance said.

Olive clapped. "Open the next one."

"I don't understand what all of this is about, but…"

He trailed off when he pulled out the second ornament. It looked exactly like his house, only decorated with Christmas lights.

Jared glanced up at both of them, an eyebrow quirked. "I guess I know where I'm heading next."

Olive pointed her finger at him and winked. "Don't fuck it up."

"I don't plan to."

On the drive back to his house, Jared found himself pushing the speed limit. He couldn't get to Anna Beth fast enough, needing to hear her say the words he'd been waiting for.

Jared pulled into the driveway and climbed out, staring at

the multicolored lights twinkling along the trim of his house and wrapping around his porch. A shadow hung by the door. He hustled up the walkway to thank Anna Beth properly.

"Santa Claus is coming to town!"

The flashing blue eyes of his mother's possessed Santa sent him jumping backward, nearly tripping down the step.

"Damn it!"

Jared clutched his chest, glaring at his mechanical nemesis. He'd noticed the prop was missing from his parent's porch earlier, but figured his mom removed it after too many complaints.

He unlocked the door and flipped the switch on the wall. The living room light kicked on, revealing a fully decorated, six-foot-tall Noble Fir in the corner.

"What do you think?" Anna Beth asked from behind him.

Jared spun around and she stood just inside his kitchen, Rip by her side. She wore a red sweater dress and Santa leggings, her hair styled in loose waves down her back.

"What do I think about the tree, or your breaking and entering?"

Anna Beth smiled sheepishly. "Both."

"I don't fear for my life at the moment, so we'll put the breaking and entering on the back burner. As to the tree, it's great, but why? And how did you know I would go to your house tonight?

"I had a feeling."

Jared's eyes narrowed. "You're in cahoots with my mother."

"Of course, I am." Anna Beth laughed. "Your sisters and brothers, too. You dad just kind of went along for the ride."

"And sending me all over town looking for you?"

"I needed time to get things perfect."

"Perfect for..."

"You."

Jared's stomach flipped. "Anna Beth, why the big show with the ornaments and the tree?"

She crossed the room and stood next to the tree. "Because Christmas trees tell stories about the people who decorate them. How families change and grow." She touched one of the green branches lovingly. "This tree is us. What our life could look like together."

At a loss for words, Jared stared as she pointed out a couple of ornaments, including a Scooby-Doo one he'd had as a kid.

"Your mom let me have them for the tree. And these are some of mine from when I was a kid." She took an ornament of a dark blue jacket off one branch and held it out so he could see clearly. "This represents the day we met, when I fixed your coat. I even drew little stitches, see?" She put the coat back and pointed to a black long horned cow ornament. "And this? Remember when we cut school because Tyler Hicks broke up with me and I didn't want to face him? You took me over to Garrett Ranch to see the calves, and we didn't know the bull was out there." Anna Beth giggled. "We ran so fast."

His heart raced, dazzled by her excitement as she showed him every special decoration.

"Here are the two from the White Elephant, and this sled, chainsaw, and pine tree? I guess you can imagine what day those represent. There are so many more I want to show you but the ones in this box are extra special. I just didn't have time to hang them."

She handed Jared a brown box of ornaments and inside were all of their friends and family. "We got everyone together yesterday and Olive took the pictures."

Jared stared down at all of the smiling faces, his eyes stinging. He picked one of his mom and dad and hung it on the tree. A sparkly glass ornament caught his eye, trimmed in black and silver glitter. He set the box down and plucked it from the branches.

I LOVE YOU.

Jared held it out to her. "What about this one?"

Anna Beth's cheeks turned red. "I think that's self-explanatory."

"Still, I'd like to know." Jared stared at her, afraid to blink for fear he might wake up and realize this was just a fantasy. "Say it. Please."

Her eyes met his, swimming with tears. "I love you, Jared. So very much. And I'm sorry. I was an ass and I just—"

Jared pulled her into his arms and kissed her, cradling her face in his hands. He poured every ounce of love into the melding of their lips, kissing her until they were both gasping. When they parted, he placed his forehead against hers. "Me, too. I'm such a stubborn idiot."

Anna Beth released a wet laugh. "Yeah, you are, but I still adore you."

Jared caressed her cheek. "Anna Beth..."

"Do you like the tree?" she whispered.

"I love the tree. I love...I love you, A.B."

"Jared," she whispered.

He kissed her again and the world exploded. Fireworks. Violins. Angels singing.

Wait, he wasn't imaging that. People were actually singing.

He broke the kiss and glanced around. "Do you hear that?"

"Yeah, that's another surprise for you, in case the tree didn't convince you."

"I'm afraid to ask."

"Come on." She took his hand and dragged him over to the door. When he opened it, on his front lawn stood their family and friends, caroling.

"We wish you a Merry Christmas…"

Anna Beth wrapped her arms around his waist, grinning. "They knew how much I love you and offered to help."

"You did all this for me?" Jared asked, holding her against him.

"There isn't anything I wouldn't do for you."

Jared kissed her temple as his arms tightened around her. "You really are the greatest gift."

"So are you."

About the Author

Codi Gary loves writing books almost as much as she loves outings with her family and snuggling with her adorable fur babies. An RWA Honor Roll author of more than twenty romance novels and novellas, her goals are to make her readers laugh one minute and cry the next in the best way possible. When she isn't glued to her computer, she can be found reading fantastic books, catching up on all the shows she loves, and taking pictures of her beautiful kids. To keep up with her releases, cover reveals, and crazy antics, just go to her website at www.CodiGarysBooks.com and sign up for her newsletter.

Follow me on...

Instagram @authorcodigary

Twitter @codigary

www.facebook.com/CodiGarysBooks

www.bookbub.com/authors/codi-gary

Acknowledgements

To my family, for being my support system and cheerleaders. You are outstanding and I love you. A very special thank you to Tina Klinesmith. I have an amazing best friend who fits me in a way no one ever has. She is funny, kind, sassy, and smart. She is an amazing mother, wife, and friend. I love her. She is my person. I would take a bullet…okay, maybe not a bullet, but a knife in a non-vital organ, for her. Thank you, Tina, for everything you do! You complete me. Victoria Colotta, my beautiful, talented friend. Thank you so much for the amazing graphics you design and my gorgeous cover. Your work is always impeccable. Thank you to Killion Publishing for cleaning up all of my grammatical errors. I appreciate you! And as always, thank you for my readers. You are wonderful rock stars and I wouldn't be here without you.

Made in United States
North Haven, CT
29 November 2024

61244186R00147